I0576020

ETHAN A. GERBER

Islorr's Blood

Volume I of the Voltaris Saga

First edition

ISBN (paperback): 979-8-9942752-1-4
ISBN (hardcover): 979-8-9942752-0-7

Editing by Gary Smailes
and Ben Espach

Cover and map art by
Elyse Royer

This book was professionally typeset on Reedsy.
Find out more at reedsy.com

To my sister, who put up with my shenanigans for all these years.

PART 1

The Beginning of a New Age

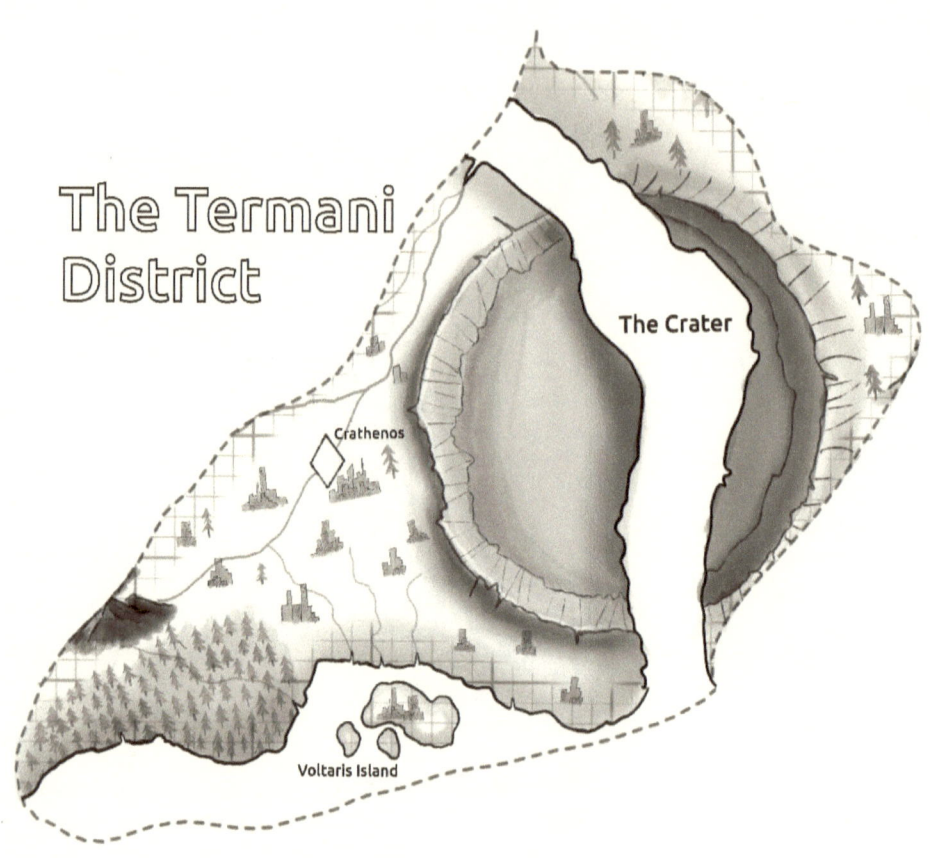

The Termani District

The Crater

Crathenos

Voltaris Island

CHAPTER 1

LUKAS

The holographic screen flickers with a performance from my favorite band. Usually this song, this exact live performance, has me belting along at full volume. Today it's just noise. Still, I can't afford to look away. I grimace and pull at my hair with clenched fists. Damn it. Why does Axle have to go to that stupid party?

The chorus hits my ears and I force my foot to tap with the beat. I drop my shaking hands from my hair.

Stop thinking about Axle. You told him to go.

The chorus finishes with a deafening silence. A new song begins to play. Damn it.

I tap my earpiece to kill the music.

"Notifications," I grumble.

A high-pitched robotic voice enters my ear.

"You have no new notifications," the voice says. The music roars back at full volume.

He wants to be there. Otherwise, he'd leave.

I sigh.

What am I talking about? Seriously, he just graduated upperschool. Of course he's happy. We'll leave Termani the moment he's back.

The music cuts out. The performers disappear from the screen, leaving a pitch-black projected screen hanging in front of my eyes. That's weird; it's not off. Just black. Static fills my ears, replacing the silence. Accompanying

3

it is a new voice. It sounds robotic, but with a lower pitch and an organic wavering that I've never heard in a synthetic voice before. "Thank you for electing me, I will ensure your safety."

The guy with the mask won then. Not that it matters anyway.

I click my earpiece to switch to another musician, but the same black screen remains with the same message looping in that unsettling voice.

What?

I switch again, and still the same message.

How many people did Prime Termani pay to broadcast this message? He probably didn't even spend a ferring. Anything for the safety of Termani.

I press another button on my earpiece and the screen fades out of view

"Enough of that," I say out loud.

I step forward and something bright yellow shoots out from my right, nearly knocking me off my feet. I stumble and just barely catch myself with a heavy step backward. I right myself, take a step forward again, and slam my fist onto the top of the mechanism. Unhindered by my outburst, the traffic blockade completes its extension, the other end attaching to another light pole on the opposite side of the wide street. Both light poles bathe the area in orange light, but with the noonday sun overhead their glow isn't too blinding.

I lean forward into the intersection, searching for people. No one is there. The automated system doesn't care.

Come on.

I glance up at the poles; their lights still a stubbornly deep orange as possible—no sign of changing to blue. I check both ways again; still no one.

Screw it.

I grab the blockade and hoist myself into the empty street. A loud beep from the light poles warns me to stop walking. I spare a glance at the camera on one of the poles behind me, turn back, and hop over the barricade, waving at the flashing red dot with the back of my hand.

I reach the other side and make my way over another blockade; the orange light on the ground turns blue. Machinery clicks and whirs behind me—too late now. I continue to walk forward.

I take a moment to look as the towering buildings rise on either side of me. The same smooth concrete used for the roads adorn their faces, interrupted only by large rectangular windows. One window has a small crack made glaringly obvious by the yellow paint plastered over it and the metal 'X' over the window. The street ahead is littered with large yellow signs posted in the middle of the street. I pass them without bothering to read the warnings. To my left, a ramp drops away beside me, descending into darkness. The SpeedTunnel. A sleek train emerges from the shadows, brakes hissing as it slows on its rails. The SpeedTrain makes a familiar ding, and streamlined doors slide open to the side.

I turn to the right, away from the stopped train. I force a chuckle. I'm used to Axle being right next to me.

I stop staring into nothing and pick up the pace, walking past the ramp. The two sides of the street merge back into one.

"Thank you for electing me; I will ensure your safety." I reach up to double-check my earpiece, but the sound dial is still set to zero.

What?

"Thank you for electing me; I will ensure your safety."

I look up to the buildings on either side of me. While mostly identical to the buildings back the way I've come, these host large holographic screens that span from end to end. All of them are blaring the same propaganda I tuned out earlier.

"Thank you for electing me; I will ensure your safety."

On the screens are the newly elected Prime of the Termani District. The new Prime Termani is wearing an unnaturally wrinkle-less dress suit fitted expertly to his slim frame. Golden buttons hold the slim fit perfectly in place, and the red accents, consisting mainly of a long tie and thick gloves, are clearly meant to command attention. However, it's the red prominent on the man's face, a cloth wrap that covers anything that could be remotely recognizable, that truly catches my eye. His eyes are obscured by large black goggles, and his mouth is covered by a metal plate pinholed to let air flow in and out.

The Prime, albeit strangely dressed, is not dissimilar from many other

Primes that came before him. Just like them, he preaches the same Terman doctrine: safety above all else.

"Thank you for electing me; I will ensure your safety." A pause. "Thank you for electing me; I will ensure your safety." Yet another pause. "Thank you for electing me; I will ensure your safety." Prime Termani speaks with the same modulated voice that I heard in my earpiece earlier.

I turn away from the screen and once again tune out the message.

"Hello," a voice says, deep and crackling with lifeless static. I whip my head around to turn back to the screen. Prime Termani is still standing there, but he is no longer repeating the same message. "Thank you for electing me"—I turn away as the familiar message begins, "—and I am honored that you chose me to be your new Prime."

I spin right back around to stare at the screen. I check all the other screens in my view; they're playing the same video. I step closer to the screen, just as Prime Termani steps closer to the camera. "One hundred and thirty-five years ago, the Union of Ayzol-Carkun was indisputably transformed into the nation it is today. One hundred and thirty-five years ago, this continent was turned into a bastion of freedom and peace. One hundred and thirty-five years ago, Saberrens and Cortenians were finally considered equal under the law. Today, I stand before you, on your screens, in what should be a celebration. It should be a celebration of our endless strive to improve our lives, and to honor those who died for our freedom. It should be a celebration of the peace in Ayzol-Carkun, and the safety that previous Primes of Termani have brought to this district. It should be a celebration of a brighter future for all of us. But it is not.

"You all know how the Saberren War of Independence ended, how the Saberrens utilized new weapons that gave them the ability to overcome their Cortenian enslavers. Well these weapons never disappeared. There is an uprising of people who intend to find the weapons made for good and use them for evil. These people call themselves Primordialists, after the very Primordial Stones that won the war. These people want to rip open the closing divide between Cortenians and Saberrens, forcing us apart once again, and I regret to admit that I have been unable to stop this group from infiltrating Termani.

"This is why I am here, broadcasting across all wavelengths. This is why I cannot wait for a more opportune time. This is why I am prepared to fight back. Effective immediately, I am implementing a new protocol for all Termans. This protocol will involve mandatory testing of the populus, starting with smaller groups and working outward until all of Termani has been tested. We cannot let this Primordialist threat spread unchecked. It is the beginning of a new age for Termani, and we will not stop fighting until we are free from the threat to our safety." The screen flickers, cuts to black, and then turns back on. Prime Termani is once again in a loop, repeating the same message from earlier: "Thank you for electing me, I will ensure your safety."

"What?" I murmur, stepping back from the screen. Images flash through my head from books I read in school. I knew the Primordial Stones still existed, but I never expected them to be the center of attention.

Prime Termani's looped message rings in my ears, even when I try to block the voice out. I grasp my head with my hands and pace back and forth. It keeps playing louder and louder in my head, though the volume remains constant. I look up again at Prime Termani, then back down.

By the blood of Islorr, mandatory testing? Primordialists? The Primordial Stones? Prime Termani was just elected.

A ding reverberates in the distance. I recognize the sound and begin walking in that direction. I break into a jog and move toward the source of the ding. Prime Termani's message slowly fades away, leaving only the pounding of my feet echoing in the street, and I know I have finally passed the screens. The road in front of me diverges, and I look down the ramp toward the SpeedTunnel. The tracks are barren, the empty tunnel carrying no sound or sign of an oncoming train. Too late. I close my eyes, hearing the faint sound of Prime Termani drone in the distance. Opening my eyes, I turn away from the tunnel and continue jogging down the street.

I hoist myself over the yellow blockade once again, cross the street, and finally draw within view of my house. On my right, an abandoned screen sits propped up by a few posts. An angry buzz in the air betrays the thick wire connecting the screen to larger wires overhead. Despite efforts to siphon power to the screen, a few scratch marks keep the archaic display permanently off. The lifeless screen is nevertheless covered in vivid still-wet graffiti. Most of the old art is hardly visible, but the freshly dripping paint captures an undeniably realistic portrait of the new Prime Termani—albeit with large 'X's on his mask's eyes. I force a chuckle, then turn slightly left toward home.

My house is not easily distinguishable from those around it. It is a large concrete cube, surrounded by identical cubes on either side and on top of it. An angular staircase on the side of the complex enables access to the upper units' balconies. Luckily, mine is on the bottom layer—no need to climb stairs after that jog. The concrete was once painted bright white, but a large portion of it shows the gray of the concrete beneath. I vividly remember the day Axle and I scratched most of this paint off to remove a display of 'public art'.

I clench the handle and swing the unlocked door wide open. Once inside, I slam the door shut behind me and flick the lock. I take a step, my foot catching on something, and fall sprawling onto the ground. I turn on my back with a groan, straining to see what tripped me up. My once neatly packed suitcase is now open, with my clothes flung all over the dirty floor.

"Dammit." I stand up, pacing back and forth. I should've zipped up the damn thing. I throw myself on the bed, shove my face into a pillow, and let out a brief muffled exclamation. After a couple of seconds, I stand up, leaving my face and some spent frustration imprinted on the flimsy pillow. I scramble across the room, furiously tossing stuff on top of the neatly folded clothes that remained in the suitcase. I shut the suitcase and shove it in a corner where it won't be a tripping hazard. I walk down the short hallway toward my and Axle's bedrooms. Going past my room, I peek through Axle's bedroom door and see a pile of clothes on the floor. He hasn't even started to pack. I walk in and start tossing his clothes into a large open container by his bed.

We won't be let out of Termani until the testing is over.

I pause, dropping Axle's clothes on the floor again and storm back into the main room. My hands shake.

There's no way we're getting out for at least another season.

"Fuck Termani."

I lunge forward at the wall, slamming my fists into the cheap composite material. The material bends behind my punch, leaving a hole that reveals the framework of the building. I step back. There's blood on the rim of the hole. I lift my hands; blood is streaming from deep cuts on my knuckles and along the outside of my palms. My body quivers. The initial numbness fades. Pain blossoms sharp and hot through my hands.

Why did I do that? Why the fuck did I do that?

I pace back and forth, staring at my hands. Blood drips from my wound onto the floor, marking a pattern that follows my footsteps. My hands shake uncontrollably. The pain now dominates my mind, commanding all my attention. I try to move my fingers, but they barely respond.

I swing my fist at the wall again but stop myself just before my hand hits the composite. I grab my hair with my hands and pull. However, the pain of the sudden movement and slick blood cause my hair to just slip between my fingers.

What do I do? I don't have any medicine. I could wrap it up. Do I have any bandages? Not sure. I bet there's medicine at the store. I could buy some, but I don't want to leave. Don't leave. I should fill the hole before Axle gets back. He'd be mad. I'd be mad. I need to sleep. Axle would tell me to get some sleep. Axle would know what to do. Who am I kidding, he would have no idea. The pain doubles. I cannot even control my hands. They spasm, and I almost hit the wall again. My hands seem to have a mind of their own. I step away from the wall and force my hands into my pockets.

I stumble backward and collapse over onto the couch.

CHAPTER 2

LUKAS

'Thank you for electing me; I will ensure your safety.' Prime Termani's speech echoes through my head. I stare up at the ceiling, waiting for it to stop.

Safety means shit if you can't do a damn thing.

I force a chuckle. It dies in my throat. My fists clench, causing the ache in my fingers to sharpen. I hold them up to the light fixture above, revealing dried blood caked to my knuckles. That light is so damn bright. I track the cool light of the fixtures, the brightness creeping even into my peripheral vision. I force a chuckle again, resulting only in a coughing fit. I pitch forward, swinging my legs off the sofa's edge. The room tilts as I sit up.

The jagged hole across the room stares accusingly at me.

Bracing my hands on my knees, I push myself up and walk over to confront the hole. I lean in close. The composite is warped and cracked; its edges bite at my fingertips when I touch it.

That's not going away on its own.

My legs tremble. I reach my hand into the hole and tug at a bent piece of composite. Carefully, my injured hand shaking in protest, I bend it back toward me. The piece snaps with a loud crack, and fragments scatter across the floor.

Dammit.

I step away from the hole and head over to the closet in the hall. I open the closet to rummage through my disorganized supplies. There's a drill, but that won't be of any use to fix the hole. A plasma torch for melting metal together rests unplugged on the bottom shelf. That wouldn't work, I'd probably set fire to the house. A blade saw could work, but I'd need to track down some scrap composite to replace the hole, and it still wouldn't be very secure. I would need liquid composite to fill the hole, which is hard to come by. I can't fix this myself.

I close the door and march back over to the hole, tapping my earpiece. My fingers scramble to enter a number on the numpad that I memorized long ago. The earpiece barely rings before the automated voice pops up.

"Thank you for calling Voltaris Repair, a subsidiary of Voltaris Industries. Please hold while we connect you with a customer service representative." The message stops. A typical corporate melody loops endlessly.

What is it with people and their looped messages?

I roll my eyes at the melody; I still tap my foot with the beat though. My eyes jolt back to the dent in the wall, and Prime Termani's looped message plays in my head unbidden.

Fuck safety.

I tap my foot twice as fast.

Hurry up.

The hold melody tangles with Prime Termani's voice in my head, bleeding together like a bad remix.

Does it really take that long to pick up the damn phone?

The melody swells. Louder. Louder. A sudden ringing in my ears makes my heart drop into my stomach. I freeze. My foot stops tapping, and my eyes dart around the room. This isn't the hold music. This is something else entirely.

Not now.

The ringing drowns out the melody and Prime Termani's haunting message.

Please, not now. Don't be here now.

I grab my ears with my hands and crouch over as the ringing persists.

Please. Get out of my head.

"Hello, this is Voltaris Repair. How can I help you?" I rip off my earpiece and hurl it across the room. The device hits the floor and cracks. "Hello?" the now muffled voice says. "Hello?" I ignore the voice, pressing my palms against my ears. The ringing still doesn't stop.

Go. Away.

"Hello Lukas," another voice says. This one doesn't come from the earpiece.

Go. Away.

My hands shaking against my ringing ears, I turn to the hole in the wall. The jagged edges of the hole no longer resemble a fist. They blur and twist into the shape of a head.

"Lukas, you need to calm down."

"Get out of my head," I shout, my voice cracking. My trembling hands fall from my ears. The ringing finally stops. "What are you doing here?"

"Your head, your rules," the voice says.

"I was trying to call Voltaris."

"To fix the hole that you created?" she asks.

I grunt. "Alright, last time you were here, it took me an hour to get rid of you. I'm not doing that again."

"What do you suppose we do?" The silhouette shifts, textured composite rippling as her 'shoulders' shrug.

"I have a list of questions for you. Answer each one, and that should get rid of you."

"Go ahead."

"Question 1: why are you here?" I ask, my hands still trembling.

"I answered that already. Your head, your rules."

"Worth a shot."

"Was it?" she asks. I grimace, turning away from her taunting silhouette. I glance briefly at the dead earpiece.

"Next question. Are you mad at Prime Termani?"

"Well, you are, so I'd assume I am as well."

"Not helpful."

"Prime Termani might restrict your travel plans. And Axle's at that graduation party, so you can't discuss this with hi—"

"Shut up about Axle."

"I'm trying to help."

"Fuck you."

"Is that really how you speak to your mother?"

I whip around to face the ghostly silhouette. "You're not my damn mother."

"Your head seems to think I am."

"She left. You're here. See the difference?" I clench my fists, marching over to the earpiece on the floor. "I'm calling Voltaris. When they pick up, you better be gone."

"That's not how this works."

"Then how does it?" I demand. "What do I have to do to get rid of you?"

"Maybe try distracting yourself. You and Axle always loved the woods."

"I'm not going to the woods," I snap. "I am going to call Voltaris so they can fix this damn hole."

"Axle doesn't want to travel, does he?"

"I said stop talking about Axle." I shove the cracked earpiece back on my ear.

"He wasn't packed when you got back. You were. Maybe you should talk to him about it."

"You don't decide what I do. I do." I type the first number in.

"How many times do I have to tell you? This is your head. It's your idea."

"Fine. I'll go to the damn woods." I turn away from my mom's rippling figure and head over to the door, fidgeting the metal lock open. I swing the door open. I step outside onto the moonlit road; the brisk air offers a brief moment of calm. The residential street is silent compared to the chaos of the blaring screens on the main street earlier. It's also less empty. Seven guards patrol the street. The guards step down in unison, their heavy boots pounding against the ground. I'm surprised the concrete doesn't crack under their heavy steps.

A guard strides over to a light pole, reaching for its bulb. The segments of his bulky metal armor grinds on itself and restricts his movement. The guard grabs a switch and pulls down. The light flickers off. Another guard does the same thing for the light pole across the street.

What use is a light if everyone is always inside?

13

My gaze locks on to the brightest light in the city, aside from the moons. The building towers over the rest of Crathenos, the Termani district's capital city. Its rectangular shape is identical to most other buildings on Crathenos' skyline. Identical, that is, except for the massive glowing purple diamond crowning its peak. The signature glass ornament marking it a capitol building. I briskly turn away from the light, back toward the cramped complex of stacked apartment units. Looming behind the complex is the darkest area of Crathenos, if it can even be considered part of Crathenos at all. As much as the city tries to push the forest away, the host of trees still dominate the horizon.

I walk around the side of the stacked cubes, where the clean, smooth concrete abruptly gives way to dirt and grass. Trees spring out of the ground, dwarfing the concrete jungle behind me. Their turquoise leaves shiver in the wind, wrapping me in a calming rustling sound. I enter the peaceful chaos of the woods and leave the harsh order of the city behind. The dirt is packed where it meets the concrete, but gets looser as it strays away from the road. Weeds attack the complex from behind, their vines sharing the back wall with faded graffiti. I head away from the complex, following a well-tread path leading to a gap in the trees. With each step deeper between the trees, the packed ground becomes more overrun by grass and weeds. The circuitous path is barely visible, but I remember it clearly. I hardly look down as I follow the course that Axle and I spent years packing down with our feet.

"That took you a while to make." My mom's voice jolts me out of my reverie. I spin around to face her silhouette lounging on the side of a dying tree. Many branches have fallen in the area, and the scattered mess lies withering and rotting away.

"I thought I got rid of you."

"Unfortunately, you did not."

"Why'd you come back?" I ask, turning away and slowly continuing down the faded path.

"Your head, your rules." She fades from the dead tree and reforms on the tree ahead of me. Her head tilts up, and I follow her gaze up the massive tree,

14

past its sprawling branches to where the three colorful moons hang shining in the dark. Vermaiye, the largest of the three, casts an orange glow that contrasts against the turquoise of the leaves. Rosaea, the pink moon, is the brightest and has no trouble piercing the canopy of the trees. I could barely make out Lokx, the smallest and dimmest of the moons. "Very calming. I've always loved the moons." Her soft voice sounds almost reminiscent. "I fondly remember the times we watched the three moons when they were all full. Like they are tonight." Yeah, right. I think I'd remember that.

I scoff and continue along the path, kicking fallen leaves out of my way. I glance down at the packed dirt beneath my feet, dirt that has been stomped on for years.

"I showed you through these woods once. Before you met Axle."

"I'm aware of my own memories. It was more fun with Axle. Always has been."

"Axle's your age. That likely makes a difference." I stop walking, turning to the tree to face my mom's silhouette.

"You know that's not what I mean."

"Yes. You know, I would rather us not argue."

"We wouldn't argue if you didn't speak."

My mom lowers her voice. "Your head, your rules."

"Can you stop saying that stupid phrase?" I shout.

"I really can't. I don't have any free will in this. It's all you."

"Lovely."

"Let's talk about Axle. About Prime Termani," my mom's silhouette says. I glance down at the scabs on my fists, reminded of my reaction to the new Prime's election speech. "Termani was always a joke," she continues. "'I will ensure your safety.' What a bunch of hypocrites."

"If it weren't so ordered—"

"You expect to find freedom in chaos," she interjects.

"What?" I step toward her shadow-like silhouette. "I don't understand." My mom doesn't respond, instead her silhouette fades to look more like an actual shadow than like a person. "What do you mean?" I plead, hanging my head. "Dammit. Fuck." I slump against a tree with my head in my hands. A tear drips down the side of my face before I can wipe it away.

"Lukas," my mom's voice whispers behind me. "Do you really believe in anything at all?"

I swing around and smash my fist against the tree. I look down at my quivering right hand. Dammit. The pain had *finally* started fading. The wounds from earlier are deeper now, with fresh blood streaming over my knuckles and down my wrist. I don't notice any pain. My numb fist just quivers.

"Why do you want to leave Termani?" my mom asks, her voice even softer this time.

I slump further as another tear runs down my cheek. I taste its salt in the corner of my lip. Silence surrounds me, broken only by my own sobs and the wind rustling the trees. I look around as I sniffle up my tears. Her silhouette is gone. It's just my own shadow cast on the tree now. I lean my back against the bark. I can wait a little longer. Then Axle and I can leave Termani together without looking back.

I look back at the trail disappearing into the dark woods and let out a deep exhale.

"Screw it, I'm going back home."

I stand up, wipe the tears from my eyes, and begin the trek back to the city. A twinge of pain shoots through my right hand. Both fists are bruised and torn, but my right hand looks torn from hitting the tree. A tear drips into an open gash, stinging my knuckles.

"Dammit."

I grab the hem of my shirt and tear off a long strip, leaving the remainder of my shirt looking cropped and dyed red at the bottom. I rip the strip in two and wrap one around each of my fists, wincing as the fabric bites into raw flesh.

CHAPTER 3

LUKAS

uildings pierce the sky like knives in the horizon. The angular faces
of Termani's capital are a far cry from the curving branches and
vines in the woods. The closer these towering edifices are to the
center of Crathenos, the more angular they become. The most prominent
buildings are all shaped like scepters pointing to the zenith of the horizon —
the capitol building itself. While the capitol mirrors the sharp architecture
of the surrounding city, its angular curves jut out of the building like vines.
They wind around the otherwise rectangular building, creeping up to where
the capitol ornament rests, shining like a lighthouse. The three moons orbit
around the ornament. It would make an imposing painting indeed.

I glare at the building. Underneath that purple beacon is the office of
Prime Termani. The same office where the Prime decided that freedom
wasn't as important as safety.

A faint vibration tickles my ear. I press the main button on my earpiece's
numpad, and a high-pitched robotic voice pipes up.

"One new message: unrecognized contact."

Interesting. Shaking my head, I turn away from the bright city's skyline to
use the dark backdrop of the woods. I click the display button next to the
numpad. A blue tinted screen projects in front of me, obscuring the forest.
A wooden background shows up first. The perfectly parallel lines of the
paneling are a poor imitation of the bark on the trees in my peripheral. The
school's walls are unmistakable. The projector builds the rest of scene in

three-dimensional layers. First, a wooden table materializes in front of the wall. The table is stained with different colors, and is covered in half-eaten food, scattered chips, and overturned cups spilling blue Serotonic.

Five people begin fading in on the last layer. The person in the center fades in first. She's well-dressed, despite slightly messy hair and a small blue stain at the bottom of her button-up shirt. On her left ear is an earpiece with a bright blue light illuminating the scene, marking her as the unrecognized contact that sent the photo. I don't know her.

Just as I reach my hand back to turn my earpiece off, the other four people snap into focus. One of them looks young but has a scrappy beard that contradicts his youthful appearance. Another is dressed like she is at a funeral, with a perfectly fitted all-black dress and straightened hair. The fourth wears a baggy shirt and supposedly fancy khakis that really just look like they haven't been washed in days; he's grinning from ear to ear. The gaps between his teeth have fragments of chewed food in them. I don't know any of these people, but it's the appearance of the final person that stops me from disabling the photo projection. On the far left, with his curly black hair, obsidian skin, and bright blue eyes, is Axle. His arm is wrapped around the woman dressed for a funeral, and his other hand is frozen mid-wave. I smile at the sight of my best friend's happy face, even though I know that Axle won't see it.

I press the main button on my earpiece and the screen fades away.

I soon reach the boundary again where the concrete of the city marks the edge of the woods. My apartment complex appears on the right, but I head past it toward the unmistakable creak of those damn rollers that the safety department uses to perform their checks. What are they up to now? A drilling noise whines ahead, and curiosity gets the better of me, pulling me past the last of the complex's apartment cubes. From the woods I could make out almost the entire city. Now my view is blocked by the towering structures surrounding me.

The tall overarching light poles are all dark now, and I rely almost purely on the light of the moons and the sound of the nearest roller to guide me. The only other faint sources of light come from inside the residential buildings on either side of me. Through the windows of countless housing complexes, the soft blue glows from screen lights escape instead of the warm yellow light of the lights along their ceilings. Many silhouettes lean back to stare at their screens for a dose of effortless entertainment. Some windows are just dark, obscuring the residents from my view.

I continue strolling down the empty moonlit street; my only company is the sound of the roller up ahead. I stop watching the silhouettes of the city's citizens and focus on the lifeless street in front of me. Against all odds, I spot a lone sapling protruding from between two slabs of concrete. Even in Crathenos, where trees are removed for "safety reasons," some still manage to sneak themselves into the city. Stubborn as weeds.

I continue walking down the street, and a small vehicle—rolling on thin rubber conveyor belts—arrives at the scene. The creaky roller is painted a dull gray, with the acronym 'CSD' plastered on its side in an equally dull navy blue. The Crathenos Safety Department. I hope Prime Termani isn't able to take over the CSD. The guards are bad enough.

A single windowless door opens, spilling out workers carrying a large metal drill. The drill's 'CSD' marking is poorly placed, allowing the original metal logo to peek through: a large 'V' with a diagonal lightning bolt slicing the letter in half. The safety department workers hoist the drill over to the sapling's base. It screams to life and grinds away at the concrete around the young tree. I press the upper button on my earpiece, turning on some music. Although I can still hear the drill's roaring with my right ear, the music in my left helps me tune the noise out.

I step past the sapling and look around for the remaining rollers that I can still hear. A side street opens up ahead where a group of kids are running around and jumping over a vine torn from the budding tree. The kids swing the vine in a consistent loop, small flashlights strapped to their wrists casting wild shadows. They each take turns hopping over the vine before it hits their feet. One of them glances at me with a quizzical face, and I remember there's blood staining my torn shirt and hands. Shrugging, I smile at the kid, and she returns to play with the rest. The drill sound fades behind me as the workers grab the sapling and rip it from the ground. The kids, unfazed, continue playing their jumping game in the street.

I spot a guard walking down the street toward the kids. He's wearing thick dark gray metal armor. On the guard's waist is a leather belt, with a shining silver weapon tucked in a holster. Guards like him haunt every corner. Overkill in a place where people actually leave their doors unlocked.

The guard briefly surveys the area, then his gaze settles on me. He closes the distance, one hand already gripping the handle of his holstered weapon. I freeze in place. His eyes move from my torn bloodstained shirt to my wrapped hands.

"You gonna keep looking at me or are you gonna say something?" I ask, eyeing the new weapon in his holster. The same 'V' logo from the drill is engraved on the weapon's grip. Someone, likely the guard himself, has sprayed a red 'X' over the engraving. I turn my eyes back up to the guard. He's staring right at me.

"What happened to you?" he asks.

I ignore his question. "Is that new?"

"What?" the guard asks. "I asked you a question."

"I was in the woods," I say. "That's an EM-Plasmar. Those things are expensive." The guard turns to the Plasmar in his holster, grunting. I continue. "I didn't know Voltaris was working for the government now."

"Voltaris isn't working for the government. They provide the energy to power the Plasmars. That's it. Why were you in the woods? Were you injured?"

"Because it's fun," I reply, glancing over my shoulders at the woods. My house instantly draws my attention; it's the only cube in the complex with all the lights still on. I turn around to head back home, but the guard grabs my shoulder, pulling me back to face him.

"Do not return there again," he commands. I bring my hand to my forehead in a mock salute. I drop my hand as the guard rolls his eyes, and walk back toward my house.

"Give me that," the guard orders from somewhere behind me. I glance back in time to see him rip the vine from out of a kid's hands. "It's not safe." The guard heads back down the street toward me, leaving the kids staring down at the ground. One of them, the same one that had looked at me earlier, begins to cry. The guard meets my eyes as he passes, and I whip my head back around to face my house. I slowly walk home, leaving the saddened kids in the street behind me.

I arrive at my front door just as the lengthy song in my ear finishes. I swing the door open, step in, and slam it shut, pressing the button on the handle to make sure it's securely locked. I flick the lights off. Yawning, I wipe my eyes, step into my room, and collapse onto my bed.

CHAPTER 4

AXLE

"I think we've taken enough photos…" Jeremiah growls over the loud music. I turn to look at him just in time to see him scratch his scraggly beard, sending chunks of food to scatter on the floor.

"Fine," Aurela sighs. She tugs at her oversized buttoned shirt so that it twirls like a dress around her knees. "But if your family and friends are mad that they didn't get enough photos, that's on you."

"Fine by me," Jeremiah grins. Aurela presses a button on the side of her earpiece and the blue light turns off.

"Come on dude. I put so much effort into my outfit," Lyra whines. I glance over at the tight black dress clinging to her thin body. Her usually wavy hair has been straightened out for the evening and reaches down past her shoulders.

"Who died for you to wear that?" Nikolas chuckles, causing the fat on his upper body to jiggle underneath his baggy shirt.

Lyra rolls her eyes. "Maybe you should wash your clothes before saying anything."

"Hey," Nikolas says.

I turn away from the group and glance around the room. The walls of the massive conference room are typical composite covered in a facade of perfectly lined-up wooden planks. But the wood isn't even real, just more composite with a careful paint job. The room is stuffed with hundreds of people, but there are still patches of empty space as conversations draw people into tightly packed groups. A couple of people hover around the banquet table at the center of the room, reaching over each other for the remaining scraps of food.

"Hey Axle, what's Lukas's number?" someone calls from behind.

I turn around. Aurela has her finger on the numpad of her earpiece, eyes on me.

"Six-nine-zero-one-four-seven-three-six."

I turn back around, pretending to listen to the group's conversation. The music is loud, but I have mostly tuned it out. My eyes wander to the door. Its transparent glass window is surrounded by a metal frame and a glowing orange 'exit' sign above it. I can make out the long hallway lined with metal lockers through the glass door. At the far end is another glass door. The door leading outside. The moons' lights glare through the distant exit, casting three colorful hues onto the unlit hallway floor.

"Hey man, how's it going?" I shudder as a warm sweaty arm wraps around my shoulders and neck. I look to the side at a grinning Nikolas. Sweat drips down his baggy shirt and onto my side.

"I'm alright." I turn around so he's forced to take his arm from me. I shudder as I resist the temptation to wipe his sweat off my neck. "How are you?"

"I'm fantastic, man," he chuckles. "Overschool's gonna be a blast. I'm gonna build so many cool things."

"That sounds awesome," I say, staring at his wide brown eyes.

"It will be," he says, grinning. "You sure you can't join us? It'd be great to have you."

I sigh. "Lukas and I are going to travel for a bit. He really wants to see the rest of Ayzol-Carkun."

"Enough with Lukas." Nikolas nudges my shoulder. "What do you want?"

"I—"

"Hey everyone, Prime Termani's speech was just published online," someone calls out. The loud music stops. Nikolas and I turn around to face a stocky guy holding a drink. He takes off his earpiece and props it up on a scratched wooden chair. While he messes with the numpad on his earpiece, people fetch and drag chairs from the corners of the large conference room. Nikolas rushes away to push the snack table closer to the chairs. I glance back at the door and the moonlit hallway behind it. Sighing, I make my way over to the makeshift theater people are making. Most students take a seat and wait for the projection, but others lounge over several chairs. Those left without seats sit down on the floor. I choose to stand behind everyone.

Blue light shines from the propped-up earpiece, bathing the fake wood paneling on the wall. A blue-tinted picture of a man wearing a suit materializes layer by layer. His suit is pale, but I can't tell if it's white or gray with the blue light from the projection. The tight suit clings to the man's slim body. Golden buttons adorn the jacket, and more golden accents creep up his suit and over the man's mask. A vibrant purple elliptical mask of acrylic obscures his features. The mask surrounds the man's purple eyes with deep black circles, with golden teardrops gliding down its sides. In place of his mouth are four equally spaced vertical cuts. I can just barely make out pale skin and dull pink lips behind the cuts. The lips move, but no sound comes from the projection.

"Anyone have an amplifier?" the stocky guy calls out. "My earpiece isn't loud enough."

"Why can't we just do a mesh projection?" someone asks.

"Not everyone has an earpiece," Aurela says, pointing in my direction. I feel my cheeks burn as several eyes turn to me. A short woman waves her hand to draw the stocky guy's attention, and she tosses him a small metal rectangular device. He places it next to the in-ear section of the earpiece. It briefly flashes a bright blue before emitting a constant dimmer glow.

"Here at Voltaris Industries, we believe that everyone deserves a shot at life," the man says, walking over to a set of double doors. The camera follows him as he pushes open a set of heavy doors and walks into a room filled with more masked people. They're all wearing black-and-white masks and knee-length lab coats. Everyone is fidgeting with different machines at their workbenches. "That's why we created Voltaris Laboratories. To help you help yourself." A woman in the back tilts her head up, and I can barely make out her similar purple eyes. The woman next to her taps her shoulder, and she looks back down at her workbench.

"I thought this was supposed to be Prime Termani's speech," a woman next to me complains. I glance over at her and back to the projection. The masked man continues to speak, but I can't hear him over a rising series of shouts from the people around me. The screen flashes to black, and then to the image of a woman standing in Crathenos' main street, her long hair blowing in the wind. The cacophony of students yelling ceases. A microphone curves from the woman's earpiece to the front of her face. Behind her, the massive projected screens on the city's buildings display a different masked man. He also wears a tight white suit, but with blood red accents instead of gold. Also unlike the man in the Voltaris advertisement, red cloth wraps his face instead of a solid acrylic mask. His eyes have similar black circle coverings stitched into the fabric, and his mouth is covered by a metal filter. All the screens in the background blare, but the video's audio is poor and sounds muffled. An edited blue banner slides across the projection, reading: 'New Prime Termani gives election speech'. The woman begins to speak.

"Today was a wild day for Termani," she says. "This is the toughest election since former Prime Termani's first win a decade ago. Many were convinced that former Prime Termani would win in a landslide for his third term as Prime. However, the new Prime Termani narrowly secured victory over the former Prime. Remarkably, the new Prime has never held political office before now." The woman looks down, then back up. "Without further ado, here is Prime Termani's first address to the public as the newly elected Prime."

The projection flickers to black again before assembling into the same image displayed earlier behind the reporter. The cloth-wrapped man stands in front of an ornate chair. The room behind him is dark. A single light from above illuminates his masked face.

"Hello," he says. His voice is deep but distorted by a slightly screeching static. "Thank you for electing me, and I am honored that you chose me to be your new Prime." Prime Termani steps closer to the camera, tilting his head to look down at his viewers. He cuts quite the imposing figure.

"One hundred and thirty-five years ago, Ayzol-Carkun was indisputably transformed into the nation it is today. One hundred and thirty-five years ago, this continent was turned into a bastion of freedom and peace. One hundred and thirty-five years ago, Saberrens and Cortenians were finally considered equal under the law. Today, I stand before you, on your screens, in what should be a celebration."

As the new Prime continues to speak, I turn away, my eyes drawn back to the glass exit door. I wrap my fingers around a drink from the table, pick it up, then set it back down with a sigh. Taking a deep breath, I walk away from the crowd of viewers and toward the glass door. I've stayed long enough that the others can't complain if I leave now. I reach the door, press the unlock on the handle, and slide the door partially open.

I jolt, jumping away from the door as a sudden loud crashing noise rings in the air. At the far end of the hallway, glass shards reflect the moons' lights in front of the exterior door. I lean my head in through the gap in the door to peek at what caused the glass to break. A black boot steps through the broken entrance, crunching it into finer pieces. I trace the boot upwards to the man it belongs to. He's a city guard, wearing bulky dark gray armor on his chest, legs, and arms. On his head is a helmet with a harsh blue light streaming from the side of it. The blue light sweeps over my face. I raise my hand to shield my eyes. He marches down the hallway with more guards rushing in behind him. The armored guard glares at me as he advances toward the door I'm holding open. I release the door and scurry out of the way. He hits the glass door with his armored elbow, sending shards flying into the conference room. People behind me scream as guards swarm the room.

The guard in the center, who had broken the glass, pulls out a silver-tinted weapon. The Plasmar is angular, formed in a long 'L' shape with the handle at the short end. On the handle's back, a 'V' shape is engraved next to a glowing blue dot. The guard raises the Plasmar, aiming it at me and the students around me. With his other hand, he pulls out a ball, flicks a switch, and rolls it along the floor. Orange gas pours out of the gas grenade, and my eyes are forced shut.

CHAPTER 5

SAPPHIRE

T he lock is too small for the door.

On any ordinary day, I'd report this. The insert for the knob is a fingernail's distance too large, so it wobbles when flicked from the inside. The doorknob itself is a bit rusty but, glimpsing through the tiny gap at its side, I can tell that the metal of the lock looks brand new. The lock must have broken, and someone used the nearest replacement they could find. The idiots used the wrong size. I expect better from the largest company on the continent.

Tonight, I'm grateful someone at Voltaris has been cutting corners.

I reach into my pocket and pull out a small metal pin, bent into a 'U' shape. The pin barely fits as I slide it into the gap with the bends of the 'U' pointing toward the knob. I fidget it around a bit until I hear a click, then quickly reverse the direction of the bend and carefully twist the pin the other way again, I force the pin and hear it grinds inside the lock before it clicks again. I pull the now 'S' shaped pin out of the gap, grab the knob, and pull the door open.

I step into a room with evenly spaced metal desks arranged so that a person just barely has enough room to work behind their desk. Each desk has an optic microscope, a vial sealer, and a bunch of glass vials organized by size in a large container. The vials are empty, and all the machines are powered off.

I press the door shut behind me, locking it again. The light fixtures above are turned off, and the room is dimly lit by the few windows scattered around. The three moons' rainbow light seeps through the glass panels, casting intricate shapes through the empty vials on desks. Someone walks past one of the windows. I spot black shoes, a lab coat that reaches his knees, and a too-tight hat squeezing his head.

Oh shit.

I duck down, scurrying across the floor and between the desks. My hands clutch the handles on either side of my waist.

I can't believe they forgot to close the blinds.

Eyeing the unaware bystander, I scramble from under one desk to the other, sneaking through the lab toward the double doors on the far side of the room. The doors on this side are painted white, blending with the white walls, floor, and ceiling. A few smudges mark where countless hands push and pull the doors every day. I'll make sure they're cleaned tomorrow.

Above the doors, the large 'Voltaris Laboratories' sign gleams. It's painted on the wall in the teal-ish Voltaris Blue. Typical Voltaris, claiming a color as their own. Brand awareness, I suppose. But who hasn't heard of Voltaris? It just seems like a waste of money.

Speaking of a waste of money, the label shows signs of wear. The word 'Laboratories' is partially scratched, and faded letters beneath 'Voltaris' hint at an older lab name. Before Voltaris Industries bought the lab and built Voltaris Tower. Before they bought the whole island.

I push open one of the double doors and step through to the spiral staircase on the other side. Taking a deep breath, I run up the staircase.

This better be worth it.

At the top, the main entrance to the engineering floor is a heavy wooden door with scratches up the edge that keeps hitting the wall. Its label is scratched beyond readability. Everything about this room screams importance. Holding my breath, I grab the doorknob and yank it. The door doesn't budge. Something next to the door starts beeping. Loudly.

Damn it.

A flashing orange light draws my attention to a sensor bar along the right side of the door.

How did I miss this?

I run over to the nearest window, as the beeping continues. I stare out the open window at all the civilians walking past the tower. Going to party after a long day at work, most likely. Everything looks tiny from up here. The beeping stops. There's no way they'll know it was me. No way. But what if they suspect something?

I have to get out of here.

I turn back to the stairs, glancing down at the ground floor. I can barely make out the steps with only slivers of the moons' lights coming through the windows.

I can't leave with nothing.

I pull out the large glass vial I stole earlier. Its translucent green fluid contrasts with the colorful moonlight, casting eerie shadows down the stairwell. Why were none of the tests successful? We were given the exact measurements to use. Something's off. It won't be long before they discover my meddling. I need to figure this out soon. I pocket the serum and run down the stairs. I carefully push open the lab door and sneak inside. If I'm going to analyze this, I can't risk someone seeing me. I crawl to the windows lining the wall and peek over the glass pane's bottom edge. There's no one out there. I push the blinds buttons and wince at the motor's sound, soft as it is.

I pull out the serum again and head over to my desk. I turn on the microscope, and a bright laser illuminates the plate below the scope. I move to smash the vial's edge against the side of the desk, then hesitate, placing the vial on the desk. I rummage in a drawer where two lab coats lie stuffed inside. I pull mine out and put it on. The lab coat is too short, but it covers enough of my body. I pick up the vial again and smash the tip on the edge of the desk. Slivers of glass scatter onto the floor. Green fluid sprays onto my lab coat. I kick the fragmented glass under the desk.

I tilt the vial, letting a small drop of the serum fall onto the plate under the scope. I squint into the scope's eyepiece and look at the serum. Just like during normal lab hours, I can't make out any compounds; they're too small to recognize I turn the dial, zooming in as far as it goes. Nothing. The compounds remain invisible. They made it impossible to analyze. They don't want us to know what it's made of.

I turn away from the microscope, looking around the room. I grab the microscope from the desk next to me and unscrew the bottom part of the scope. I bring the magnifier over to my scope and position it beneath the one already attached. I peer through the makeshift double magnified scope. Two compounds float in the base fluid, which is presumably salt water. I was only expecting to see one. The larger compound is as expected, black powder that has dissolved into the water. The powder reacts with the saline, producing a green glow. This was mentioned in the descriptions. It's not unusual. I was never told about the smaller compound, however.

I see something move a tiny bit out of my focus. I shift focus, searching the fluid for the movement. The smaller compound is too small to see in detail. I would have to grab another magnifier, and I don't even think that would be enough. I can't be here much longer anyway.

One of the smaller compounds moves again. Short spasms, like a living organism swimming in water. I jerk away from the microscope, panting. Did they put bacteria in the serum? Or a virus? A parasite? I screw the borrowed magnifier back onto its microscope. I turn my microscope off, remove the plate, and toss it underneath the desk with the shattered glass fragments. I turn the vial sealer on and it begins heating up. I place the vial with the remaining serum in the sealer to remelt the opening closed.

Why would they put something organic in the serum?

I furiously open the drawers at my desk and scrounge around in them for anything sharp enough to pierce skin. There's a narrow tube with strong acid inside one of the drawers, but I can't risk denaturing the proteins in my blood. No luck. Nothing in these drawers is meant to draw blood. I quickly grab another plate and close the drawers. I carefully position the plate underneath the eyepiece of the microscope. I reach over to the vial sealer and yank free the partially sealed tube. The light on the side of the sealer flashes orange, but I ignore it. Ensuring none of the green serum gets anywhere near the sharp tip of the vial, I press my finger against the glass and let it pierce my skin. I immediately pull the vial away as my blood drips from the cut. I smear my finger on the plate beneath the eyepiece.

Grabbing the magnifier from the other microscope again, I carefully reattach it beneath my own. I peer into the eyepiece. The enlarged blood cells look huge through the ocular. Around them float even larger cells, their surfaces studded with segments that latch onto unfamiliar organisms and particles. Immune cells. I slowly drop some of the serum onto the plate. I watch the saline solution carry the dissolved black powder particles and foreign organisms towards the blood sample.

Now I wait. The saline solution settles in place, flowing between blood cells like a river crashing into rocks. The black powder collects on the basins of the flow, sticking to the sides of the blood behemoths. The smaller compound springs to life, wiggling between the large red blood cells way faster than it had moved in the serum before. One of the immune cells notices the intruders. It pushes through the green salt water toward the nearest invader. The black powder blocks it. What? As the immune cell presses forward, the black particulates solidify around the attacking cell. Islorr's Blood. The organism continues onward. The immune cell attempts to eat through the dissolved powder, and it rapidly decays, as if the powder is draining the life out of it.

More immune cells attack, and eventually, a few of them are able to get to and kill the intruding organism. I step away from the microscope and place the serum-filled vial back in the vial sealer. Whatever the powder is, it can block immune cells. So that the organism can get through. The serum is meant to be injected into the bloodstream. But why? Why allow these strange organisms through the body?

CHAPTER 6

LUKAS

A loud noise outside rips me out of my sleep. I jolt up from my bed, sending my blanket flying. I moan, lying back down. "Axle," I call out. Silence hangs in the air. Ah, right. The party.

I stand up and make my way over to Axle's room. I glance in, seeing only his messy clothes on the floor. I step out into the main room and wince at the bright sunlight streaming through the windows.

He should be back by now.

I go back down the hall to the bathroom at the end, but the door is wide open.

"Axle?"

I run into the main room, still not seeing him anywhere.

"Axle?"

As I shout, a loud sound erupts just outside my door. I march toward the door. As I swing it open, I find out exactly what woke me up.

A horde of people are marching past my open door. They wear modified earpieces that create massive projections above their heads. I am not able to make out the text at this angle. A man wears a large shirt that hangs on his knees. Prime Termani's face is sprayed on the back, with 'X's on his eyes like the graffiti I saw earlier. The man screams 'Fuck Termani', punching his fist in the air. The projection disappears above his head and reassembles above a small woman next to him. The woman wears a similar shirt. She screams the same phrase, and the projection continues to move along the makeshift mesh

32

network that the protestors have created. I glance around, and a hundred people wear similar shirts. The projection hops across through the crowd from one protestor to the next while they march like they're going to war.

I step out the door, shutting it behind me.

What is going on?

I walk alongside the crowd toward the capitol building. More doors open and more people, wearing the same shirts, join the crowd. Soon I'm caught up in the middle of everyone. Another scream follows, and I'm smacked in the back of the head. Turning around, I see someone with the projection above his head. It reads, in a graffiti style, 'Free the kids!' The projection flickers, attempting to connect to my earpiece. When it fails to find the mesh network on mine, it moves ahead to someone in front of me.

Guards flank the crowd on both sides, all wearing the same dark gray armor and holstered Plasmars. Just like the guard that I saw last night, they all have red 'X's painted over the butts of their weapons. What is happening? I grab the shoulder of the person in front of me, and she whips around to face me. Her face is drenched in sweat and thick black eyeliner streaks down her face from spilled tears. She stares at me with wide eyes.

"What's going on?" I ask.

"They took our kids," the protester shouts in my face, turning her body away from me. I grip her shoulder tighter, pulling her back toward me. I notice a small hash mark tattoo on the shoulder I grab. She's served a prison sentence before. I look around and find that a lot of the protesters share similar markings.

"Which kids?"

"The school," she says. "There was a graduation party at Crathenos Upper. The guards just swarmed in. I saw it myself—" People nearby begin shouting in agreement.

Axle was at the graduation party.

A drop of sweat glides down the side of my face. The tattoos make sense now. These are parents who don't want the same fate for their kids. Everyone's heard whispers of the brutal 'reintegration' programs used in the Termani Prison.

33

"Did anyone escape? Was anyone able to leave the building? Did the guards take everyone?" I shake my head with more questions, but she's already gone—lost in the crowd. I clench my fists and push through the throng of protestors. Unlike with the guards barricading the edges of the crowd, most protestors let me pass. I move forward, pushing people aside as they swear and grumble at me. I break into a run, shoving through the crowd with a growing ferocity. I pass the SpeedTunnel and enter the center of the city. The capitol building looms in front of me, its artificial vines stabbing at the sky. In front of the building, a stage has been erected and surrounding it is almost a hundred more guards. These guards have their Plasmars in their hands, pointing them at the crowd. No shots have gone off yet. The Plasmars emit blue glows from their handles.

At least the Plasmars are still on stun then. They probably want to keep people alive to 'reintegrate.'

Shit. What's gonna happen to Axle?

The crowd continues screaming, passing hundreds of signs between them. People press against me on either side as I stare at the stage.

The door to the capitol building swings open, and a man steps out. Prime Termani. Dressed in the same white suit from his election announcement, now layered with a long white trench coat. The crowd yells as Prime Termani makes his way to the edge of the stage.

"Hello." It's even worse in person. His voice, although easy to understand, is filled with layers of screeching static. He sounds inhuman, terrifying. This is a man far removed from the civilians around him.

The crowd silences immediately, almost everyone taking an involuntary step back. Prime Termani paces back and forth, his masked eyes seemingly scanning the crowd even though it's impossible to tell underneath that cloth mask. With each step he takes, the crowd takes a deep breath. The rhythm feels hypnotic. The Prime's suit clings to his thin frame. His movements look like they are programmed to seem natural but are missing certain human subtleties. His trench coat billows behind him with his steps. His hands reach forward toward the people, and the crowd responds with whimpers of fear.

"I understand all of you are upset. You have every reason to be upset. Your newly elected Prime just forced a group of innocent individuals into mandatory testing. But I encourage you to redirect that anger, that fear, at those who caused it. Because the Primordialists are still out there, and they are growing in number." Prime Termani enunciates each word, and his loud voice reverberates in the city square. "Our forefathers used the Primordial Stones for good so that all of you can live without fear. They are the reason why all of you can openly protest in front of me without significant repercussions. They are the reason none of you even know whether you're Cortenian or Saberren at all. They are the reason it does not matter." Prime Termani stops pacing and turns to face the crowd. He takes a deep breath, which echoes through the crowd.

"The Primordialists are planning to use the Stones to destroy society as we know it. They want to rob you of your freedoms. And they have already attempted to infiltrate the testing center."

"What are the tests?" a voice shouts from the crowd.

Prime Termani pauses, and sighs. Static crackles with the sigh. "While I cannot tell you the details of the testing environment, I will tell you what we are testing for. The Primordialists intend to separate Saberrens and Cortenians, and they themselves consist of mostly self-proclaimed Saberrens. If we want to save the people and stop the Primordialists, we have to be able to distinguish between Cortenians and Saberrens before they can. The testing will allow us to classify people based on the differing immune systems that separate the two groups."

"You didn't have to kidnap a bunch of kids," another voice yells. Prime Termani's hand twitches.

"In order to perform an effective test, I have to ensure that all other variables are the same, or at least similar. By selecting the recent graduates of Crathenos Upper, I am ensuring that the only significant difference between the Saberrens and Cortenians among them are their immune systems. Since they're all approximately the same age, they'll share similar physical development stages. Although tradition states not to interrupt affairs such as graduation celebrations, your safety is my priority."

The protester wasn't lying. They took Axle. My mind flashes to an image I saw a long time ago. A bloodied man chained to a wall. Guards beating him with chain whips. Reintegration programs.

But is Axle in the prison? Prime Termani didn't mention where the testing site was. I need to know. I shoot my hand up to get the Prime's attention.

"They're kids," someone screams, the words echoing across the crowd. I keep my hand raised, waiting for Prime Termani to acknowledge me.

"They. Are. Not. Kids." Prime Termani paces back and forth across the stage. "They're sixteen, making them adults by law."

"What about those who skipped ahead in school?" another crowd member screams. My vision blurs with tears.

Prime Termani hesitates. "That was an oversight. If I took anyone under sixteen, they will be returned."

I wipe sweat off my head. My heart is pounding in my ears, drowning out the crowd. I sway unsteadily back and forth.

"What about the rest? How long will they be imprisoned?" someone asks. Imprisoned.

"I do not know," Prime Termani sighs. "It depends how long the testing takes and how long it takes to find the Primordialists and eliminate them."

"You took my daughter," a parent screams.

"I'm sorry."

"My kids," another one screams.

"I'm sorry for that as well."

"Why?" a voice demands from the crowd.

"I already told you. It was necessary."

The crowd is so loud, I can't distinguish between the questions being thrown at the Prime and his answers.

"Where is the testing site?" I shout. I can hardly hear myself over the crowd. I push forward through more people. "Where is the—" A protester slams into me from the side, running toward Prime Termani. He shrieks and throws his earpiece at the stage. It carries the projection with it. Another protester soon follows with her earpiece. Then another. The crowd erupts as protesters scream and throw their signs. Some tear off their shirts, tossing them at the stage. On the stage, Prime Termani steps away from the flying earpieces and shirts. The projections from the earpieces crowd together on the edge of the stage.

People charge at the stage, but the guards point their Plasmars at the charging protesters. The protesters stay back, but continue screaming at the guards and at Prime Termani. Prime Termani retreats carefully, never taking his eyes off the crowd as he steps back. I step forward, trip, and catch myself with hands and knees on the ground. My injured hands scream in protest. The crowd runs on either side of me, jostling me as I try to get back up. I have to do something. I need to know where Axle is.

The sheer mass of the crowd is too much for the guards to stop. Guards stumble backward, pressed up against the step. All I can do is stare at the filthy concrete and wait for my senses to return. I feel tears crawling down my face. The shouts and shrieks around me unite into one roar. The crowd attacks as one. I feel my forgotten earpiece on my head. It's partly chipped, from when I threw it back at home. I force myself up, eyes on the stage.

A wild protester crawls up onto the stage. I yell a warning as a guard moves up on the stage to block him. The protester runs at the guard, but the guard doesn't even flinch as she shoots him with her Plasmar. The air crackles as the energy blast hits the man in the chest. His body goes limp. The man tumbles backward, rolling off the stage.

"Fuck you," a protester screams, and soon the entire crowd chants the curse at Prime Termani and his guards. The crowd pushes forward and more protesters clamber onto the stage. The guards array themselves across the stage, stunning the protesters with their Plasmars. Stunned protesters fall off the stage, immediately replaced by more clambering bodies.

One of the guards shoves unconscious bodies off the stage's edge. A protester spits at him, and his finger hovers over a switch at the back of his weapon. The angry woman hoists herself onto the stage. Instead of attacking the guard immediately, she throws a torn shirt at him. The guard throws up his arm to bat it away. The Plasmar now gives off a soft orange glow. Shit. His finger must have slipped and pressed the button. The guard doesn't seem to notice as the Plasmar makes a faint hum. The woman takes a step toward him, and he shoots her with the Plasmar. The energy blast blows through her body and blood spatters surrounding protestors. She flies off the stage and hits the ground with a sickening crunch.

Fuck.

Everyone freezes, even the guards. The guard who just shot the protester steps away from the dead body, his Plasmar shaking in his hands. The rest of the guards quickly regroup, allowing Prime Termani to turn and bolt for the door of the capitol building.

What the fuck?

The crowd recoils as one. Everyone scatters, screaming and fleeing from the stage and Prime Termani as possible.

I step back, turn, and sprint through the crowd. I spare a glance behind me. Prime Termani steps through the door, leaving the guards outside. The crowd tramples each other, stampeding in their panic.

I reach for my earpiece and start a message to the woman who sent the photo with Axle.

"Is Axle with you?" The message sends, then fails. A beep tells me that the receiving end has been disabled.

Shit. Islorr's fucking Blood. What now?

The crowd carries me down a slope in the street, and rails appear on either side of me. I'm inside a large SpeedTunnel station. Swarms of people queue in scattered lines. The walls, floor, and ceiling are all painted the same sleek white. The only things hinting at depth and distance in the massive room are holographic signs. Large translucent screens hover near the ceiling, listing destinations in big bold text: 'Lusia,' 'Fendar,' 'Wylak'. They are all of Termani's neighboring districts. Alongside these are much smaller signs listing the names of cities in Termani. On either side of the large room are magnetic tracks along the ground. A small line of people in the center of the station is queuing before a vaguely person-shaped robot. The robot has thinner eyes than Prime Termani's mask, and its hands somehow move more naturally. I get in the shortest ticket line. I need to get out of the city. I glance up at the signs again, my eyes settling on the one I know the most about. I can go to Lusia, that's safe. Wait. Axle. I can't just leave him alone in Termani. But the streets here could be a bloodbath soon. What if I came back? Maybe. I don't know. Should I go to Lusia? I don't have my stuff. My ears start to ring, and I instinctively glance around for her silhouette. Not now.

"Where would you like to travel?" the robot asks me. I can't tell what kind of accent his voice is trying to emulate. The line moved fast.

"Uhh…" I glance around. The ringing increases. I notice a silhouette start to take shape on a pillar. I glance at the exit to the SpeedTunnel. I can't just leave Axle.

"Hurry up," someone barks behind me. To my left, a streamlined, gray-painted train pulls into the station. A small sign above the train reads 'Voltaris Island.' My mind flashes with an image of the guard's Plasmar that I saw earlier, the logo covered with red paint. The guards hate Voltaris. I look back again, then focus on the robot in front of me. I won't have a chance at convincing the Prime with the protests going on. Once that calms down, I'll come back. I will come back.

"Voltaris Island," I say.

The robot's eyes flash blue. "That will be twelve ferrings."

Damn. It used to be nine. I press a button on my earpiece, activating a blue laser that interacts with the scanners on the robot's flashing blue eyes.

The silhouette fades away.

CHAPTER 7

I grab the knob of the lab door inside Voltaris Tower, eyeing the mismatched lock. Turning the unlocked knob, I swing open the old door. The lab somehow looks bleaker in the daylight as I take in the scientists at work behind their desks, mixing the serum with acids and bases, and leaning over their microscopes to check that the powder has properly dissolved. These idiots don't even know what they're making in here. I step into the room and shut the door behind me. Heads lift, and I'm greeted by a room of blanks stares. All of the scientists wear black and white acrylic masks over their faces. The masks are mostly identical, with black rings around their eye holes and dark mesh coverings over their mouths. White acrylic fills the gaps. The masks aren't entirely identical though. They're roughly molded to represent the person underneath. Acrylic cheekbones, brows, and jaws are all that hint at the people underneath. Renna, standing at our desk, points at me. Heat floods my cheeks, and I reach up to my bare face. I forgot my mask.

Casting my face down, I hurriedly walk over to my desk to stand next to Renna. I lean down to rummage in the bottom drawer where I keep a set of spare generic masks. I scoff, picking up one of the extra masks. I place it on my face, the hard acrylic pressing into my skin. This mask is not designed for my face.

"This is the third time this season you've forgotten your mask," Renna says. I close the drawer and open the one above it. Only one lab coat waits in the drawer, with the new green stain. I remove my overcoat and swap it out for lab coat from the drawer.

"Well, I don't understand why we have—"

"Woah, what happened to your lab coat?" Renna interrupts. "This wasn't there yesterday," she says, lifting the edge of my coat. A couple of people glance over at me, but I don't get a good look at their expressions.

"I spilled some serum on it," I snap, tugging the coat free from Renna's grip. "What are we working on today?"

"I didn't see you spill anything yesterday." Her voice cuts across the lab. A few more scientists look up from their desks, then lean back down to work.

I grab Renna's shoulder and peer down at her. She's a lot shorter than me. Her curly hair spills out from behind her mask, giving her a slightly wild appearance. Today it's messier than usual, and the well-tailored clothes under her lab coat reveal mismatching patterns. Renna moves away from me as I lean over her. I can overhear others muttering under their breaths.

"Listen," I lower my voice. "I will explain everything when I learn more. For now, just tell me what we're working on today, and let's get to work."

I can almost feel Renna's unwavering gaze behind her mask. "What were you doing?"

"Renna, please. Not right now."

Renna hesitates, looks around the room, then turns back to me and sighs. "We are making more serum."

"Again? How much damn serum do they want us to make?" I ask, looking around the desk. The quota container is overstuffed with dozens of empty vials. Renna opens a supply closet next to our desk and hoists out a large metal canister with glass sides. Black powder swirls around in the acidic liquid, kept moving by a fast-spinning stir bar attached to the bottom of the canister's interior. An eerie green light emanates from the mixture as the powder slowly dissolves. I look over at the other desks; everyone is mixing fluids together with robotic efficiency. "This is ridiculous. They're paying us to do grunt work that they can easily automate with machines."

"Maybe they don't want to buy machines," Renna says, unscrewing the cap of our canister. I turn back to the closet, pulling out a glass bottle labeled 'base.' I undo the cap and dump the contents into the stirring fluid. Renna screws the cap on and turns the dial at the bottom of the canister up. The stir bar hums even louder than before.

"We're talking about Voltaris Industries, the biggest company on the continent." I grunt. "They have more than enough money to spend."

Renna shrugs. "Maybe they're avoiding registration laws. Registering a machine in Termani? Paperwork nightmare."

"Once again, it's Voltaris Industries." I turn the dial even more. The noise is now akin to a drill. The green light intensifies. The curves on Renna's mask take on harsh shadows. "Besides, if they don't want to register machines in Termani, they could just manufacture the serum in another district without those regulations."

"Then they have to register the imports into Termani," Renna adds.

"So Voltaris is just lazy? That doesn't sound right."

"No, Termani is just stupid," someone says at the desk next to me. The desk that I borrowed the scope from last night. I don't even know how he heard us over the noises of the mixing serum. Renna and I turn to the scientist. He has gray hairs that flop over the front of his mask. His lab partner looks away and remains silent. "Did you hear about Prime Termani's mandatory testing?" He leans forward conversationally, resting his arms on his own canister. "I think it's nonsense. They just want to control our lives. I bet the Primordialists don't even exist," he continues.

I sigh. "Then leave Termani…"

"And go where?" the scientist chuckles. "The hippies in Lusia aren't much better."

"They don't have regulations in Lusia," I say. Renna and I start walking toward the double doors to grab more powder and acid. The scientist shifts as if to follow, and his lab partner throws her hands up.

"Calm down," he says to her, walking over to us. "Besides, I can't abandon the lab. We're doing good work here." I roll my eyes. "We just have to vote better in the next election."

"Nothing will change," I mumble. I kick open one of the double doors and Renna shuffles through sideways. I walk through the door and the scientist tries to follow us. I face him. "Why don't you get back to work?" He shudders and scurries back toward his desk. The door swings closed behind me. "Idiot."

"You're the one who entertained him," Renna says, and we start walking up the spiral staircase. They still have yet to fix the lifter. We only go up a couple of floors, then walk over to the door labeled 'Oven.' Renna shoves the unlocked door open with her shoulder.

Heat floods my body, despite the huge fans surrounding the metal oven at the center of the room. Through the glass opening, streams of plasma attack the usually black powder, now glowing bright green under the extreme heat. The powder rests on ceramic sheets. Renna hands me a heat-absorbing cover that I clip onto the mask that I already wear. I reach for two sets of thick gloves, tossing the other set to Renna. I head forward toward the oven and turn the dial off. The plasma streams immediately dissipate into the air. With our thick gloves on, Renna and I carefully open the oven door. Scorching dry air bathes over us. We grab the heavy ceramic sheet from the oven.

"Grab the acid," I say to Renna. She nods and lets go of the sheet. Renna opens a freezer filled with canisters of strong acid. She pops off the cap and places it and the canister on top of the freezer. She kicks the freezer door shut and grabs the ceramic sheet again opposite me. We carefully bring the sheet to the canister and hover the corner above its opening. We slowly tilt the sheet, and the hot powder slides down grooves in the sheet into the acid. It sizzles as it transfers its heat to the cool acid.

While Renna deals with the stir bar, I place the ceramic sheet back in the oven. I press a button on the side of the oven door, and black powder pours from a chute onto the sheet. I close the door and turn the dial back to maximum heat.

Renna grabs the canister with the acid and powder mixture. I flick off the lights and we step out of the room. I shut the door and we head back downstairs, but I stop before we reach the lab's floor.

"What are you doing?" Renna asks.

"Asking a question."

"Whatever," Renna says, straining. She continues heading down the stairs. I walk down a hall of the current floor and approach the door labeled 'Laboratory Office.' This door is old, like the front door, and must have been part of the original building. I grab the handle and yank it. It doesn't budge. I shrug and knock on the door.

"Who is it?" a man calls from the other side. He has a familiar, gruff voice.

"Sapphire," I say. "Can you let me in?"

"What do you want, Sapphire?" he asks.

I pause, clenching my fists. "What is in the serum?"

"You've asked me this before. I will not give you an answer."

"I am your daughter. You should trust me."

The voice scoffs from behind the door. "You may be my daughter, but at work, I am your boss. I am not telling you what is in the serum."

My nails dig into my palms. "Then tell me what it does."

"I will not do that either."

I grit my teeth, and start to turn away, but stop myself. Not this time. Not without an answer. "The serum does not respond to any of the tests as it should. The information given about it must therefore be incorrect. We can't run accurate experiments blind. We should know what the serum is made of."

"Right now, your job is to make more serum, not to perform experiments," my father says flatly. "You may leave."

"This doesn't make sense."

"You may leave," he repeats. I shudder.

"You are wasting my time. Wasting everyone's," I say, my voice raising. "Is this about Termani's registration laws? Why are you so afraid to draw attention with this project? You're too lazy to register a machine, so you make us do manual labor? Is that it?"

"Sapphire… If I have to ask you one more time—"

"I deserve to know what I am making."

"You *do not* deserve anything," he yells. "If you do not want to work under the conditions provided, then you may quit your position at Voltaris. Is that clear?"

I stomp my foot. "I will figure out what this serum does."

"Sapphire, you are a smart girl," my father says. "But I assure you, you will not."

CHAPTER 8

LUKAS

L ight floods in from the right. Yawning, I turn toward it. Large blinds slide open to gently wake passengers, revealing an expanse of ocean and sky. The sky is a washed-out turquoise bleeding into the richer, more saturated hue of the ocean. Enormous cell towers jut out from the water, following along the train's path. The train's tracks are raised high above the ocean, and I peer out the window at the undisturbed water zooming past me.

Voltaris Island rises from the flat horizon, an island covered in artifacts of its history. Buildings span its surface from end to end, and I can barely glimpse open ground between them. The city's rapid growth looks like it will claim the sea next. The buildings are different from those of Crathenos. While Crathenos has sharp points at the tops of the buildings, the island city's buildings are much more rectangular. The few gaps in the skyline are littered with poorly concealed rubble. A remnant of the island's history as a prison. The cliff edges of the island are bombarded with so much white spray I can't spot many flat beaches. The teeming aquatic life here made the island a busy fishing industry long before Termani joined the Union of Ayzol-Carkun.

Shrubbery thrives in the humid climate, claiming back metropolitan areas despite people's attempts at clearing the overgrowth. Unlike Crathenos, Voltaris Island isn't plagued with its own safety department roaming the narrow streets. Ever since Voltaris Industries bought the island from

Termani, they have defied nearly all attempts of government intervention. In addition to nature being allowed to persist unchecked, the island refuses to install light poles or monitoring cameras too.

One thing this island does have in common with Crathenos is an enormous central building. Giant 'V' signs struck through with lightning bolts cover all four sides of this building. Voltaris Tower is the newest development on the island, as is evident by the lack of plant growth anywhere near it. From the train's vantage, I can just about make out people running in and out of the double doors of the surrounding complex. Many wear large white coats, beckoning unwanted reminders of Prime Termani's trench coat. Although these are probably meant to protect them from hazardous materials.

I turn away from Voltaris Tower and back to the ocean and sky. All I can see is Axle, hanging from thick metal chains tied to either side of a wall. They can't just chain him though. Why would they? It's just a test. It'll be over soon. As my vision flips between the view out the window and images of Axle, Prime Termani's crackling static sigh echoes through my mind. It's just a test, a damn test. The sigh's static screeches until I can't tell it apart from Axle's scream. I instinctually clamp my hands over my ears, but the sound continues haunting my mind. Why would they chain him for a test? They won't chain him for a test.

My ears start ringing.

Oh no. I pull at my hair, pressing my head against the cool glass. They can't chain him for a test. I tug at my hair so tightly that it hurts. Prime Termani surely has someone he cares about. Perhaps I can use that to convince him to free Axle. I can't wait until the protests are over. I should go back now. Plead him to release Axle. I shift in my seat. No. That won't work. But maybe I could take Axle's place. That could work. What am I thinking? I release my hair and lean my head back, staring up at the train cart's ceiling. What would Axle do? What would he do? I can't just abandon him. Why did I think it's a good idea to go to Voltaris? I look out at the island, slowly drawing nearer to dominate my view. I've always wanted to explore the place. But not now. I'm not staying on that island. I have to go back. I have to.

"Hello."

I whip around, expecting to see her silhouette. Instead, a large blue projection assembles itself on the wall away from the seats, near the door. All the people around me turn to face the screen as well. Prime Termani sits in front of the camera, in the same dark room that he recorded his election speech in. "Earlier today, there was a protest near the capitol building. During that protest, a number of people were fatally wounded. Postmortem investigations revealed that these protesters were none other than Primordialists. The Primordialists are more involved than I had previously thought, and it is unfortunate that they were able to do as much harm to Termani as they have. It is due to the quick actions of the guards that I am still here to speak to you today. I can assure you that the guards will be rewarded, and that the Primordialists will no longer compromise the safety of Termani."

The screen flashes off and the train buzzes in a hushed noise as people shift in their seats, grumbling and swearing under their breaths.

"That's all you have to say for yourself?" I mutter.

Just as I'm about to lean back, a series of bangs against the ground clambers through the train. Chatter dies out. I twist my neck toward the sound. From the left, a large man strides through the train's hallway. He wears a chestplate made of deep gray metal. A guard. I look up at his face. The man is bald, with an overgrown, scruffy beard and thick eyebrows. Despite the armor he wears over his chest, his arms are bare. His whole body is muscular, but his arms are massive, with veins meandering all over them. I scoff in amusement, glad to have a distraction.

I glance down at the other side of the and see more guards in the distance. "Fucking murderers." I force a chuckle. "Does Prime Termani think Primordialists will be on a SpeedTrain?" I say, my voice rising. The absurd image of the woman's body blowing to bits surfaces in mind. The Prime lied so casually about that. "What's gonna happen on a fucking SpeedTrain?" I yell, my body shaking. The muscled guard snaps around to face me. I tremble as he stares into my eyes.

"What did you say?" he asks. His eyes scan the rest of my body, squinting as he notices my wrapped hands and the blood on my shirt.

"I, uh..." I stare up at the guard.

"Stand up," the guard orders.

Sighing, I step up from my seat. The passengers around me stop whatever they're doing to watch me and the guard. I am taller than the guard, but that doesn't make him any less intimidating. My eyes flit down to the Plasmar strapped to his belt. I shudder as I recall that blast at the protest again.

The guard paces around me, examining the sorry state of my clothes and hands. My fists clench unintentionally, and the guard draws his Plasmar, pointing it at my face.

"Were you involved in the protest in Crathenos?" he asks.

"No, I was not," I say, glancing around at the other passengers, who continue to watch the confrontation. "But if I were, it would be within my rights."

"You have no rights as a terrorist." The guard's thumb hovers over the mode button on the back of his Plasmar. He notices me watching and removes his thumb. "If you are not a Primordialist, then why are you covered in blood?"

"It is my own blood."

"Your own blood?"

"Yes, sir."

"Why would you be covered in your own blood?" the guard stares at me, waiting for an answer. His finger rests on the trigger. Thankfully the Plasmar is still set to stun. He wouldn't believe me if I said I punched a wall and a tree.

A soft lurch and a ding echoing across the SpeedTrain signals our arrival at Voltaris Island. The doors scattered across the train slide open, and the passengers begin shuffling off. I turn back to the guard, whose eyes narrow at the open doors. The guards are not allowed to set foot on Voltaris soil unless absolutely necessary. I remember when Voltaris bullied the former Prime Termani into making that deal years ago. I have always wanted to go to Voltaris Island for that reason.

I need to get off the train.

My whole body shaking, I jump backward and run, ducking behind disembarking passengers. The guard stumbles in his pursuit and fires a shot from his Plasmar. The shot misses me and hits one of the passengers instead. He collapses from the shot, leaving the guard with wide eyes. He shouts something incomprehensible at me, aiming to fire another shot. The remaining passengers scream and push each other out the door to get away. The flow of the crowd takes me with it, and I shoot one last glance at the guard before running off onto the platform with everyone else.

What have I done?

CHAPTER 9

AXLE

I lean against the wall of the crowded room, my whole body trembling. The room is small and cold, and over a hundred students are tightly pressed together so tightly I can barely breathe. Vents above us supply barely filtered air, and I have to look down to stop the dust from entering my eyes. Many of the students around me have dust caked on their cheeks from crying. Their eyes are bloodshot. I know what it's like in these prisons. I shudder as I recall rumors of the intense 'reintegration' process. I don't blame them for their tears.

Everyone's screams of defiance have long since died out. Now only whimpers of fear cut through the near silence. Most of the time I can only hear my own heartbeat. Each beat follows in rapid succession, and my lungs work just as fast to keep up. I don't know what this testing is that the guards spoke of, but I hope that it doesn't last much longer. I already despise this room. I don't know how long I've been here, but it's long enough that I'm missing my bed. And Lukas. I haven't even finished packing yet. He must be worried about me.

"Please let me out of here," a student pleads, banging on our cell's metal door. This is not even close to all of the students they abducted, so there must be more rooms just like this one. I wonder how much space Prime Termani dedicated to this testing. I haven't seen anyone I know yet. I hope my friends are faring better than I am.

The student eventually stops banging on the door and slumps down in front of it. But it doesn't take long for the door to actually open. The student falls backward, and other students stampede over her toward the door, but they don't get very far.

Four heavily armored guards step into the room holding large Plasmars. Everyone shuffles back, and the trampled student forces herself up to limp away from the guards. I notice the blue lights on the Plasmars and let out a sigh of relief.

The guards survey the room, their Plasmars pointed at us. One of the guards steps forward, and everyone tries to move in further back, huddling into a tight mess of bodies. I am shoved back against a student with rancid breath. I resist the urge to gag and keep my eyes on the four guards.

The lead guard follows the trampled girl. She's covered in footprints and, although I can't see her face, I can hear her muffled sobs. The guard grabs her, she whimpers in protest, and the four guards exit the room. The metal door slams shut behind them.

It only takes a few minutes before the guards return. The student doesn't return with them though. It's just the guards.

One of the guards grabs another student. He resists, and his button-down shirt wrinkles as he tries to shrug his arm out of the guard's grip.

"Where is the other girl?" he asks, standing still. Well not completely still; I can see his body shaking.

"She completed her testing," the guard replies with a gruff voice.

"So she was let out of the prison?" the student asks.

"That information is classified," the guard says, tightening his grip on the student. "Let's go," he says to the other guards, and they drag the student out of the room. He looks back at us with pleading eyes.

"We need to know what happens in this test," someone sporting an oversized pinstriped tie says, pushing past everyone to stand at the front of the room and face us. "Alright everyone, here's what we're going to do. One of us is going to attempt to see what's going on and then run back here."

"Are you insane?" another student yells. She wears a flurry dress. "There are four guards with Plasmars. We'll be killed."

The student with the tie grins. "No, we won't. They need us alive for the testing. Whoever escapes just has to leave before the testing happens." He looks around the room. "Any volunteers?"

Someone bursts into tears at the front left corner of the room. The tie-wearing student turns to the one in tears. "How about you?"

"Please, no, don't make me…" he pleads. The tie-wearing student walks up to the crying student and grabs his arm. The crying student tears his hand free. "I'm not going," he screams, sending spit flying into the air. The student with the tie looks around.

"Guys, I need some help here," he says. A couple of other students grab the crying student and drag him to the door.

"Please, don't make me go," he yells. "Please!"

"Be brave," the tie-wearing student smiles. "This is for the greater good."

"No, please," the crying student yells, trying to scramble away as the door opens. Just like last time, the previous student does not return. As expected, the guard grabs whoever's unlucky enough to be closest to the door. The kid turns back to us with tears as he's dragged outside. The door shuts behind him with a hollow thud.

"Now we wait," the student says, adjusting his tie.

"Why did you do that?" asks the student who had objected earlier.

"I already explained," he says. "It's for the greater good."

"Good for who?" the other student fires back. He doesn't answer her question.

A minute passes in tense silence as everyone listens for the sacrificed student to give us any clues. Everyone jumps at a sudden banging on the door. It must be the crying student. He screams something, but I can't hear what he said. I hear a blast, and the screaming cuts off. I stiffen. Is he dead?

Immediately the room erupts into chaos. Students wail in indignation, and others start shoving themselves toward the back of the room. I step back too, ignoring the bad smell of the dude behind me.

"Guys, guys. It's okay," the first student says. "He's not dead. The Plasmars were on stun."

"They could've turned the stun off," someone says.

"I told you already. They don't want us dead. Just wait until they open the door. There won't be any blood."

"But why was he screaming? The testing must've scared him," someone else says.

"What is the testing?" another student asks.

"How are we supposed to know?" yet another says.

The door opens, and there really isn't any blood on the floor. I let out a small sigh. All of the students are pressed tightly against the back of the room, and the four guards all enter the empty space. There isn't anyone at the front for them to select. One of the guards locks eyes with me.

My heart pounds as the guard pushes through the crowd and grabs my arm. Resistance clearly doesn't help. I let him drag me out of the room. Beyond the door stretches a long hallway lined with more doors. The guards drag me toward one final door at the far end. One of them pulls out an empty syringe and shoves it into my arm. I wince as the syringe sucks blood from my vein. The guard quickly pulls the syringe away and places it in a bag attached to his belt.

Turning back to me, he and the other guards shove me against the wall next to that final door and wait. Faint sounds leak through the door. I hear muffled footsteps scuffling around. Sounds like the kid they dragged away earlier, but it could just as easily be someone from another room. One of the guards cracks the door open, peers inside, then lets it draw shut on its own. I shoot a quick glance to make sure the guards aren't looking, then ease my foot into the door's path. I carefully crane my head around the door's edge.

My breath catches. The gasp dies in my throat.

Piled up in the corner of the otherwise empty room are bodies upon bodies of dead students, limbs bent at surreal angles. There are so many students, more than I remember being at the party. Blood and saliva pour foaming out of their gaping mouths. Their eyes are rolled back into their heads. I try to look away, but I'm rooted in place. The student is strapped to a chair in the middle of the room, tears streaking down his cheeks. A shadowed figure looms over him. I can't glimpse any of his features.

"Please, please, I don't want to die," the student whimpers. The shadow-man holds up a glowing green syringe, pressing the plunger to purge air bubbles at the thin needle's end. "I don't want to die," he screams as the shadow-man closes in on him. "Please…" He lurches, straining against the leather straps of the chair. His eyes are locked onto a body lying at his feet, white foam pouring from its mouth. "P-p-please."

The shadow-man jabs the needle through the student's shirt and into his arm, pressing on the plunger. The green fluid drains completely, and the shadow-man steps back. Tears pour from his eyes as he convulses. I flick my gaze between the foaming mouth of the dead student and the still living student spasming in the center of the room. His arm blackens near his wrist, spreading across his palm, and smoke rises from his uniform. The shadow-man's head tilts as he studies the green flames bursting from the student's charring hand. I nearly stumble backward but catch myself against the door frame.

The green flames slowly change hue to more standard orange flames. The student's convulsions stop, sweat pouring from his face. "I- I'm not dead…" He looks up at the shadowed figure with a face full of hope. "I'm not dead," he exclaims, staring at the flames dancing across his palm, licking at the fabric of his shirt. The shadow-man steps toward him, unsheathes a knife, and slashes through the student's neck. I shudder, and have to gulp down my vomit. His head topples off his body and thuds to the floor, rolling. The shadow-man unstraps the limp body from the chair, pushes it to the ground, and drags it to the pile of dead students. He turns back to grab the severed head when his gaze snaps up to me. The details of his face remain hidden, but two deep black angular eyes stare at me.

I yank my foot free from the door and slam it shut. My heart hammers in my chest.

CHAPTER 10

SAPPHIRE

I turn away from the door, fists clenched so hard my nails bite my palms. I descend the stairs. My father's words echo in my head. I *will* figure it out. I will. I have to.

I hit the landing at the bottom of the stairs and shoulder the double doors open. The doors fly open, and I stumble into the main laboratory. The lab looks the same as when Renna and I left to get more supplies; everyone's bent over their stations, mixing serum. Renna leans her chest against the steel-and-glass canister we left stirring earlier, carefully pouring the mixed serum into separate vials one at a time. The canister trembles as the serum streams through the vacuum spout. The other canister that we had just grabbed is out of sight, put away in the closet as it mixes.

Renna looks up from her work; her eyes turn to face me. She pulls back from the desk and the canister tips to the side. I rush forward, shoving a passing scientist out of the way. He throws his hands up, but I shoot past him and grab the canister to steady it on the desk. A drop of serum spills onto my hand. I whip around and head to the far edge of the desk, yanking open a narrow drawer with a faucet inside. Cool water washes over my hand, disposing of the serum. I wipe my hand dry on my lab coat.

"Did you get the answers you wanted?" Renna asks. I hold the canister still as she fills the remaining vials and sets them on a stand to rest.

I shake my head. "Nothing."

Renna scoffs. "What I expected." She pauses, her eyes scanning my stained lab coat just like she did earlier. "You didn't have that yesterday."

"You already pointed that out. You probably just didn't notice me spill."

"You didn't spill. I watch you all the time, Sapphire. The only reason you spilled a drop just now is because I was clumsy. When you're focused on a task, you don't mess up." Renna steps closer to me. "You're up to something. Were you at the lab after hours?"

I grab her shoulder, pulling her in close to whisper in her ear. "If you don't stop asking questions, I'm going to have to do something about it. I told you I'd tell you when I learned more. Right now, I just can't risk it. If I'm wrong, then I might get in trouble. At least right now there's no evidence to get me in trouble for anything."

"You might get in trouble now," Renna hisses, her glare cutting. "Tell me everything, or I'll tell your father you broke into the lab."

My stomach drops. "You don't have evidence. I'm not saying anything."

"Ok..." Renna smirks, ripping her shoulder from my grasp. "Empty your pockets."

I shake my head. "You don't know what you're talking about."

"Remove your lab coat then," she orders. My hands move under my coat, fingers finding hidden handles. "It's no secret that you have something you're not supposed to have. Look around, everyone knows it." I glance around the room; a few scientists dart quick glances in our direction. "The only reason you're here is because of your father. I don't think Prime Termani wants dangerous people like you in the workforce."

I clench my fists tighter on the handles. "Prime Termani cannot do anything. This island is owned by Voltaris."

Renna's smirk slips. "There's a new Prime now. Old agreements can be overturned." Renna reaches for my lab coat, and I step back to keep my belongings concealed. "Now tell me what's going on." I look around again, and all the scientists are now openly staring at us. I meet their stares until they return to their work out of discomfort.

I step closer to Renna and whisper, "Fine, but you must not say anything." Renna's demeanor shifts. Her body relaxes, and she smiles. "I promise."

"Good." I open the supply closet and grab the mixing serum canister.

Opening the cap, I pour an alkaline solution into the canister. I crank the dial to its maximum until it sounds like a construction site. "No one can hear what I'm about to say except you." Renna nods. "I know about something in the scrum," I whisper. Her breath catches. "Partly anyway, but I know that what Voltaris is telling us is a lie."

"What do you mean?" Renna asks.

"I mean, there's something in the serum that they never mentioned. An organism. And the black powder prevents the immune system from getting to it. At least it tries to."

"Do you think this serum is supposed to be used on people?"

"It's likely." I step closer to Renna. "Voltaris wants it to be a secret. They won't register machines to make it, and they won't make it outside of Termani because they'd have to register the imports into Termani. And they won't even tell the people making the serum what they're making. Whatever Voltaris plans to use this serum for, or whoever they plan to use it on, they don't want anyone knowing about it."

"How do you know about this organism?" Renna asks. "They aren't letting us look too closely."

I spare a glance around at the scientists. None of them look like they're listening in. I lean in closer to Renna. "You were right. I snuck into Voltaris last night. I used the equipment to analyze the serum."

"I knew it," Renna exclaims. I shove my hand over her mouth. A couple of scientists glance over, then turn back to their work.

"You cannot tell anyone about this."

"I have to turn you in." Renna pushes me away and walks away from the desk. I grab her arm and pull her back. "What are you doing?" she snaps.

"Give me a day. I can prove that I am right."

Renna yanks her arm free from my grip. "And how do you intend to do that?"

"There's a door at the top of the tower that is unlabeled. I believe that the answers lie behind that door."

"And how are you gonna get behind that door?" she asks.

I grab the canister from Renna and place it down on the desk. "I'll figure something out." Renna presses her hands flat against the desk, ready to argue her point. She stares at me and sighs, her hands falling to her sides. She walks away from me.

"Renna please..."

"I'm not gonna say anything," she says, throwing her hands in the air and leaning against the wall.

Hinges squeak and I turn to glance at the double doors. They swing open as several men in suits with identical black and white masks haul a large gray box into the lab. One of them kicks the doors shut. They use the box to shove equipment aside on the central desk. Two scientists scramble to pull the equipment safely to the corner of the desk. The men step away from the box. One unfastens two flaps, throwing the lid open. The man who kicked the doors shut reaches up and taps his earpiece.

"We have the first batch," he says. He lowers his hand and gestures the other two toward the door. They both scurry around the desks and vanish through the doors. The remaining man looks from one scientist to the next, scanning the room. His deep indigo bow tie and matching indigo shoes distracts from his serious demeanor. "You may collect your samples one at a time." The scientists shuffle forward to line up, and Renna and I place ourselves roughly in the middle.

The first person steps forward and pulls a rack of five small vials from the box. The scientist in front of me blocks most of my view, but I catch sight of something red. It's not serum. Vials in hand, the scientist heads back to her desk. I crane my neck to see what's in the vials, but I still can't make out much.

The next person steps forward, grabbing their rack of five vials. One by one, the lab's scientists claim their racks without saying a word and return to their desks. Their masked faces stare in silence at the man in the middle of the room. The man's posture commands the room—spine straight, shoulders back.

The large scientist in front of me finally moves out of the way. I walk up to the box to claim my vials. They're filled with dark red fluid and their small white caps are numbered. I pick up one of the vials out of a rack and rotate it against the light. The semi-viscous burgundy liquid clings to the inside of the vials.

"Please take your vials and return to your desk," the man says. I look up at him, still holding the vial.

"Why are you giving us blood?"

"That is classified information," the man says. "Now place that back in the rack, take the rack, and leave the line."

"Where did you get this blood from?" I ask. "Was it from volunteers?"

"That is classified information," he repeats. "Return to your desk now."

I place the vial back, grab the rack, and step out of the line. I look back at the line as Renna steps up to the box. She grabs her rack and pauses, turning to me. I tilt my head to the side and Renna walks up to me.

"We were just talking about the serum being used on people," Renna whispers, placing her rack on the desk. I place mine right next to hers.

"That's what concerns me."

We wait until the last scientist returns to his desk. The man paces the room, grabbing stands of serum-filled vials and placing them into the box one-by-one. He reaches up to his earpiece, whispering something, and the two other men return. They struggle to lift the box, but eventually manage to carry it through the double doors and out of the room. The well-dressed man steps back toward the exit.

"Thank you for your good work making the serum. For a much-needed break, you will examine the blood samples that I have supplied. You are to sort the blood on a spectrum from Cortenian to Saberren, by examining the number and type of immune cells mixed in with the blood. Record the results."

The man spins around, presses one of the double doors open, and strides through. The door shuts behind him. I turn to Renna, who holds one of the vials in her hand. She looks up at me, worry creasing her brow.

"Now do you want to know what's in that room?" I ask.

Renna sighs. She unscrews the cap from one of the vials and drops a sample on the clean plate underneath the microscope. She caps the vial and returns it to its slot in the rack. Renna shoots me one last quizzical look, then leans her mask against the scope.

"What do you see?" I ask. "Pay attention to the immune cells. You won't see the organisms with this weak magnifier, but you should be able to tell that the immune cells are reacting to something. If I'm right, this blood came from test subjects exposed to the serum."

Renna shakes her head, facing me again. "Nothing."

I take her place at the scope and, as she said, there is no movement. I step away from the microscope again. "Must be a sample from before the serum was introduced."

"Maybe you're wrong about this," Renna says.

"I'm not wrong," I snap. "Let me show you. I just need the sample I made." I lean under my desk to grab the glass plate that I tossed away when I broke into the lab. There's nothing there.

Oh, shit. I knew I should've thrown them away. Or hidden them better.

"What's wrong?" Renna asks.

I stand up straight again, grabbing Renna's shoulder. "Listen, whatever happens next, I need you to trust me."

"What?"

"Just trust me."

Renna nods and returns to looking at the scope. It won't be long before Voltaris comes for me.

CHAPTER 11

LUKAS

The Voltaris SpeedTunnel is very different from the one in Crathenos. Firstly, it's significantly smaller. The section that I stand on only has two sets of rails, both heading to and from Crathenos. The tunnel is also more fortified than Crathenos. Despite the lack of safety regulations that apply to Voltaris, the tunnel still has multiple barrier pillars between the two sets of rails. I squeeze between the pillars to wait for the train heading back to Crathenos. The scared passengers pressing against me make it worse, bodies everywhere, nowhere to move. At least it helps keep me hidden.

The other set of rails already has a train calibrated to head back to Crathenos. The passengers waiting to board this SpeedTrain are dressed entirely differently from those who just got off it. There's only a handful of them, dressed in all-black suits. They lug around large metal boxes engraved with V's crossed through with lightning bolts. Voltaris.

Though they face away from me, something's off about their faces. They wear something black and white that covers their skin. I step closer to the train, but also so that I can get a closer look at their strange faces.

I shoot another glance at one of the employees. On his face is a mostly black mask sporting white accents around the eyeholes. My breath catches. I've seen people wearing these masks in Voltaris advertisements, but I thought that was just for privacy. I didn't expect them to wear these out in public.

The train dings. Doors along its length slide open.

"Hey," someone calls from behind me. I spin around. The panicked crowd has finally cleared out. Leaving me in the open. The guard who interrogated me earlier stands right outside the door of the SpeedTrain that I was on. He's flanked by four other guards, two on each side. All five point their Plasmars at me, blue lights glaring.

Oh fuck.

I spin back to the open SpeedTrain I was about to board. The masked Voltaris employees back away slowly as they board the train, their cold stares fixed on the guards. I step back too. The lead guard fires a blast at me. The shot misses and hits one of the Voltaris employees. The woman collapses, dropping her metal box. She and the box hit the ground with a clatter.

"Your aim sucks," one of the other guards says, stepping in front of the central guard. She raises her Plasmar at me. Before she can fire, the Voltaris employees all clamber off the train, set down their boxes, and advance on the guards.

"What are you idiots doing?" one of the employees yells. "You just knocked out one of our own."

"We don't have time for this. We're meant to be looking for her," the new guard mutters to her colleagues. She faces the Voltaris employees again and points at me. "This man ran away from a guard. That is illegal." She aims her Plasmar at me, but the angry employee shoves me aside, walking toward the guard. I make for the SpeedTrain, but the other employees are in the way. The nearest unblocked door is out of reach, and the other guards have me pinned with their eyes.

"I don't care what your job is. You are not allowed to get involved with Voltaris affairs," the employee spits, walking closer to the central guard.

"I apologize for any harm my fellow guard may have caused. Now please get out of the way."

"I'm not going anywhere until my coworker wakes up."

The guard turns to the other guards, sighs, and fires a blast. The stunned employee flops to the ground in front of her, leaving me in her line of sight. The other employees all draw their own Plasmars. Their Plasmars are bulkier than the ones wielded by the guards. They don't have stun lights. The guards' eyes dart between me and the Voltaris employees. One of the employees fires a blast at the nearest guard. Another guard pushes his comrade out of the way, leaving the ball of plasma to fizzle past and sear the side of the SpeedTrain. The guards turn as one to face the employees.

Now's my chance.

The door behind me is still blocked. I bolt for the nearest exit instead. One of the guards moves to intercept me. A Voltaris employee clips him with a right hook, and his attention snaps back.

I reach the exit just as the SpeedTrain in front of me leaves for Crathenos. There goes my ride.

Shit. Now I have to wait for the other one to calibrate.

The guards shoot the last Voltaris employee, who collapses next to the others. The guards leave the metal boxes, turning to face me.

Islorr's Blood. I'm screwed.

I turn to the stairs behind me leading down. It's the only way out of here. The guards sprint toward me, their Plasmars aimed at my face. I bolt down the stairs, out of the tunnel, and into the streets of Voltaris Island.

Now that I'm actually on the ground, the island is massive. The large buildings stretch in every direction. While smaller than their Crathenos counterparts, they loom above me. The rectangular buildings are evenly spaced throughout the city, forming a grid. The streets of the grid are also wider than they appeared from the train, but still narrow compared to Crathenos. A crowd would have to move in rows of five to comfortably squeeze between the edifices and vehicles around them. Personal rollers push through the crowd with little care for pedestrians that happen to be in their way. And that's without accounting for the shrubbery lining the streets. Shrubbery is an underestimate—these are basically trees punching through the brittle concrete. Vines spill from these unkempt trees and strangle the surrounding buildings. I step forward and trip, my boot catching on chunks of jagged concrete. The remaining rubble of the old prison serves as the pavement of the road. A poor alternative to the more expensive smooth concrete of Crathenos. The surprisingly derelict road contrasts with projection advertisements along the buildings, which rival the numbers used in Crathenos.

"What am I doing?" I mutter under my breath, my legs shaking. I glance back at the elevated SpeedTunnel as the five guards race down the stairs. I force my shaking legs to straighten and sprint down the gravelly road. One of the guards fires a shot at me. The blast grazes my left leg. The side of my leg becomes numb, forcing me to limp slightly. The guards gain on me. Adrenaline floods through me, fueling my flight despite the numbness.

As I bolt through the island city, more and more people get in my way. Despite the narrower streets, these people push past and dodge around one another without breaking their stride. People turn as I speed toward them, confusion flickering across their faces. Then they see the guards, and their eyes go wide. Most people part for me, sneering at the guards. Some of them wear T-shirts with the Voltaris logo. A few try to block my way, but angry Voltaris supporters yank them aside.

I glance back. The guards are closing in. Another guard fires a blast, and I duck behind vendor stands. The blast sails over my head. Someone collapses ahead of me. The vendors yell at the guards, but they ignore them.

I have to go somewhere. Where won't the guards go? I scan the street. Another Plasmar blast grazes my leg. My leg buckles. I can't feel where I'm stepping with my limp leg. I'm forced to slow down significantly. They want me awake to interrogate me.

My ears start ringing. I don't bother looking for her silhouette.

Come on Lukas, where won't the guards go? To the left of me, one building stands taller than the rest. It is surrounded by a massive complex that looks like what the cubed housing in Crathenos might have looked like if it were actually cared for. The puzzle-piece-shaped complex bristles with metal pillars along every edge and corner, all pointing toward the tower at its center. At the top of the tower, illuminated with a vibrant blue glow, is a giant V with a lightning bolt that cuts it in half. Voltaris Tower. The ringing stops.

Despite my numb leg, I'm able to shuffle over and reach the nearest door. The door is metal, with a small glass window at the top. I don't have time to look inside. I wrench the door open and slip inside.

CHAPTER 12

LUKAS

"Welcome to Voltaris Industries," a high-pitched robotic voice booms in the entrance way. I turn toward the commanding speakers as sleek glass double doors slide open, and swarms of people crowd around a security scanner.

Glancing behind me, I notice a large orange 'EXIT' sign above the door. I can't hear the guards outside, and I don't see them enter through the main entrance either. Did that really work?

I limp toward the crowd of people who eagerly await their tour of the largest company on the continent. Many of them are kids, wearing gray T-shirts adorned with the Voltaris 'V' and lightning bolt. Their parents urge them to stand still, but quite a few of the kids cannot contain their excitement, screaming and jumping in place. At the scanner, people place their bags and items in a container that shoots through on a conveyor belt toward the other side. Lights above the belt flash blue, signaling the customers to pass through. One at a time, people shuffle through the larger scanner.

Lined up along the walls of the extravagant room are glass displays holding various artifacts of Voltaris' history. Kids scatter toward different exhibits, their parents struggling to catch up. One of the artifacts displayed stands out, the EM-Plasmar that the Termani guards now wield. This display is on the far-right side of the expansive room, so I assume the oldest artifacts would be on the far left. Turning to the left, I weave through the crowd and barely avoid a running kid from bumping into me. My guess was correct.

The first thing displayed on this side of the room is old mining equipment. Behind a glass barrier against the wall are two items. The largest of them is a metal arm made of what looks like scrap metal welded together. Visible through the cracks of the old mining arm are bulky yellow nerve-wires, with orange and blue transmission wires snaking around them. The smaller item is a tiny fragment of a deep black metal that absorbs almost all light. If I hadn't known any better, I would have thought it was a hole in the wall.

A small kid steps onto a button outlined in blue on the floor in front of the display, and the same high-pitched robotic voice from earlier pipes up again.

"Voltaris Industries started during the Saberren War of Independence as a defense contractor called Islorr Manufacturing. The company was known for mining and refining one of the strongest and most durable metals on the continent, Akorth." Islorr's Blood. I knew I recognized the material. The voice continues. "Islorr Manufacturing first discovered Akorth deep in the mines of—"

A loud scream from behind me interrupts the rest of the message. I whip around toward the main doors as the five guards who chased me enter the building. Kids and adults alike move away as the guards near the scanners. They won't be let in. They have Plasmars. The guard in the front steps forward toward the scanner. The light flashes orange. The guard steps back, raises his Plasmar, and fires a stun shot at the sensor bar. The spark arcing from the weapon hits the sensor, and the orange light flickers before turning off completely. The guard smirks, and all five of them proceed through the broken scanner. Their heads jolt around as they step between screaming kids and their worried parents. I make eye contact with one of the guards.

Shit.

Staring at me, the guard signals for the others, and they all advance, raising their Plasmars. I check the lights. They're on blue. But I still can't go to prison. I whip around. The main entrance is still blocked, and I can't go through the same door that I came from. They probably have backup waiting for me out there. In the back of the room, to the side of a display housing some sort of electricity-absorbing device, is a small metal door labeled 'Employees Only.' I sprint toward the door at full speed as the guards gain on me. One of them fires a shot, and the crackling electricity barely misses my other leg. I sigh in relief, grab the door handle with both hands, and yank it open.

The room on the other side of the door is very different from the impressive one I just left. It is not only much smaller than the previous room, but it is crammed with rows of cubicles stacked next to each other. The lower ceiling illuminates the employees typing on screens at their small desks. They don't seem to notice my presence. They all wear earpieces and talk over each other on different calls.

"Hello, this is Voltaris Repair. What seems to be the problem?" the person nearest to me says. The door behind me opens again, and I scurry out of the way as a guard steps into the cramped room. She fires a shot at my head, and I duck into one of the cubicles. The employee turns around, wearing a finely-molded acrylic mask with black accents around the eye holes. What's with that? She screams, plucking her earpiece off and jolting up from her seat. A faint "Hello?" crackles from the earpiece on the desk.

"What are you doing back here?" she demands, as another guard fires a shot at me. It hits her instead, in the chest, and she flops limp over her desk. Other employees peek up from their workstations, wearing similar masks. They all turn to face the door as the five guards crowd into the entrance. Another shot flies past me, but I duck back into the cubicle. I glance around for another door as I weave between the cubicles across the cramped room. More blasts crackle through the air, but I keep my head ducked. Employees stand up around me as I run, then immediately sit back down at the sight of the guards. Hoping to stay out of trouble, I assume.

I take another glance around the room. The guards move between the cubicles, none of them have spotted me. I turn back and eye another door. It's close. I zip out and shimmy to the door. I carefully swing it open, and step into a wide hallway that splits left and right. The hallway is populated with more employees, wearing various unique masks and ordinary attire. Nothing special. They walk past me, sparing no more than quick glances at my bloodied, wrapped hands. I keep my head down and use my hands to shield my face from their view. Everyone seems engrossed in their own things. I can't let them know I'm not one of them.

A man steps out of a door on my right and walks past me toward the left. Unlike the rest of the workers, he wears a dark gray suit similar to those in the SpeedTunnel. The guards really didn't like them. He must be important. He could be going somewhere the guards won't dare to go. Staring at the ground so that no one can see my face, I follow the man's footsteps down the wide hallway without looking back. A door swings open and the man's feet disappear through it. I pause, waiting a few seconds to ensure it's not obvious that I'm following him.

Sighing, I open the door.

I don't know what I was expecting, but it wasn't this. Rows of scientists in matching lab coats brood over evenly spaced metal tables across the room. The tables are crowded with microscopes, various test tubes of different sizes, and other equipment I don't recognize. Bright white lights blaze from above, bleaching everything in the room.

I step forward, and all eyes turn to me. Just like everyone else working here, their eyes are surrounded with glossy acrylic masks. Why do all the employees wear masks? I take another step and make my way past the tables. Sets of cold eyes track me across the room. I shudder, looking away in hopes that the scientists will go back to work. I need to find a place to hide soon. Halfway across the room I can't help but glance back at the scientists; everyone's still staring at me. I look around the room, desperate to avoid locking eyes with anyone wearing one of those masks. Written on the distant wall are the words 'Voltaris Laboratories.'

The metal door swings open behind me and the five guards storm the room.

I thought they wouldn't come in.

The scientists turn as one, abandoning their workstations and flocking toward the guards.

"You're not allowed in here," one of them says.

"Yeah, get out," another yells.

The guards shrug, ignoring the order. Their eyes lock on me, they charge.

I bolt backward, weaving between the tables. The guards are unperturbed, flipping tables out of their way in pursuit. One guard runs straight into a table, pushing it to the ground. The scientists yell at the guards, getting in their way. The guards fire blasts from their Plasmars, knocking a few scientists out. Enraged, the scientists run and tackle the guards, but they just shove through them in pursuit.

"Hey guys, this has gotten out of hand. Let's just talk about this." I stutter as they approach, still looking around for a means of escape.

"You can talk as much as you want when you're in prison," a guard says. She turns to another. "I haven't seen her yet. Prime Termani said she'd be here."

A door squeaks behind me. I spin and come face-to-face with a masked employee donning a gold-accented white suit. This one is different from the rest, wearing a strikingly purple mask. Two golden stripes pour like tears from the cold black outlines of the mask's eye holes, accentuating his startlingly vibrant purple eyes. He steps toward me, forcing me back in the direction of the guards. Two of the guards seize my arms. Three more form a wall around me. I struggle against their grip, tugging my arms. Their grip doesn't budge. All I can do is stare at the purple-masked man in front of me.

"What are you doing in my lab?" the head scientist asks, standing completely still.

"Uhh…" I begin.

"He ran away from us," a guard says.

"That does not give you jurisdiction to enter my lab," the masked-man says. "Now take him and get out."

The two guards spin me around and drag me to the door. Something purple-silver flashes across the room and one of the guards stop dead. The same guard with the impeccable aim.

"What are you doing?" the masked man exclaims. "I said get out."

She eyes a specific scientist with a green-stained lab coat, whose hands hover inside her coat as if ready to spring into action. Her eyes are vibrant purple just like the head scientist's.

"Well, well. That's convenient. I think we've found who we're looking for," the guard mutters just loud enough for me to hear. "I am under explicit orders to detain any threats to Termani," she says to the lead scientist, but her eyes remain fixed on her quarry.

The masked-man follows her eyes to the scientist with the stained lab coat. "You are not taking her. If you do not leave right now, I will have you escorted out."

"I will repeat myself. Prime Termani ordered us to bring in any threats." The guard raises her Plasmar at the purple-masked man. "Let us do our job."

CHAPTER 13

SAPPHIRE

"I cannot do that," my father says. He barely finishes his sentence when the guard fires her Plasmar point blank at his head. The crackling energy blast snaps his head back. His mask recoils upward, revealing flickering purple eyes and a gaping mouth.

My father's whole body is thrown back in an arc as if picked up by his head. His head strikes the ground with a sickening crunch. Blood pools beneath his head, forming a puddle on the floor. A guttural scream rips from my throat.

I rush over to my father's fallen body, grabbing his head and lifting it up. Blood pours from a gash at the base of his skull onto my lab coat and hands. I tear his mask away, tossing it to the side.

"Get up," I yell at him. Saliva flies out of my mouth, plastering the back of my mask. "Get up. Now. You can't leave me yet." My father doesn't move at all. I look around frantically. All the scientists stand frozen, watching me. The lead guard nods to the two on either side of her, and the three of them advance toward me. The strange man's green eyes stare in horror at my father, his body trembling in the other two guards' grips. The man's hands are caked in dried blood; filthy rags wrap around his knuckles and thumbs. His shirt is ripped and stained from blood.

My eyes lock on to the guard with her raised Plasmar. Her eyes widen slightly. She looks as shocked as their captive by the sheer amount of blood pouring from my father's head.

"Why?" I scream at the guard.

The guard hesitates, watching my father's blood run down my forearms as I hold his head. I move my fingers toward his neck to check his pulse. She sighs, pointing the Plasmar toward me. The blue light is still on. "Stop what you're doing. You are coming with us."

I glare back at the guard. Heat flushing my body. I lower my father's head, and grip the handles attached to my belt. Bent low and ready to pounce. "No, I am not."

I launch myself forward, yanking the weapons from my belt. The leather handles are round and slightly curved, like a predator's fangs. I flick the handles toward the ground, and curved blades snap into place with a metallic click. The Arcblades shimmer like liquid silver tinted a strange purple. The fugitive's mouth gapes. The scientists stare, frozen in place, still in shock over the shooting of their boss. Of my father.

I lunge right at the guard who shot my father. She fires a Plasmar blast right at me. I intercept it with my sword, which emits a faint glow as it absorbs the energy. I stab between gaps in her armor, and she spasms as the electricity transfers back to her. Her body recoils, and I slash through her neck with my other sword. The guard crumples to the ground, armor clanging in the air. The two guards not gripping the now struggling fugitive advance on me, weapons raised. Still on blue. They don't want me dead. Why was that guard intent on capturing me?

I charge forward at the two guards, swinging my twin blades at both of them. I cut through the arm of the one on the left, causing him to drop his Plasmar. He grunts and dives down for the Plasmar, but I kick him in the gut. As he hits the ground, I step on his head, pivoting my heel on his face to slash at the second guard again. He fires off a blast, but I deflect it with my other sword. I thrust a blade under his chestplate and twist. He promptly falls to the ground.

I pivot around again, the first guard's skull crunching underfoot. There are two left. The one leaves her comrade to restrain the captive alone and fires a shot that goes wide. The other still grips the strange man, watching me decimate his fellow guards. The free guard fires several consecutive shots. I dodge and deflect as I lunge toward her, stabbing with a now charged blade. The electricity arcs over her body, and she falls convulsing onto the ground. The scientists seem to recover from their shock as they scream and dive under their metal tables.

"Fuck," the last guard shouts, pushing the strange man away to aim his Plasmar at me. The captive seizes the opportunity to limp toward the door leading deeper into the tower. The guard presses a button and the blue light turns orange. His shaking hands point at my face. I dive down and slam my body into his legs. The legs contort to the side, and we both topple toward the ground. His finger slips, and a stray Plasmar blast shatters the skull of an incapacitated guard. The blast sprays blood, brains, and scull fragments across the lab. I pass the Arcblade in my right hand to grip both with my left. With my free hand, I grab the guard's trigger hand, wrap my leg around on his arm, and arch my back to pull. I hear a crack as I snap his thumb joint. He gasps in pain and drops the Plasmar. I drop his hand, snatch the Plasmar, and jump to my feet. I fire a shot right through his chest. The shot rips through his torso, sending his body skidding over the white floors.

I walk past the lifeless guards and fire shots through their heads, exploding them all. I switch the Plasmar back to blue and attach it to the back of my belt. I return my second Arcblade to my right hand and I flick their switches. The blades telescope inward, revealing carefully placed intricate joints, and rest back inside their handles. They lock into place automatically, and I return the hilts back to my belt.

In my peripheral, I see the strange limping man at the door, reaching toward the handle. I walk toward him and grab a second Plasmar from a dead guard rather than drawing the one on my belt. It's on stun. I aim the Plasmar and shoot it at the stranger's limping leg. The leg buckles and he falls to the ground. Using his other leg, he tries to push himself up to no avail. The man turns around to face me, as I approach him.

"Why did you do that?" he groans. Sweat drips from his messy hair.

"If I let you leave, you will die on your own." I approach the man and reach for his arm. He pulls away.

"You just killed five guards. How do I know you won't kill me?"

"You don't. But, as far as I'm aware, you've done nothing wrong. You don't deserve to die." The man stares at me, then past me at the carnage. Scientists peek from under their tables. I look away from the man and face the other scientists. "If any of you spill a word about what happened here, I will kill all of you." The scientists raise their hands and nod to show they understand. I turn back to the stranger. "That blood on your hands, it's your own. I can tell by the scabbing peeking out from your shoddy bandages. You don't seem like the kind of person who would purposefully provoke the guards," I add, grasping his forearm and pulling him up. "I take it they assumed that you were dangerous because of all the blood? And you running from them didn't help." I pause, giving him another look over. His earpiece is damaged. Either he fell, or he dropped the earpiece. Probably related to the blood on his hands. "Why did you come to Voltaris Island?"

"How did you know I'm not from here?" he asks.

"There aren't guards on this island. They came from a SpeedTrain, the same one that you came from. What were you running from? No one comes here unless they work for Voltaris or are escaping from government control."

"There was a protest..." the man sighs. "I got scared. I need to go back."

I notice dirt smeared along with the blood on his shirt. He fell during the protest. I heard the Crathenos protest took an ugly turn earlier today.

"You know someone who was at the graduation party."

"My best friend. Prime Termani took him..."

I pause, looking back at my father's corpse. Prime Termani wanted me as well. These guards were sent on that train to go after me. I didn't think he knew where I was. How did I piss him off this much?

"I'll help you get your friend back. But first, I need you to come with me. Guards will storm the building any minute now. We can't be here when that happens."

"You just killed five guards on your own," he argues.

"Do you want to save your friend or not?" I ask. The man reluctantly nods, and I wrap his arm around my shoulder. Together we shuffle through the double doors leading to the spiral staircase. I turn to Renna, who silently watches me behind her mask.

I spare a final look at my father. The blood has stopped flowing, and coalesces into a thick, sticky puddle on the floor around him. His eyes stare unseeing at the harsh lights above him. I didn't get along with him well. We certainly have a complicated history. But he didn't deserve this. My vision blurs. I can't look away. His skin has always been pale, but now it's a sickly gray. His last words to me echo in my head. *But I assure you, you will not.* I will figure it out. I'm not giving up. Not now.

Leaning down, I carefully pull his blue ID card from his pocket. The strange man leaning on me staggers, but I stand back up just in time. "Renna, let's go. I'll show you the room. And grab me a new lab coat."

Renna hesitates, taking in the state of the lab. She grabs a spare coat from her drawer, steps out from behind her desk, and follows us toward the double doors.

CHAPTER 14

AXLE

The door's slam echoes in the narrow hall. The nearest guard whips his head toward me, taking a step in my direction. He reaches for my arm, but I bolt away from him and the guards and that thing in the room. All I can see in my head are the shadow-man's two pitch black eyes. Whoever he is, he is killing us off one by one. That's why no one returned to the room.

The four guards pivot to me, Plasmars raised. The lights are still blue, which means they don't just want me dead. I remember the flames bursting from the student's hand. The last time I saw anything remotely similar was in an outdated history textbook I read years ago. I just can't remember what caused the flames.

My head feels fuzzy. My heart is pounding. I want to throw up.

A guard fires just as I near the door to the room I was kept in. Unlike the student who slammed on the door, I bolt past it. The guards didn't expect that. The blast hits the door, sparks crackling and spitting as the energy diffuses into the metal.

I keep my focus pinned in front of me, urging my legs to move faster. I'm pretty in shape, but those four guards have trained for years to be stronger and faster than the average person. The longer the chase drags on, the smaller my chances are of escaping. I watch the ground speed by as I sprint down the seemingly endless hallway. I reach a turn. Another guard fires a shot in front of the turn. This time he hits my arm.

I've never felt worse discomfort in my life. Thank Lokx he didn't hit my chest. I can't feel my left arm. It flops about limply as I run, and I feel a burning tingle right above where the blast hit. The tingle sensation intensifies, nerves screaming at the barrier between searing pain and complete numbness. It feels like my arm was just cut off. I have to keep glancing at it to make sure it still exists.

I look back at the guards, who slow down periodically to fire off more shots. Energy crackles on the walls and ceiling as the barrage continues around me. They keep their Plasmars raised while running, aiming directly at me. In unison, they fire a wave of shots at me. I turn the corner to the left to avoid the blasts, which all hit the wall. The air sizzles behind me, and the hairs on my head stand on end.

I gulp for air and redouble my sprint down this new hallway. I glance back to see the guards turn the corner in hot pursuit. Despite their fast physical superiority, I think their bulky armor is taking a toll. I can hear them huffing as they run. I look forward again and almost collide with another guard walking toward me. I catch him off guard, and he takes a moment to spin around and take in what's happening. My lungs burn, and the rest of my body feels like it's overheating.

Another corner. A left again, just like the previous one. Shit, this might be a loop. I don't have time to think about it. I near the corner and spare another glance behind me. Not only are the four guards gaining on me, but the fifth guard has joined them in their pursuit. Unlike the other four guards, the fifth's Plasmar light is orange. His Plasmar is not on stun.

I whip my head back around and lean forward into my run, nearly slamming into the wall. My ankle buckles, but I ignore the pain, continuing down the hallway to the left. As much as I don't want to, I force myself to look back again. This time, only the newest guard rounds the corner behind me. He has his Plasmar raised at me for a second, but quickly lowers it, attaching it to his belt.

"Hey," he calls out. I don't understand why he didn't shoot me when he had the chance, but I don't intend to find out. I focus on my escape route again. There's another corner ahead, veering left like the others.

It is a loop. I'm screwed.

"Hey!" the guard yells even louder. I speed up and quickly turn the corner, but I'm out of breath. My lungs scream for air, and I stumble, almost falling. I stare down at the ground, catching my breath. The shadow-man's black eyes stare at me in my head. There were so many dead bodies in that room.

All I can manage is a slow jog. I lean over, pressing my non-numb hand against a flaring side stitch. I picture the green fluid forced into my arm, haunting black eyes hovering over me. I double over, sucking in air and coming to a stop. My legs are leaden. I hear a deep crackling sigh and feel a cool breeze brush my shoulder. The breeze tingles down my numb left arm. I freeze in place, slowly tilting my head upwards in the direction of the cold sigh.

Standing in front of me is the shadow-man, those dark eyes that watched me escape now uncomfortably close. But he doesn't look like a shadow anymore. He looks robotic in his strange black metal armor, so dark that it doesn't reflect any of the harsh lights in the hallway. Peeking out underneath his armor is a thick bodysuit made of blood-red fabric stitched in a diamond-shaped pattern. Where I saw shadowed eyes earlier, I now see a pitch black, angular, full-face helmet. Sharp pieces of black armor ridge the lines of the helmet's features, making the cheekbones and chin sharper and more menacing. On either side of the mask's forehead are spikes that seem to serve no real purpose beyond being intimidating. A vaguely nose-shaped armor piece is flanked by two smokey black eye covers. I can see my face in their reflection. The mouth is a series of vent slits spewing out cold air with a crackle of static.

I shudder as the man studies me with his mask's pure black eyes, staring at me like they're looking right through my body. He sighs again, and wisps of chilly condensation cascades around my body, swirling to the ground. His presence towers over me more than his actual height should allow. He lets out a deep groan filtered through so much static that it sounds uncannily robotic. I hear an indrawn breath as if he's about to say something when someone grabs my right arm, causing me to stumble. I look over, and it's the guard from before. He nods to the shadow-man, who stops mid-vowel.

The robotic man's head turns away as the guard pushes me past him down the hallway. I look back, and the shadow-man is standing completely still; I shiver as I still feel his cool breath. I look up and get my first good look at the guard. His face is deathly pale, nearly paper white, and I can see his jawbone through his thin skin. The man has dull blue-gray eyes and thin, bone-white hair peeking out from underneath his helmet.

The guard takes me to the end of the hallway. I was wrong about the corner. It does turn to the left, but there's a passage to the right, leading away from the testing room. The guard turns me to the right, and we move away from the testing center and the remaining students.

"Why are you taking me the wrong way?" My breaths are shallow, and my fear is all but spent.

The guard ignores me, pushing me forward down the hallway. He reaches up to his earpiece, pressing the button on the side.

"One of the prisoners escaped. I am bringing him with me." He lowers his hand again and continues escorting me down the hall. We turn a corner.

"What happened to the other guards?" I ask. My legs barely work after my sprint, and he drags most of my weight.

He scoffs, then stops moving. While still holding my arm, he turns his whole body to face me.

"I killed them."

I pause, looking at him. His eyes are cold, showing no sign of remorse. The man is a pale statue.

"Why?" I ask, watching his face for some kind of change of expression. Nothing.

"I'm saving your life."

"What?" I look back down the hallway, but there's no one pursuing us. "You're not a real guard, are you?"

"Correct," he whispers.

"Well then what are you here for?"

"Doesn't matter," he says. "I'm saving your life."

CHAPTER 15

LUKAS

My leg burns with pins and needles as Sapphire, still gripping my arm, guides me beneath the large 'Voltaris Laboratories' sign plastered on the wall. My left leg drags along with my right, but I can't put any weight on it. One of the scientists looks up at us, but another taps his shoulder and he looks down again.

Renna reaches the double doors, steps in front of Sapphire and I, and pushes them open. We step through and Sapphire pulls a door closed behind us, her hand leaving a bloody smear on the pristine white paint. The doors slam closed behind us.

Beyond the doors lies a short, empty hallway. A massive spiral staircase, lined with thick black rails, dominates the space. Underneath the spiral is a blinding white light that illuminates the entire stairwell from below. Sapphire ushers me over to the stairs. Renna hesitates, stealing glances back at the lab doors. As we reach the stairs, I look up. They spiral all the way to the top of the tower; glowing signs mark each of the fifteen floors.

I turn to Sapphire, her lab coat is a mess of green and red stains. Her hands are still covered in blood, which she quickly wipes off on the coat. Renna's lab coat looks brand new in comparison. Pristine white and neatly buttoned to fit her frame, where Sapphire's disheveled coat flaps as she moves about. Renna hands Sapphire the clean lab coat, and Sapphire quickly swaps it out with her dirty one. She tosses the old, stained lab coat into a trash chute against the side of the wall.

I hear a loud bang behind me, and the three of us whip around to face the closed doors. The thud of footsteps follows. Someone screams.

"Where is Sapphire ajj Termani?" someone yells from behind the door.

Sapphire turns back to me, to Renna, and then to me again. "That's the guards. We have to move fast." She releases my arm, pushing me toward the stairs. "You go first. You'll be captured by the guards if you get stuck behind."

"My leg..." I mutter.

"Go," she demands. I grab the rails of the staircase and pull myself up onto the first step. My left leg drags behind me. A twinge of pain shoots up my calf. Gripping the rails tighter, I begin hopping up the steps with my right leg.

I hear footsteps behind me as Renna and Sapphire follow.

"If we get caught, I have to turn you in," Renna says.

"The guards don't care about Voltaris." Sapphire grunts. "They'll take you in for questioning because you're near me."

Renna sighs. "Why are they after you?"

"I don't know."

I find a rhythm and hop up the flights as fast as I can, urged on by a growing commotion downstairs. With one last push, my right leg screaming in protest, I crest the top floor of the tower. I sit down to catch my breath, and I can actually feel my numbed left leg making contact with the floor. The increased blood flow must be speeding up my recovery. Sapphire walks past me, stepping up to the door. The door is solid wood, unlike the doors of the other floors, which are all made of metal. There's a label engraved into the door, above what looks like a name, but it's all been mostly scratched away. Sapphire swipes the blue card that she took from her father's corpse on a small sensor to the right of the handle. A light turns blue on the sensor, and I hear the lock click open. She grabs the door and swings it open.

"Let's go," Sapphire orders. She grabs my arm again and drags me through the door into a small intermediary room with three metal doors, one in front and one on each side. The door directly in front of me is larger than the other two, with a piece of paper labeled 'Head Office' plastered at the top. I can't believe I'm actually at the top floor of Voltaris Tower.

The door to the right is labeled as 'Projects.' The door is worn down, especially the handle, which appears to be coming off. I step toward the door, but Sapphire pulls me back, turning me to face the door on the left. Smaller than the rest, this door is unlabeled. Renna shuts the door behind us and reluctantly steps forward to grab the handle. She turns back to Sapphire.

"You're sure this is the right door?" she asks.

Sapphire nods. "I'm certain. Everything points toward this being the most important room in the tower."

Renna grabs the handle and pulls it open.

At first glance, the room is unassuming. A small office maybe used when there's no space in the main one. A small wooden desk sits in the center, paired with a matching chair. The room is windowless, and the overhead lights cast a dim yellow light instead of the overbearing white lights in the rest of the building.

"Woah," Renna says, closing the door behind us.

"What?" I ask. She points toward the wall in front of us. What I took for patterned white wallpaper is actually hundreds of scribbled drawings posted on the walls. One of the drawings depicts a knife with a strange mechanism inside it. Next to the knife is a sword containing an identical mechanism. Another drawing shows a small device fitted against the "mouth" of a head-shaped scribble. Yet another showcases one of the masks worn by the scientists. However, one specific drawing directly in my line of sight catches my eyes. Roughly scribbled on the page is a drawing of an armored suit. In dark black ink, sleek and angular armor plating is depicted around the chest, shoulders, waist, knees, and feet. Red scribbles fill the spaces between armored plates, hinting at a bodysuit underneath the metal. But the mask. By Islorr's Blood, that mask is intimidating. It shares some design elements with the masks worn by the scientists in the lab. But this mask morphs into a full helmet, wrapping around the head in harsh lines and armored spikes. Big black eyes dominate the front, and a large vent-looking object covers the mouth. Just like with the armor, red scribbles line the inside edge of the mask.

"What?"

"Who is that?" I ask.

"I don't know." Sapphire finally releases my arm. She steps closer and tears the drawing off the wall. She lays it out on the desk before us and rips another off of the wall. She turns to Renna. "Take as many as you can carry." Renna nods, and starts ripping the drawings from the wall.

"Who do you think he is?" Renna wonders.

"I don't know. I think whoever wears that suit knows everything about Voltaris," Sapphire says. "Someone high up, maybe even the person who runs the company."

I spot a side profile sketch of a similar suit on the wall; I step forward and tear it away. The scribbles are all black, lacking the red coloring of the first. Big bold letters at the top of the drawing reads 'The Seeker Mark 2.' I examine the drawing for a moment, before Sapphire tosses it on the desk too.

"Where's Mark 1?" I wonder.

"I don't know," Sapphire shrugs. "Could be in there." She points to a closet in the corner of the room. "You can look if you want. I don't know why else there'd be a closet in here." She leans back against the wall on my right, wrinkling the drawings against her back. She sighs, reaches up, and pulls her mask off, tossing it on the floor. Underneath the mask, Sapphire's face is shockingly pale. Even her lips lack much color. Against the stark paleness, her hair is a dark, rich brown, pulled up in a bun. Two stray strands frame the sides of her face. But her eyes demand all my attention. I had noticed them earlier, but without her mask, her unnaturally bright purple eyes are hard to look away from.

"What do you want?" Sapphire demands. I shake my head, heat rising to my face. She leaves the wall and paces in tight circles, stepping on her mask as she walks. "Why do we have to wear these stupid masks anyway?"

"It's protocol," Renna responds, still pilfering drawings from the wall.

"I know it's protocol, Renna. It was rhetorical," Sapphire scoffs, turning back to face Renna. "Why are you keeping yours on anyway? Protocol?"

"Hmm," Renna mutters, pulling her mask off. She walks over and carefully places it on the empty desk. Renna's face is darker than Sapphire's, deeply tanned and scattered with moles and freckles. Her eyes are dark brown, and her hair curls in ringlets that fall across her face.

"Wait, why do you have to wear those masks?" I ask. "Everyone in here seems to be wearing one."

"Protocol," Renna repeats. "It's a requirement of all Voltaris employees. It's to protect your identity."

"What's so important about your identity that you have to hide it?"

Sapphire walks over to one of the few drawings remaining on the wall, a sketch of the mask. She places it on the desk, pushing the other drawings aside. The mask looks hollowed out, showing an interior view of the hard acrylic. In the middle, near the eye holes, is a small device reminiscent of earpiece projectors.

"Actually, I don't think it is to protect our identities," Sapphire murmurs, picking her mask up from of the floor. She places it on the desk face down, and her fingers move to the location of the device. With her other hand she draws one of her Arcblade handles and swings it down. The blade telescopes outward and snaps into place. With the tip of her blade, Sapphire carefully cuts an incision in the back of the acrylic. It slices with barely any resistance. She reaches into the hole and rips out the device. She turns back to Renna and me, holding it for us to see. I was correct in my initial assumption. It is a projector. A camera.

"They were watching us the whole time..." Renna mutters. "Can you remove mine as well?" Sapphire nods, grabbing Renna's mask from the desk and cutting out the camera.

"Why do all this?" I ask.

"I think this 'Seeker' might know the answer to your question," Sapphire says.

I hobble over to the closet, finally able to put weight on my left leg without falling immediately. I swing the doors open. A black and gray jumpsuit hangs in the closet, an attached helmet facing me. The empty black eyes feel like they're watching. The jumpsuit shares similar traits with the red and black drawing, with impossibly dark armor plates on its shoulders, knees, chest, waist, and feet. Islorr's Blood, it's just like the Akorth fragment I saw on display. I run my hand along the fabric between the pieces of armor; it's a coarse, tough material. "Why the armor?"

Sapphire and Renna move to stare at the suit.

"Looks like I was right about the location of Mark 1," Sapphire says, tilting her head. "I don't know why he has armor. I don't even know who he is. The real question is: where is Mark 2?"

CHAPTER 16

"Why?" I ask. The false guard looks around, then slams me against the wall of the hallway. Pain blossoms across my back from the blow against the cold, hard wall. The wall itself is made of metal, unlike the composite material that's commonplace. The metal is painted dark gray-brown and covers the ceiling, walls, and floor of the long hallway. The hallway is poorly lit by small light inserts scattered unevenly on the ceiling.

"Listen here," the man says, his voice lowered and gruff. "If you keep asking questions, I won't be able to take you with me. I'm already gonna be in enough trouble for bringing you at all."

"Trouble with who?"

"Did you not hear a single thing I just said?" The man sighs, then steps back from me. I move away from the wall, watching his eyes. He squints down the hall. I can't figure this guy out. My gaze falls to the Plasmar strapped to his belt. The light is still on orange.

"How do I know you're not gonna shoot me after you're done with me?"

"I said I'm saving your life."

"You can save my life and end it later."

The false guard sighs. His left hand delves into a pocket and pulls out a vial; glowing green fluid sloshes against the glass. The same fluid that was inside the shadow-man's syringe.

"Do you recognize th—"

I snatch the vial out of his hand and smash it against the wall behind me. The glass shatters onto the ground; the green fluid drips down the wall and along my pant leg.

"Why do you have that?" I yell. "What are you going to do with me?"

He reaches to grab my hand. I yank my hand away, then slam my fist into his upper chest. The man recoils, and I use the moment to slide out from his arms. He grabs for my arm, but I'm already running, my arms tucked tight as I sprint down the hallway. I look back toward the false guard, who just stands, watching me flee with a blank expression.

"Voltaris is here. Abort the mission," the man says, still staring at me.

A pause. I slow down to a brisk walk, still winded from my sprint earlier. I keep my head turned to watch the strange man. The man's eyes widen in a frantic expression; hand raised to his earpiece.

"What?" he yells.

Right then an alarm pierces the air. I freeze in place, spinning back to face him. The alarm shrieks at a frequency that pounds on my ears. I clap my hands over them. I can no longer hear anything except for the high-pitched whine. The man's eyes snap to something behind me.

The man draws his Plasmar and runs at me, his pace quickening with each long stride. Still covering my ears, I whip around to come face to face with three guards. Behind the heavily armored men, the dim lights flicker between white and red with the alarm. The hallway extends past them, and I can barely make out where the hallway turns. Each guard has their Plasmar drawn, aiming at me. I raise my hands to surrender when a blast of energy rips right through the stomach of one of the guards. The guard's torso explodes, spraying me and his men with blood and guts. The guard's upper half flops to the ground with a thud. His legs tip over moments later. I force down my rising vomit, and bolt in the opposite direction. The false guard reaches with his free hand and grabs my arm.

"What are you doing?" I scream.

I kick at his legs, which buckle slightly, but he maintains his grip. The other two guards both fire blasts at him. Their Plasmars' indicator lights now glow orange. He dodges the blasts, leaving two red hot spots on the metal wall. One aims his Plasmar for another attack, but the man shoots the guard's posted leg. The blast tears away a chunk of the guard's leg. The remaining leg looks like something took a bite out of the calf. The guard lets out a blood curdling cry and topples over backward. The remaining guard shoots at the man, but he nimbly swerves out of the way, shooting the guard in the small space between two armor plates. The resulting explosion is contained by the armor, but I still see mangled flesh and blood gush through the gaps in his armor. Blood pools down at my feet. The limp body hits the ground with a thump.

"Is this what you do?" I exclaim. "You kill people? You could've used stun."

The man shoves me against the wall. He flicks the Plasmar light back to blue and points it at me. "If you move a muscle, I will not hesitate to shoot."

I watch as the man leans over the most intact dead guard. He grabs the guard's helmet first, tearing it off and letting the limp head fall back with a crack. The man tosses the helmet at me. Next, the man reaches underneath the chestplate and slides it off of the guard. As he tugs at the chestplate, the bloodied body flails in response. The man throws the chestplate toward me as well. It barely misses my leg. He removes the leg pieces and boots last and adds them to the pile of armor.

"Put it on," the man shouts over the din of the alarm.

"What?" I stare at the three dead bodies on the floor.

"There will be more of them."

The man steps back, giving me room to move. I stare at the armor, and at the bodies. I had never seen a dead body before today, and now I have seen more than I can count. I take deep breaths. The alarm's shrieks feel like a constant assault; I can't think. My vision blurs, and I feel hot tears dripping down the sides of my cheeks. I slowly pick up the chestplate and slip it over my sweat-stained shirt.

"Voltaris Industries is more than an energy company," the man says, standing close so I can hear him over the noise. "I'm sure you know that they are involved in other things. Been that way for a couple of years at least." I turn my stinging eyes to the man as I reach down to pick up the knee pads. "The serum that you destroyed. The serum that Prime Termani ordered to be injected into the prisoners. That's one of Voltaris' side projects." I freeze in place, my hands holding the boot just below my raised leg. I force my foot into the boot and straighten to face the man.

"What?" I stare at the man. "What is it for?" Sweat and tears continue down the sides of my face.

The man evades my question. "That serum has killed a lot of people. It's dangerous."

"Fine."

I place the helmet over my head. The man stares at me, grunts, and turns to look down the hallway. He grabs my arm again and pulls me down the corridor. As he leads me away, my eyes remain locked on the three limp guards who had tried to stop me from escaping. My skin feels cool as sweat starts to dry, but there's a pervasive wetness on my leg where the green fluid spilled. My mind flashes back to the shadow-man and his glowing syringe. Behind him lie strewn all the bodies, the lives, that he and that fluid had ended.

The false guard shifts his grip to the back of my armor plate, spins me around, and pushes me through an open door. He kicks the door closed behind us. The man leans back against the door and releases me from his grip.

He finally speaks. "You really tried to escape the testing. No one else did. I admire that." One person did. Other than me. That poor student was forced to try.

I scoff, rubbing my aching wrists. "Who are you?"

"Adrius," the man replies flatly.

I pause for a second. I hadn't expected him to answer my question. I eye the doorknob next to Adrius' back. I look around at the empty hall, over at Adrius's bloodied hands, and back at the door he's blocking.

"Axle."

"Enough resting. The exit's not fa—"

The door slams into Adrius's back, and he sprawls onto the floor. I scurry to my feet as the door swings fully open. Eleven guards occupy the corridor. I stumble backward as all the guards swarm into the bigger hall, surrounding

Adrius and me. The guards form a tight circle around us, lit up by the still flashing red lights. The lights reflect against their faces. Adrius stays on the floor, unmoving. His eyes don't even flick toward them.

"You are both under arrest for obstructing the operations of Prime Termani," one of the guards proclaims. "Axle ajj Termani, you will be returned to the testing facility at once. Adrius ajj Lusia, you will be subjected to interrogation and then termination. Do you both understand these terms?"

I slowly nod in response. Adrius, on the other hand, still doesn't budge.

"Adrius ajj Lusia, do you understand these terms?" Adrius remains dead still. The guard walks forward and grabs Adrius by the armor, pulling him up and slamming his face into a wall. The guard punches Adrius in the gut, then spits at his feet. "Do you understand these terms?" Adrius chuckles softly and spits blood from his mouth. The guard punches Adrius again, this time across the jaw. Adrius wiggles his jaw a bit, and blood stains his teeth red.

"Who did you get these orders from?" Adrius asks.

"What did you say?" the guard yells in Adrius's face.

"Who... did... you... get... these... orders... from?" He glances at me, then locks eyes with the guard. "Prime Termani... or Voltaris Industries?"

"What?" the guard screams.

Adrius exhales. "It's your turn to answer my question. Prime Termani or Voltaris?"

The guard snarls and opens his mouth to speak when a flying dagger embeds itself in his side. The guard reels over, clutching the knife. He stumbles backward and hits the wall, falling onto the ground. His limp body rolls to the side, and his unseeing eyes glare in the direction of the throw.

At least twenty newcomers storm the room, all wearing matching tan cloaks. The guards draw their Plasmars, pointing around frantically. One of them fires a shot at a hooded figure. It hits her arm, which visibly flops down by her side. Unperturbed, she pulls a long handle from a tight leather belt with her other arm. The handle is wrapped in a similar brown leather. She flicks her wrist, and a curved silver blade telescopes out, locking in place with a snap.

Another guard fires a shot. I glimpse the Plasmar flaring orange. The energy blast streaks through the air at another hooded figure. He unsheathes and extends his own sword just in time to block the blast. The plasma hits the Arcblade and melts right through it. Molten metal sprays onto his chest, and he stumbles backward, screaming. While the momentum was absorbed by the blade, the slag melts right through his body.

Another blast fires at a hooded figure. Someone else grabs him and yanks him out of the way.

"They're not on stun," someone shouts, running at a guard. She stabs her sword between his armor plates, and it wedges stuck as he stumbles backward. The guard falls onto another guard, and they both tumble down onto the floor.

"We have to leave," Adrius whispers into my ear. He grips his Plasmar with both hands, pointing it into the fray. I glance around the hallway. Most of the guards are either dead or incapacitated. Many of the hooded figures are out as well.

A deep, crackling sigh echoes through the hall. The robed men spin around at the sound, but Adrius and I, as well as the guards, freeze in place. The sigh is inhuman, distorted by the alarm's shriek into something akin to a chuckle.

CHAPTER 17

LUKAS

A loud bang shakes the door, jolting me back to reality. I spin around to face the wooden door behind me. It's still intact, unaffected for now.

"They're here," Sapphire murmurs, picking up her mask from the floor. "We have to get out of here." She grabs Renna's mask from the table, handing it to her. Renna places it over her face. Behind her mask, Renna's eyes search Sapphire, waiting for a course of action. I turn to Sapphire seeking direction too. I don't know this building very well.

"Is there another way out?" I ask, as another bang comes from outside this door.

Sapphire shrugs. "I've never been up here before, but I doubt it. If there were another exit, I think we would've seen it already."

"Can't we just walk past the guards?" Renna asks. "All the guards who saw you fight are dead. These guards wouldn't know it's you."

"What about him?" Sapphire points at me. "He doesn't have a mask. If they see him with me, they'll know I helped him escape."

"My name is Lukas," I interrupt. They ignore me.

"What if we just let him be captured? Maybe he did something wrong," Renna says.

"I doubt it. I did nothing wrong and the guards still went after me."

"You broke into Voltaris. They definitely had a reason to bring you in."

Another bang. "The guards couldn't care less about what happens at

93

Voltaris." Sapphire sighs. "Prime Termani must've told the guards to go after me."

"Why would he do that?"

"I… don't know. Until now he and the guards didn't know where to find me. But they know what to look for. I think that guard recognized me the moment she saw my swords, or that I was gripping something." Bang. "Or maybe they recognized my eye color. If that's true, I doubt I'd be able to bluff my way past them." Bang.

As they continue to argue, my eyes shift back to the Mark 1 Seeker suit hanging in the closet. Something about Sapphire's earlier words stick. *I think whoever wears that suit knows everything about Voltaris. Someone high up, maybe even the person who runs the company.* The Seeker is high up in Voltaris. It would be perfectly normal for him to be on this floor. The guards wouldn't have a reason to suspect otherwise.

I stare into the eyes of the Mark 1 suit. The Akorth-glass eyes of the suit stare back at me. This could work. Then I can get out of here. I can go back to Crathenos and free Axle. The reverberations from the door blend with a completely different ringing rising in my ears.

"That's not going to work," her voice says.

"Shut up," I yell, my eyes jolting in search of my mom's mocking silhouette. She isn't there. Renna and Sapphire stop talking.

"What do you want?" Sapphire asks. I clench my fists, then turn to face Sapphire and Renna again.

"I can wear the Mark 1 Seeker suit."

"That's stupid," Sapphire remarks. "What happens when the Seeker comes back and finds out that his suit was stolen?"

Renna nods. "I agree with Sapphire. If the Seeker is high up in Voltaris, he could track you down. We need to find another way. You can't wear that."

"I don't think we have a choice." I step closer to the suit, letting out a deep breath. "I don't have a mask and, as far as we know, there isn't another way out. If I wear this suit, we have a chance of escaping without having to fight any more guards."

Bang.

I hear something cracking and giving way with a thud. Heavy boots pound on the floor outside the room.

Sapphire sighs, putting her mask on.

"Fine."

I reach forward and pull the suit out of the closet. It disassembles, pieces scattering across the floor. The helmet rolls by Renna's feet, and she picks it up, placing it on the desk. I lean down and pull a suit made of tight black fabric free of the mess. I stretch the suit, shoving my aching legs through the holes. As I pull the fabric up my body, it snaps in place around me, the opening at the back fusing closed seamlessly. Voices thunder outside the door. I hurriedly slide the armor pieces into place. The black armor snatches at the fabric as it molds itself around my muscles and joints. Each piece of armor settling in place as if perfectly designed to fit my body.

Renna hands me the helmet, and I slip it over my head. It's hot, and stinks to wear. My vision is tinted slightly green. I turn the handle and swing the door open. The three of us step out of the cramped room and emerge into the open expanse of the top floor. Immediately, seven guards spread out to surround us. Every guard raises a Plasmar, training them on Sapphire, Renna, and me. The Plasmars are lit blue.

I take a deep breath, and I can hear a static sound as the breath passes through the mask. My face drips sweat from the poor ventilation.

Huh...

I slowly turn to face each guard in turn, waiting for them to squirm or shuffle under the helmet's intense gaze. I step closer to the nearest guard. He raises his Plasmar, hands shaking, to point at my helmet. He doesn't fire a shot.

"What do you want?" I ask. I'm taken aback by my own voice. The voice that emerges is unfamiliarly deep, modulated, and robotic. I force myself to not react physically. The guards seem shocked by the modulated voice as well.

"Someone, uh, attacked and killed other guards..." the guard stutters, still staring at me. It helps that I'm much taller than him.

"Who gave you permission to enter this building?" I ask, stepping even closer to the guard, his Plasmar almost touching the suit. I tilt my head downward, forcing the guard to meet the dead-eyed stare of the helmet.

"Prime Termani, sir," the guard blurts.

I sigh, but the mask warps it into a deep crackling chuckle. "Prime Termani does not have jurisdiction over this island. Everything here belongs exclusively to Voltaris."

"Prime Termani told us to enter, sir," the guard repeats, his teeth chattering. I can't believe this is working. What do I do now? I reach forward and grab the Plasmar from the guard. Another guard fires a stun blast point blank at me. The energy hits the armor and diffuses. Thank Lokx. I can still feel my body where the Plasmar hit. The stun didn't work.

Gears inside my arm whir as I wrench the Plasmar from the guard's grip. I spin to face the one who shot at me. "I can have you arrested for that."

"You attempted to disarm a guard," she says, unfazed by my modulated voice. "That is a crime."

"That guard, and all the rest of you, are trespassing on my property without probable cause." I point to the door on the ground and the empty frame behind it. "And you damaged it as well. You would not win this case."

"Prime Termani gave us explicit permission—"

"Prime Termani is not your overlord. Would you blindly follow someone or would you rather make your own decisions? You should know better than to listen to a man that promises safety but delivers injustice."

"You're not any different," the guard snarls. "The serum is far worse."

"The what?" I say just as Sapphire taps my arm. I turn to her, and she shakes her head. I turn back to the guards. "Right, the serum."

"You don't work for Voltaris. You're under arrest for impersonation."

Shit.

The guard fires another blast at me, which diffuses like before. I step toward her, and she turns the Plasmar light to orange.

Oh fuck.

Sapphire lunges in front of me, drawing her weapon handles and extending them out into swords.

"It's her!" the guard exclaims just as Sapphire's Arcblade cuts through her arm. She falls to the ground, and the Plasmar drops. The light is still orange. The remaining six guards turn to Sapphire. The one in front of me reaches to grab the Plasmar I stole from him. I fire. The blast catches him square in the chest and he collapses to the ground.

Another guard fires a shot at Sapphire. Sapphire hurls a sword at him, the blade spinning like a spear through the air. It plunges through his chest and he stumbles back, flailing at the hilt embedded in his chest. Sapphire runs at the guard, slicing through another's neck with her remaining Arcblade. He fires a blast at Sapphire's head, and she just barely dodges it. Static crackles in her hair. Sapphire pulls her sword out of the stabbed guard and launches herself at the remaining three guards, spinning and slicing between them while dodging their attacks. The guards, spilling blood, grab their wounds and drop to their knees.

Sapphire walks past Renna and me, stepping over corpses and through the empty door frame. "Let's go confront the damn Prime."

CHAPTER 18

AXLE

I stare at the shadow-man. I'm sweating, goosebumps crawling over my skin. I am unable to move.

The man's head turns, his mask's black eyes taking in the chaos in the room. They settle on me. The guard armor doesn't hide me. Those black orbs stare right through my disguise. Cool air pools from his mask, and static crackles and pops with his slow, deep breaths.

After a brief pause, the shadow-man steps into the fray. The hooded men give up attacking the guards, and charge at the robotic man instead. The first one to reach him swings her sword at his neck, one of the few areas showing only a red bodysuit. The shadow-man grabs her hand, twists it, and flicks his arm. The mechanisms inside the suit whir as his flick launches her backward. She crashes into the wall. Her head whiplashes against the wall, and she flops to the ground. He walks on, unhurried, unaffected .

The remaining guards all point their Plasmars at the hooded men's turned backs. Adrius grabs a second Plasmar from a corpse and rapidly fires at the unsuspecting guards. The Plasmar glows red around the barrel of the weapon as searingly hot plasma plows through flesh, muscle, and bone like butter. He's gonna overload it. The Plasmar lets of a growing hum, despite Adrius' hand being off the trigger. He tosses the Plasmar at the remaining guards, and it explodes outward, spewing plasma and metal shards through their bodies. Mutilated collapse onto the ground, leaving only the shadow-man facing a roomful of assailants armed with curved Arcblades and Plasmars.

My relief is crushed as the shadow-man grabs another attacker with both hands, lifts him over his head, and bends his back until it cracks. He drops the screaming man to the ground and kicks him to slide over the floor. His screams dwindle and eventually stop. I turn away, unable to watch. When I look back, the man is still staring at me, still moving toward me.

Adrius raises his Plasmar at the shadow-man. Unlike with the guards, he stalls for a split second, timing his ragged breaths before finally firing a shot. The blast streaks through the air at the shadow-man's chest. Without pause, the shadow-man grabs a hooded man and pulls him into the line of fire. The hooded man's eyes widen, and the blast ruptures his body. Blood and guts splatter onto the shadow-man, but his pace doesn't falter.

"Let's go," Adrius whispers in my ear, before grabbing my arm and running. This time, he doesn't need to drag me. I sprint down the hallway so fast that I outpace Adrius. I almost stumble in my awkward guard boots as the ground beneath them turns uneven. I can make out bumps on the ground, but they're difficult to identify with the constant flashing red lights. I kick away at debris with each long stride. I look behind me; only a few hooded figures escaped with us. The shadow-man is gaining on us.

I turn back and almost collide with Adrius. He stands in front of a dark spot on the floor, dirt and concrete rubble piles lie strewn around it. At the edge of the dark spot, torn wires poke through the dirt.

Adrius gestures me forward, and I peer down again, trying to make sense of it through the flickering red and white light and dust suffusing the air. It's not just a spot on the ground. It's a hole. I lean forward and stare over the edge. The bottom of the hole seems to open up into a bigger area, but I can't see how big it is.

"Jump. You'll be fine," a voice calls from below.

The dark hole is lit up by a small flashlight in the hands of another hooded man. The flashlight reveals at least another hundred of them. They all wear the exact same cloaks. Adrius nods and hops down the hole. A hollow thud echoes from below as he hits the ground.

I turn back down the hallway. Through the flickering haze, I can barely see the remains of the guards' and hooded figures' limp and lifeless bodies spread down the hall. Their loose limbs splay out in unnatural formations, and the iron stench of the drying blood and body fluids is overwhelming. One of the guard's arms spasms, and blood spurts from an open gash. I vomit on the concrete rubble at my feet, sweat tracking trails down my face. I look up through tears, and standing over the carnage is the shadow-man. He hovers above the corpses, his pure black eyes staring at me. I can almost feel his sharp, cold breath along my chest, like he's right in front of me. The shadow-man speeds up his pacing, then freezes. His hand reaches up to the side of his helmet. He let's out a cry of frustration and slams his fist into the wall beside him, bending the metal. I don't wait for him to continue his pursuit. I turn back to the hole and jump down.

My feet hit the ground with a resounding boom. I take a second to look around; I was right about the hole opening into a bigger space, but I didn't expect the sheer size of it. I am not in a hole, but a massive tunnel stretching as far as I can see in either direction. The tunnel is shrouded in pure darkness, except for the dim light emitting from the cloaked man's flashlight.

The man points the flashlight up at the hole, before pointing it over at the other hooded figures. The cloaked men and women finick with a series of metal carts fitted on rusty rails that disappear down the length of the tunnel.

A hooded man snaps something into place on a cart and looks up at us. "It's ready."

Everyone hops into the carts. Adrius grabs me and practically throws me into one of them. A cloaked woman looks me over; I can't see her eyes beneath the cloak. She sighs and turns her head forward again. I look in the directions the carts are pointing. Is it all over? Adrius hops into a cart with the last of the men and women. The carts rip away with a squeal of metal, leaving the nightmare behind.

* * *

I stare up at the dirt ceiling above me; my eyes track the ghostly image of the shadow-man's gaze pursuing along the carved rock of the tunnel. My mind refuses to call up his haunting mask. All I see are two unlit holes in the ceiling, like they were carved out of the dirt. The silhouette flits over the bumps and divots scattered along the careful hand-dug tunnel, those dark eyes following my vision no matter where I look.

"We should be under the capitol by now," Adrius says, breaking the long silence.

"What?" I mutter under my breath. "What would we be doing in the capitol?"

I shudder and tilt my head down. For a second there those black eyes lined up perfectly with Adrius's. I let out a quiet sigh of relief as the image fades away. Gone from my mind, at least for now.

"Zeke said he broke part of the rail to slow us down," one of the hooded men says. "We'll stop when we're there."

I lean my head back to stare up at the ceiling again. The cart lurches as it slows, whipping my head forward to nearly hit Adrius and back further than it was. The weight of the helmet straining the tendons in my neck. I steady the helmet with both my hands, and let my stomach settle back into place.

"We're here." A man hoists himself out of the cart, boots puffing up dust on the dirt below. The tunnel is still dark, but not as pitch black as earlier. In the distance, a flashlight beam cuts through the dark, illuminating the hand that holds it. All of the cloaked figures hop out of the carts and sprint in the direction of the light. I get out of the cart and slowly follow everyone. Adrius grabs my arm and forces me to run with him.

The man holding the flashlight is short but with a somewhat lanky build. His hood is off, revealing a nearly completely bald scalp with small patches of frayed gray hair. His face is rounded, and his skin is eerily smooth. His orange-brown eyes, rimmed by dark circles and creased lids, look like they were forced to age faster than the rest of his face.

"What's happening?" Adrius asks.

"We've been able to bypass most of the security measures surrounding the Stone, but we're still trying to deal with the wires connected to it. We're concerned that cutting them may lead to other issues down the line."

"Surely it'll take out the power," Adrius adds.

"Obviously," the man says. "That's not what I'm worried about. I don't want the Cortenians among us to accidentally interact with the Stone and die."

"It shouldn't be a problem to grab the Stone."

"Probably not, but if the bugs are still on the wires and creep into cuts people didn't know they had..."

Adrius nods, and he grips my arm tighter, walking us forward.

"Welcome to the Primordialist base of operations," he mutters under his breath.

The maze of tunnels reminds me a bit of the prison, except these dirt halls are teeming with hooded figures, Primordialists, jostling past each other. The tunnels are lit by long flashlights jammed into the walls. Adrius seems to move on instinct, winding along different turns at every fork in the labyrinth. Left. Right. Right. Left. Right. Left. Left.

Alongside us, Primordialists carry a few purple-silver artifacts. A couple of Arcblades, some fragments of armor. At the end of one of the wider tunnels, two Primordialists man a furnace. Those carrying the artifacts dump them into a massive crucible. Primordialists coming from the other direction add in heaps of ordinary iron. I'm forced to turn away from the furnace as we draw closer; its immense radiating heat stings my eyes.

We turn another corner, and I can look forward again.

"What was that?" I ask.

"That's how we produce the metal to make all of our weapons," Adrius responds. "A lot of older Primordialists are descendants of Shifters, so we have small portions of Cratermetal that we can dilute to make a weaker but still incredibly sturdy alloy."

The tunnel broadens out ahead and merges with other tunnels. Its also significantly brighter now than before. Too bright to be lit by the flashlights alone. Adrius guides me to join a group of Primordialists crowded in a small cylindrical enclave of the tunnel system.

In contrast to the dirt walls of the maze, these cylindrical walls are made of metal. Each branching tunnel connects to the cylinder via melted cutouts from the metal walls. The walls are illuminated by something in the center of the room, the source of the extreme light.

I try to focus on the light, but my eyes ache and tear up. All I can do is squint in the general direction and not run into people as Adrius moves me closer to the source. My eyes adjust slightly to the glare, and I'm overwhelmed by the sheer number of wires. The room looks like an overcomplicated obstacle course inside a maze meant for a bizarre entertainment show. Wires of different colors crisscross over each other at different angles. Impossibly thick wires jut upward through the dirt and into the ceiling in a parallel pattern, but that's the only semblance of order in the room. Wires of different thicknesses scatter in all directions, wrapping around, fusing with and splitting again in no apparent order. Long coils wrap roughly around the larger wires. At first the entire setup looks rushed, but the longer I study them in the oddly perfect cylindrical room, the more certain I am that each and every wire was placed with purpose. On the ground are cameras and other mechanisms. They are cracked, and clearly no longer functioning.

Now a little more used to the bright light illuminating the room, I decide to investigate the source again. Thick vertical wires jut out from a round metal casing that could engulf a whole person. The casing is Cratermetal like the Shifter artifacts, but likely even more pure. The purple tint is so vibrant that it could barely be considered purple-silver at all. It looks like it was dyed. The metal radiates heat along with that lavender hue.

"Is that the Stone you were talking about?" I ask Adrius.

"No." He points at the center of the sphere, where a small hole reveals something else buried in its center. "That is."

I step closer, leaning in and bending my neck to get as close as I can without butting the Primordialists in front of me. That's when I see it, a small Cratermetal ball, with hundreds of tiny overlapping layers, like an unpeeling fruit. Each of the layers is as thin as paper, with thousands of hair-thin wires shooting out in all directions. The Stone glows brighter than its encompassing hollow sphere. It pulses as electricity flows along the hair-like wires.

"That's the Stone?" I murmur.

"The Lightning Stone," Adrius nods. "It took us years to find this. Voltaris hid it well."

"This will stop the experiments?" I ask.

"Voltaris doesn't just use the Stone for energy," Adrius says. "They use it as a template for the serum. Without the Stone, there's no more template, at least until they find another Primordial Stone."

I pause, staring down at the ground. My mind flashes to an image in a textbook from school. A drawing of four stones. The four Primordial Stones.

"That's a Primordial Stone?" I ask, rubbing at my eyes. "I didn't think they still existed."

Adrius nods. "They exist. And they're dangerous in the hands of Voltaris."

"And you're certain taking one of the most powerful weapons from Voltaris would stop their experiments?"

"We can't ever be certain. There are too many things to account for. Maybe Voltaris has a copy. Maybe they've already found another Stone. But taking the Lightning Stone should slow them down enough to give us a fighting chance."

"Fighting for wh—"

"I got it," someone shouts.

"Where is Zeke?" someone else asks.

"I'm right here." The flashlight man steps through the group toward the Stone. His flashlight is off. "You think you can get it without interacting with the bugs?"

The man by the Stone nods.

Zeke nods in response. "Grab it."

The hooded man grabs the Primordial Stone and yanks it free from the hair-like wires. The ultrabright lights turn off, plunging the room into darkness.

CHAPTER 19

T he image of the Seeker won't leave my head. All the papers pressed up against the wall of the unlabeled room, all of the drawings. I wish I knew why they were in there. I turn to Lukas, his head leaning back against the dark gray seat cushion of the SpeedTrain. My eyes settle on the Seeker Mark 1 helmet resting on his lap. The helmet is deep black, with large, rounded bug-like eyes. A small vent marks the 'mouth' of the helmet. Spikes jut from the top, backward-flowing like hair. The Mark 2 drawing had a similar design. Lukas's eyes flicker open, and he stares up at the bright white lights above. I look over at Renna, she's facing away from me, engrossed in the view flitting past the window. I look over at Lukas again. He's still staring at the lights.

"What's so cool about the lights?" I ask. Lukas's head, still pressed against the back of the seat, turns to face me. His eyes are surrounded by dark shadows.

"Nothing important," he says, turning his head away. I continue studying the prototype helmet in his hands. My mind wanders back to the guards in the tower. They knew about the serum. No one knows about the serum. No one except Voltaris.

"What is the serum?" Lukas turns to me, this time without dragging his head against the seat.

I sigh. I expected him to ask this at some point. "I don't really know. I'm trying to figure that out. It's a project that the whole lab has been working on for ages."

"What does it do?" he asks.

"I don't know. I know it interacts with blood, so whatever it is, it's meant to be used on people."

"Why would Voltaris make a serum to be used on people?" Lukas asks.

I pause. Why *would* Voltaris make a serum to be used on people?

"What's going on?" Renna turns away from the window. "Sapphire?"

It all makes sense now. Somehow, Prime Termani found out who I was, and that I was snooping around at Voltaris. He knew I'd find out he and Voltaris are working together.

"I know what the serum is used for."

Renna's eyes widen. "What?"

"The serum is used for Prime Termani's mandatory testing."

"How do you know?"

"The guards knew about the serum. Lukas didn't. It's not public information. The only reason the guards would know about it is if the government is involved. It also explains why Prime Termani sent his goons after me. I was too close to his project for his liking."

"And you don't know what it does?" Lukas exclaims. "That stuff is being injected into my best friend."

"Voltaris wouldn't tell us the ingredients."

"So Prime Termani is just another one of Voltaris's customers?" Lukas says, his voice still raised. "Why?"

I grunt, seeing Lukas's knuckles go white from gripping the helmet. His head rolls to stare at the lights again. Who is really in charge? Voltaris seems to have a lot more power than Prime Termani. But why would Voltaris want to run these tests? I doubt they share the government's concern over the Primordialists.

Lukas turns around again and stares at the ground. "Is it just me, or has it gotten darker?"

I look up. The previously blinding lights have dimmed enough that I can make out the wires behind them.

"Might just be a quirk," Renna says.

The lights fade further. "No. It's not a quirk," Lukas says. "They're getting dimmer."

"Something's wrong with the power." I stand up and shimmy past Lukas to peer down both sides of the train. "Just as I thought. All the lights are going down."

"Wait a minute, what do you mean something's wrong with the power?" Renna asks. "That never happens."

"It happened once when I was a kid," Lukas says softly. "But wait, why are the lights still on then?" he asks. "If the power was out, then the lights should be fully out. Hold on, why are we still moving?"

I turn back to Lukas, my head tilted. "Have you *seriously* never heard of a backup reserve?" I scoff. "Just because the power doesn't go out, doesn't mean there aren't still reserves just in case it does. But the reserves don't last forever, so the energy is being redirected to critical locations, like hospitals."

"So the lights are going out... Then why is the SpeedTrain still moving?" he asks.

"Getting people off the train would be considered a *critical location*." I look around at the other passengers. The few other people on the train look around, but aren't fazed. I close my eyes. There's a dull tapping sound coming from within the train. It's a magnetic train; it shouldn't make contact with the rails unless the magnetic field fails.

I'm thrown back across the smooth floor of the SpeedTrain. I scrabble trying to find my footing, but I'm sent gliding backward. I try to use my arms to stabilize myself, to no avail.

"Sapphire," Renna calls out, standing up. "Move out of the way." She pushes past Lukas's legs and runs toward me, gripping the seats on either side of the train as she tries to reach me. Lukas stays pressed against the seat.

As the train comes to a complete stop, I'm able to steady my legs. Lukas stands up and walks over to

"What do we do?" Renna asks. Heads whip around as a few passengers turn to me.

"You know what's going on?" one of them asks.

"Can you get us outta here?" another says.

I'm taken aback by their desperate faces. Lukas and Renna look at me. I walk past them, toward the nearest door on the side of the SpeedTrain. The door is sealed shut. But I spot an emergency switch right beside it.

"I wish I'd grabbed a Plasmar from one of the guards," Lukas says.

"That won't be necessary," I reply. I flick the switch, but the door doesn't budge.

"What about your swords?" Renna asks. I didn't think of that.

"You have a sword?" one of the passengers blurts.

"I have two." I draw one of my Arcblades and slice it through the air. The blade shoots out and locks into place. I wedge the blade in the small gap between the door and wall. Gripping the handle with both hands, I slice downward. The blade vibrates as it grinds along the seam of the door. I hear a horrible screeching as the blade shears the lock in two. I pull my sword free and the door slides open with relative ease. The two pieces of the broken lock clang onto the floor.

"Alright, everyone out," I yell, sheathing my sword and stepping out of the way. The passengers hurriedly shuffle out the broken door. I follow the passengers into the dark SpeedTunnel, with Lukas and Renna soon trailing behind me.

* * *

My eyes ache from the bright light of the sun, even looking at the ground from behind my mask does little against the glare. I had gotten used to the darkness after our long trek through the tunnel to the station. Nevertheless, I still force myself to take in the Crathenos cityscape. Unlike on Voltaris Island, the buildings here are much more spread out. Large roads cut between sky-piercing edifices.

The majority of the city, like the SpeedTrain, lacks any source of artificial light. Power has been directed away from the light poles lining the sides of the street. Similarly, the walls of buildings are bare, with no projected screens to shove propaganda down citizens' throats. Silhouettes move behind open blinds in all the buildings.

Gargantuan rollers trudge along the streets, their perfectly cleaned conveyor belts not even leaving tread marks on the mostly empty streets. The rollers are tagged with the letters 'C-S-D' along their sides, but the navy-blue letters fail to conceal the Voltaris logos etched into the rollers' walls. One roller stops at the end of the city block and people climb out, wearing bright yellow uniforms. They have the same letters patched on their shoulders. From the roller's interior, workers grab blankets and heating lamps, handing them to a newly-formed line of eager civilians. The people from the SpeedTrain rush past me to join the line.

CHAPTER 20

LUKAS

My eyes are drawn to the capitol building in front of me. Without the light of the purple ornament at the tower's top, the building appears like any other building. Just a bit taller than the rest. I look at the stage in front of the building and images of the protest rise unbidden. Bodies crawling onto the stage, stun blasts knocking people back into the angry crowd below. In my mind, Prime Termani stands on the stage, unfazed by the crowd's pitiful attempt at change. His head whips to face me. The black eyes of his mask stare at me. I shiver, and my mind snaps back to an empty stage. Alright... let's go. I stand up straight and begin marching toward the capitol building.

"Do you have a plan?" Sapphire grumbles from behind me.

I clench my fists around the helmet in my hands and keep walking in the direction of the building. I can almost see Prime Termani standing right in front of me, Axle cheering me on right by my side.

"Luk—" Renna starts but cuts herself off with a sigh.

I can hear Axle, calling for help, screaming in my mind. My hands tremble; my eyes water. I drop the helmet. I reach up to grab my hair but force my arms back down, clenching my fists hard enough to tear the scabs on my knuckles. Something warm trickles down my right hand. I look down to see blood drip between the plates of the black glove. I look up again and break into a jog. Cries fill my ears, but I cannot tell if they're Axle's in my head or my own. Wet tracks burn down my face. The cries are my own.

"Lukas," someone screams from behind me. I whip my head around, and it's Sapphire. Somehow, I didn't recognize her voice. I stand still, shivering in place, facing her and Renna. "I know you want to save your friend."

"Shut... up..." I murmur, but I'm rooted in place.

"You don't have a plan. We need to think this through."

There's no time.

"Shut... up..."

"I know it's hard to wait. But you can't just go into this blindly."

"Shut... the fuck... up..." I squeeze my eyes closed, trembling as I struggle not to clamp my ears shut with my hands.

"She's right, Lukas," Renna says. "You need to relax." Saliva drips from my seething mouth. I open my eyes again, glaring at both Sapphire and Renna.

"I thought you were on my side," I spit. "You said you'd help me."

"Lukas there's no power," Renna says. "Prime Termani is already stressed out trying to fix it. If you had a chance to convince him to release your friend, it's gone now."

"*If* I had a chance?" I cry. Fresh tears run their course down my cheeks.

"You know that's not what I meant."

"Do I?" I clench my fists and force my hands back down to my side. "I can't believe I thought anyone in Termani would choose to fight with me."

Sapphire speaks up. "Lukas..."

"Don't you want to know why Prime Termani sent his guards after you?"

"I do, yes, but it's too risky to take action yet. There's—"

"A right way to do things?" I ask. "That's fine. You can wait. But I'm not gonna wait any longer." I turn away from them, picking my stolen helmet up from the ground. I bring my helmet up, and static fills my ears. What? I grab the knob behind the earpiece and start finicking with it, but the static doesn't go away. Huh?

"Hello," a familiar voice says. My head shoots up, turning toward the nearest building. The building is projecting a screen, but parts of the hologram are missing, flickering in and out of existence. The partial image shows the same dark room as before. His pristine white suit seems more ruffled and wrinkled than usual. His face, wrapped in red fabric, fills the screen as he leans forward. His goggled eyes seemingly locking onto mine through the screen.

Prime Termani.

"I don't think anyone could have expected this rapid loss of power. But I am not surprised. The Primordialists have been on a rampage throughout Termani. They have caused a breakout, disrupting my testing protocol." Axle. "They have caused numerous protests across Termani that have led to the deaths of respected citizens. And now, they have infiltrated Voltaris Industries. This one, I fear, is the worst of their offenses. Voltaris Industries has enabled our prosperity. They have provided the Termani guards with advanced weaponry that is essential to fighting off the Primordialist threat. They have personally handled the testing facilities, which has been of great assistance to my work. Without Voltaris Industries, Termani would be a backwater district, known by little and home to no one of importance."

I grit my teeth. He admitted to working with Voltaris.

Prime Termani leans in even closer to the screen. "I have spoken to Voltaris Industries, and they will be increasing their security tenfold. I will ramp up the testing and expand it to multiple locations for maximum efficiency. No one will leave Termani until the testing is complete. No one will leave until the power is back on. No one will leave until the Primordialists are destroyed."

My breaths are ragged as I stare at Prime Termani on the screen. He stands up and turns around. The screen flickers off.

"Don't do this," Sapphire says. "It's a stupid plan."

"Either you stay out of my way, or you help me. I am *not* letting you stop me."

I turn to face the capitol building once again. I'm going to find you, Axle. I bring the helmet down over my face. It fits snugly around my head. My vision, blurred with tears, tints green from the mask's lenses. Keeping my fists clenched, I resume my march toward the towering capitol building. In my head, Axle is by my side, marching alongside me. My breaths match my pace, slow and calculated. I turn to Axle marching beside me. Blood pours out of his eyes and down his whole body. I shake my head to clear the horrifying image away.

I near the capitol building, and notice guards stationed evenly spaced around the perimeter of the stage. Others guard the entrance to the building itself. The guards wear thicker armor than I've seen on guards in the past. Armor plates protrude out so far that the exposed sections of their bodies look incredibly thin. The guards hold their Plasmars at the ready. No holstered weapons in sight. Their Plasmars are massive, requiring both hands to handle.

"Prime Termani!" I scream. My modulated voice produces a deafening static screech that hurts my ears. But it doesn't matter. Nothing matters except Axle. The guards' heads all whirl around at the sound of my voice. They stare at me, each one of their Plasmars pointing somewhere else on my body. The nearest guard walks over to me, his Plasmar trained at my chest. Orange lights glow from every weapon.

"Prime Termani is not letting anyone in the building at this time," the guard says. I snatch at his Plasmar before he can react. I tear the weapon from his hand and throw a punch with my free hand. I can hear mechanical whirring as my arm collides with the guard. His body flies backward, crashing into the ground.

"Don't move," another guard commands. I raise the Plasmar and fire a blast at the yelling guard. My accuracy isn't great, but it still catches him in the side. Armor cracks and blood spouts out of the new wound. The guard collapses to the ground. Another guard turns to him in shock. I seize the moment and shoot her as well. This time, the blast hits her leg, bending it backward at an unnatural angle. Her shrieks fill the air as she goes down.

The remaining guards fire as one. I dive down, rolling over the ground as sizzling bursts of energy streak past my body. I get up and bolt of plasma strikes me in the side. The armor cracks and bends inward. Sharp fragments tear into my flesh, sending a shock of white-hot pain through my side. I delve my hands between a gap in the plate and grab the bent and bloody metal. The suit whirs as I pry the metal outward. Tiny splinters of metal stay lodged in my skin. Another shot fires at me, and I manage to jump out of the way in time. As I twist, a fragment tears free of my wound with a spurt of blood. Another shock of pain wracks my body. I double over from pain, then force myself upright. Resuming the offensive, I retaliate with a blast at the guard who shot me. The blast misses her entirely.

Dammit.

I shoot again, and miss again.

Fuck.

I reach down, scratching in vain at the armored suit to pull a shard out of my side. I look up to see an energy blast flying directly at my face. Someone knocks me out of the way. I hit the ground, landing right on the wound, pushing the fragment in deeper. Gasping in pain, I roll off of the wound. I manage to grip the sharp edge and tear the shard of metal out of my skin. Blood puddles on the ground from where I fell.

I look up, and Sapphire stands in front of me, her two curved Arcblades drawn. Her undone hair flies in the wind as she steps toward the nearest guard. The guard fires a shot at her. She swerves out of the way, stabs at him, and knocks the weapon out of his hand. He reaches for her arm, but Sapphire swings her leg, kicking the guard to the ground. Another guard runs at Sapphire, aiming her Plasmar at Sapphire's armor-free chest. The guard fires the blast dead center, but Sapphire bends over backward, allowing the sear by overhead. She snaps back up straight and slashes with both swords, cleaving through an unarmored spot on the guard's abdomen. The guard hunches over then crumples, face first, to the ground.

"Are you okay?" I turn to the side. Renna leans over next to me.

I grunt. "Could be better." Renna shudders at my robotic voice, then reaches out an arm. I grab it, and she hoists me up from the ground. I grimace at the pain in my side.

"That's a nasty gash," Renna says. I scoff, my eyes following all the bodies limp on the ground. Sapphire pulls a sword out of the remaining guard's neck. He drops to the ground. She kicks him off the stage and walks over to us. Renna turns to the stage and hoists herself up. She and Sapphire each grab one of my arms and pull me up onto the stage. The three of us walk toward the door. Sapphire grabs it and, without pause, swings it open.

CHAPTER 21

An energy blast flies at my chest the moment I step into the building. I shift out of the way and the blast nearly hits Renna behind me. I swing my head around to Renna who, eyes wide but unhurt, points forward. I whip my head back around as yet another blast fires at me. I lunge forward out of the way, swords in hands. I slide up to the guard, knock his Plasmar out of the way with a sword hilt, and slice through his chest with my other blade. The purple-silver blade cuts through the armor like butter, and the guard collapses to the ground.

That was the first of many. Surrounding me and the severely wounded guard, eight more guards draw their Plasmars and point them at different parts of my body. I hear the footsteps of more guards in the distance.

"Drop your weapons and put your hands behind your head," the guard in the center yells. I can't dodge all of those shots. I slowly release the grip on my Arcblades, quickly grabbing a bent metal pin from my belt. The swords clang to the ground. I raise my hands and place them behind the back of my head, concealing the pin from the guards' view. Renna and Lukas raise their hands as well.

One of the guards pulls out three pairs of handcuffs and walks behind us. The guard grabs my hands and yanks them downward, shoving the handcuffs around my hands. He repeats this action to Renna and Lukas.

"I want to speak to Prime Termani," Lukas growls with his modulated voice. I can hear Lukas's deep breaths pass through the modulator. A guard

115

grabs my Arcblades from the ground and hands one to the guard next to him. They study the hilts, finicking with the extension mechanism. Their efforts are pointless.

"Prime Termani will not be having any guests," the center guard asserts, pointing her Plasmar at Lukas.

Lukas stares back at the guard. "Who do you serve?"

The guard flinches at the question. "Prime Termani."

"Wrong," Lukas says. The guard starts to speak but Lukas interrupts her. "You work for the people of Termani. Not Prime Termani. Not Voltaris. The people of Termani." I grip the pin with my fingers and start finicking with the lock on the handcuffs. "Now I want you to think really hard about what I'm about to ask, and I mean really think about it." The lock disconnects from my left hand and I start removing the other from my right. "Do you really believe that innocent people should be forcefully tested?" The center guard's eyes narrow as she stares at Lukas. The other guards turn to the center guard, as if waiting for orders.

The right cuff disconnects, and I catch the handcuffs before they can drop to the floor. Lukas glances back at me as I draw the stolen Plasmar and fire a shot at the guard holding one of my Arcblades. The plasma makes contact right beneath the guard's chin. His head explodes, spattering blood into the eyes of the surrounding guards. I lunge forward, grabbing the sword hilt as the guard drops the ground. I flick my hand and the curved blade extends. The guard holding my other sword swings the retracted hilt around aimlessly, still blinded by the blood. By sheer luck, the blade extends out. He swings it at me, but I step in close and chop off his hand. He screams and grabs his stump, his severed hand hitting the ground with my sword. I turn away and fire a blast at his head. His head ruptures apart, spewing more blood onto the guards, just as they finish wiping their eyes clean from the previous gore. I toss the Plasmar toward Lukas and Renna. Leaning over the dead guard, I grab my other sword and jump up in time to cut through an attacking guard.

In unison, the remaining guards fire blasts at me, and I duck down, slicing at their legs. Their shots crossfire and searing hot plasma shatters through their flesh, muscles, and bones. The last of them collapse onto the ground. I step away from the mess of corpses and toward Lukas and Renna.

"What did you do?" Lukas exclaims, his whole body turning around to face me. The static produced from his voice overwhelms my ears, but I try to ignore it. "I could've convinced them."

"They weren't going to listen to your stupid speech," I say. Renna stares at the bodies on the ground, speechless. I grab her hands and remove her cuffs.

"You don't know that," Lukas says.

"They're all the same. All Termans are the same."

"That's not true."

"You all voted for the new Prime Termani." I reach toward Lukas, who reluctantly gives me his hands. I remove his cuffs and drop them on the floor.

"I did not. You can't lump us all into one group. I'm my own person, and those guards were as well. If we're all the same, if we're all bad, then why bother saving me and helping my friend?"

I turn to Renna, who remains silent. "Because he doesn't deserve to die." I holster the Plasmar on my belt again. "Let's go find Prime Termani."

I scan our surroundings. The room is rectangular, with a fake wooden texture lining the composite of the walls. The ceiling has a similar wooden texture, with some of the composite peeling off at the corners. A single white circle of light hangs dead center, illuminating the red carpet below. Dirty footsteps mar the red carpet, leading away from one of two hallways in front of me. Other than the main door, several others dot the length of the two hallways, each of which end in their own large doors. I head left, tracking the dirty footprints. Lukas and Renna join me, and the three of us walk down the short hallway. I skip past the doors on the sides of the hall, following the footprints to the door at the end.

I open the door and step through into a narrow hallway perpendicular to the first. On the left is a metal lifter door with a blue arrow button pointing up. To the right is a door just like the one that I came through. Footprints track back and forth between the lifter and the other door. I crouch down. These footprints differ from the standard-issue boot prints that the guards tracked around the carpet. The grip pattern is more angular. I follow the footprints over to the door, and the floor gives off a muted clang as I approach the door. Weird. I tap on the floor with my foot, listening to the dull echo, then turn back to Lukas and Renna.

"Do either of you know where to go?" I ask. "I've never been to Crathenos."

Lukas nods, stepping toward the lifter. "Prime Termani's office is on the top floor." He presses the button on the door and it flickers from blue to orange. At least the building has enough reserve power for the lifter. The door slides open across the ground, and the three of us step into it. The metal lifter is a tight fit for us. Renna is pressed up against the back of the lifter, covering a sign. The lifter's panel glows with numbers—fifty down to one—with a golden 'P' button hovering above them.

Lukas presses the golden button and the lifter shoots upwards. The ascent is quick and the lifter decelerates within seconds. Seems the building still has some auxiliary power left. The doors slide open with a soft rasp. Lukas steps through the door into the room on the other side.

The floor here is stripped of carpet, replaced with the same composite wooden texture that lines the walls and ceiling of the bottom floor. The walls of this room are dark gray and made of a smooth plain composite. The room is empty besides a small desk in the center of the room facing a large camera mounted on the right wall. Dusty footprints mark out a path between the desk and the lifter.

"He's not here..." Lukas walks past me, circles the room, and returns to the lifter. "He has to be here somewhere."

I tilt my head, leaning down to get a closer look at the footprints. They're the same as those on the first floor, with the angular grip pattern. Why's a politician tracking in so much dirt? I walk back into the lifter. Renna hasn't moved from her spot at the back.

"We have to check every floor," Lukas says. He reaches to press the next highest button on the lifter door, and I grab his arm.

"I don't think that's necessary. I have an idea as to where he might be." I press the button labeled '1', and we accelerate downward.

"What are you doing?" he asks.

118

"Just trust me."

I stare down at the floor, my mind rushing through all of the things I've pieced together so far. There's a man called the Seeker who made a suit built for fighting. He most likely leads Voltaris. If that is true, then he was the one who decided to create the serum. But he, or Voltaris, doesn't want anyone to know about it. Not even the people making the serum. At the same time, Prime Termani created mandatory testing that's being forced upon selected people, like Lukas's friend. We got blood samples at the lab before Lukas showed up. Those blood samples were likely from those tests.

I tilt my head to the side, still looking at the ground. The tests must have been using the serum. Because it was definitely designed to be used on people. But what are those organisms? What else do we know? The power went out recently, too. Does that have something to do with it? Voltaris runs the power grid, and they run the tests with Prime Termani. There's still a lot of power in this building. There're too many factors to keep track of. I need time to think. But there's definitely *something* happening in this building. Something important. Something to do with that room on the bottom floor.

CHAPTER 22

AXLE

I stand completely still, looking in the direction of where the Stone once was. I thought the Lightning Stone was gone, hidden after the Saberren War. Apparently, Voltaris has been powering the continent with it. How long has Voltaris had it? From what Zeke and Adrius mentioned, it's been a very long time. The last time anyone lost power was when my parents died in the SpeedTrain accident. Since then, Lukas and I have been alone, together. He's probably worried about me. I'm sure he knows I was selected for the testing. But he can't know what the testing is.

I can hear people finicking with stuff in front of me. I don't know how they can see with all this dust they're kicking around.

Footsteps thud in the darkness around me. Mostly behind me, as people are getting to work. A set of footsteps get louder. A faint cool breeze brushes my skin. I turn in the direction of the cold air. The direction that we came from. Clanging sounds echo in the tunnel as a metal cart flies through the dusty air and crashes against the dirt wall, sending even more dust raining all over us. The clamor dies down, replaced by soft whispers and murmurs. And something else. Static.

Someone steps in front of me, and several flashlight beams wave around, barely piercing the dusty air. The lights eventually coalesce into one beam, illuminating the shadow-man. His gaze locks on me, but then moves past toward the Lightning Stone. He takes a step toward the Primordialists.

In the front, Primordialists rush toward the shadow-man. This time, the shadow-man pulls out two knives and starts cutting through the swarming crowd; his unnaturally fast movements are accompanied by mechanical whirring I stumble backward into Adrius. I turn around to see his eyes fixed on the shadow-man. His hands shake as he draws his Plasmar.

Adrius fires a blast at the shadow-man, whose head whips around at the crackling sound of the Plasmar. Just like earlier, the shadow-man pulls a Primordialist into the blast's path. The exploding body leaves more blood and guts all over the shadow-man's armor and red bodysuit underneath.

"Protect the Lightning Stone," Zeke exclaims, pointing his flashlight at the shadow-man. More Primordialists brandish their blades and attack the shadow-man. A river of dead bodies grows in the wake of the shadow-man's stride.

A forest of Arcblades glint in the flashlight as multiple men and women attack the shadow-man at the same time. The shadow-man nimbly dodges back and forth while drawing another set of blades. Clutching two knives in each hand, he flicks his wrists, and the four knives thud into the closest Primordialists. He walks forward, leans down, and grabs the knives. Sheathing two of them, the shadow-man spins around in a circle, cutting through the attackers. Bodies topple on top of other bodies. The shadow-man moves forward unhindered, stepping on the fallen and killing whoever's still clinging to life.

A woman circles him and leaps, stabbing toward his back. His hand snaps back, grabbing the blade in a gloved hand and yanking it free. He elbows her in the temple, spins her around, then kicks her hard, sending her crashing into the other assailants. The Primordialist men and women stumble backward, but quickly find their footing and lunge forward again. The shadow-man, still holding his knives, steps forward and stabs them into the necks of the nearest Primordialists. As they fall, he wrenches the knives from the bodies and stabs to the sides at more assailants.

Someone pulls a sword free from a corpse and throws it spinning end over end at the shadow-man. He catches the sword, still holding his knife, and throws it back like a spear at twice the speed. The sword impales him, pinning his body to the tunnel wall. The shadow-man dives forward between two attackers, rolls, then springs to his feet and yanks the thrown sword free. He spears it at the attacker to his right and turns his body to the left, stabbing through the nearest person with both knives.

I turn to Adrius, drenched in sweat. "Where do I go? Why aren't you running?"

"If he gets the Lightning Stone, it'll be years before we can find it again."

"Our lives are not worth risking for that Stone," I yell. "What about the people being tested on? You were willing to leave them behind but you won't leave this?"

"That Stone is what allows the testing to happen. Voltaris cannot have it. They don't deserve it."

I look back at the shadow-man again. Half of the hooded figures are dead, and he doesn't have any noticeable scratches. "How do I leave?"

Adrius sighs. "The fastest way is up, but you'd have to get past the fighting. Otherwise, you can take the rails. It might take a while, but you'll find a place where you can climb out of the tunnel."

I look down the tunnel, then forward again. The Primordialists are dwindling in number, maybe around thirty left maximum. A figure steps back from the fighting, climbs on a cart's edge, and shoves a trapdoor open overhead. He pulls a handle and a ladder drops down.

"Give it to me," I hear Zeke call. Another Primordialist hands him the Lightning Stone, which he quickly pockets. He flicks a button and the flashlight goes out. "Don't let him see you," he exclaims. I hear screams as more people die, and footsteps clang as others scurry up the ladder. He can see?

Adrius grabs my arm and guides me forward. My boot squashes down on something soft. A corpse. I wince, but don't slow down. I hear a clang right in front of me, and Adrius releases my arm. I reach out and grab onto a rung of the ladder. I still hear that awful screeching static and feel cool breath twirling around my legs. I race up the ladder as fast as I can.

Pushing off the final rung, I hoist myself up into more darkness. I stumble blindly around the room until my hand finds a wall. I scramble to the right, pushing against it. A slam thunders and I whirl around. My heart pounds as

I hear footsteps closing in on me.

"Zeke," Adrius asks. "Can you get some light in here?"

A pause. "Not yet. He may be able to see in the dark, but his vision could be limited. Try to feel for an exit." More footsteps resound in the room as people run toward the walls. I keep my hands pressed to the wall and continue feeling my way along it. I hear a creak and blinding sunlight floods through a newly formed crack up ahead.

"Zeke?" someone asks.

"That wasn't me," he replies. I squint at the light, a small crack in the wall. A door continues to open, letting more and more light into the room. Three figures stand in the doorway. Two women flank the figure in the middle. They wear vaguely familiar ornate, black-and-white masks that cover their faces. Their white lab coats are stained with blood and dirt, and the remaining white spots contrast against the black of their masks. The central figure wears a deep black and gray suit that covers his entire body, including his face, which is hidden by a full-faced helmet. I suddenly realize what the masks remind me of, because this man reminds me of it more. His suit is like the shadow-man's, just without the red jumpsuit underneath. This suit is much more streamlined, as if it was made for stealth rather than battle.

"Voltaris," Zeke mutters under his breath. The remaining hooded men all point their Arcblades at the three people in the doorframe.

We all step back from the door as the three figures step forward. The fully suited man heads right for me, his neck craning forward quizzically. I stumble back, but the man moves toward me at faster speeds.

"Get away fro—" I begin.

"Axle?" he says in a deep robotic voice that crackles with static. The voice forces me to cover my ears, and static comes along with the man's breaths. We left the shadow-man below us. I don't know who this is, or why he's wearing a similar suit.

"Who are you? How do you know my name?" I flounder backward. There must be more people like the shadow-man.

"Oh," he pauses. "Right."

He reaches to grip his head and pulls the helmet off, tossing it to the side. It's Lukas.

His eyes are filled with tears that stream down his face. He quickly glances around the room at the hooded figures and at Adrius, but his eyes settle on me.

"Why are you here?" he asks through shallow breaths. "What are you doing here?"

"You know him?" Adrius murmurs.

"He's my best friend." My eyes burst into tears as well. "How did you find me?"

CHAPTER 23

"What?" I mutter, my eyes blurred from tears. "I didn't think you'd be here... I'm here for Prime Termani. I was gonna try to force him to free you from the testing... I thought you'd be in the prison. I thought the testing was in the prison. But you're here."

Axle's eyes shift. He continues to look in my direction, but it seems like he's no longer focused on me. "It was in the prison." He wipes his eyes. "There was so much death. They were injected with this weird serum... it killed them. And when it didn't, a man did."

"What did he look like?"

"He didn't look like a person. Well, kind of. He was wearing this weird armor, like what you're wearing."

My stomach drops. "The Seeker," I murmur.

"What?"

"How did you get out?" I scan Axle's body, noticing the guard armor. "And what is with the armor? Where did you get that?"

"He helped me," Axle gestures to the other armored man next to him. "His name is Adrius. He told me to put on this armor to disguise myself. It didn't work though." Axle shudders. "The shadow-man still found me. He works for Voltaris."

"I know. I saw a drawing of his suit inside Voltaris Tower. It's called the Seeker."

"You were in Voltaris Tower?" Axle exclaims. "Why?"

"We don't have time for this," a man says in the back. "Let's get out of here. Fast." The cloaked figures all move toward the door that we came in from, but Sapphire steps in the way, blocking them with her swords.

"Move out of the way," the man in the front says. His hood is off, revealing a nearly bald head covered in patches of small gray hairs. He pulls out a handle just like Sapphire's, and extends it out in the same way. His Arcblade, however, lacks the purple tint that Sapphire's have.

"Not until you tell me what you're doing in the capitol building," Sapphire says.

He eyes her swords, before staring at her mask. Sapphire removes the mask, tossing it behind her. "We don't have time for this. The Seeker that your friend speaks of is below us, and he'll be back."

"What?" I exclaim, turning back to Axle. "Is this true?"

Axle's eyes shift again, and then widen. His body begins to shake. "Oh, fuck. Oh, shit."

"Axle… What's going on?"

"I talked to you for too long. It's quiet down there. Either he's dead, or he's coming."

A creak punctuates his statement. My eyes snap to a trapdoor in the center of the room. A black glove creeps through a narrow opening in the door. Axle, Adrius next to him, and all the cloaked figures whip around as the glove drop a ball-shaped device with a clang onto the floor next to the trapdoor. Hissing erupts from the ball and a plume of smoke explodes to instantly engulf the room.

A black dagger cuts through the smoke, embedding itself in the shoulder of the bald man. He gasps, and grabs the knife with his other hand. Although I can hardly see though the haze, I spot blood welling up around the knife in the man's body.

"Hello Zeke," a voice booms. The voice is unnatural, deeper than anything human. It is similar to the Mark 1's helmet modulation, but there's more crackling static warping the uncanny voice. The sound makes my skin crawl. Beside me, Axle shivers too. "It has been too long since we last met, hasn't it? I remember that protest very well. It was a valiant effort." Through the shadows, I see the silhouette of a tall man rising from the trap door and walk toward the injured man.

The injured man scoffs; his silhouette continues to grip the knife embedded in his shoulder.

"So, you're called the Seeker now. A little on the nose, isn't it?"

"Oh, Zeke, you haven't changed a bit," the Seeker says. "Now where is the Lightning Stone?"

"I don't have it."

"I know you're lying," the tall silhouette hovers over Zeke. "I found that Stone. You have no right to it. It is mine." The silhouette reaches forward and grabs the knife in Zeke's body. "Where is it?"

Zeke spits. "The Lightning Stone belongs to the Saberrens, just like the rest of the Primordial Stones."

"Primordialist scum," the Seeker says. "Your mission is pointless. Your values lack clarity. Give me the Stone, and you will earn a painless death."

"I don't have the Stone."

"Where is it?" the Seeker screams. His static-filled robot voice echoes throughout the room, triggering a loud ringing in my ears. No, not now. Anytime but now. I grab my ears, but the ringing persists. Dammit. No. Get out of my head.

"You can kill me. It won't matter. The Primordialists are everywhere. They will return, and in greater numbers," Zeke bellows. The voice scoffs, and twists the knife out of Zeke's body. He slices it across Zeke's neck, and his limp body drops to the ground.

The cloaked figures—Primordialists—all point their own swords around aimlessly through the smoke cloud. The ringing in my ears gets louder. I whip my head around, looking for a silhouette. I turn to Axle, whose wide eyes meet mine. I turn away.

Where is she? Why is she in my head?

"You Primordialists won't give up," the voice booms. He throws another flying knife at a Primordialist, who collapses under the shock of the blade. More move in the direction that the knife came from, and they're met by long black swords that cut through the smoke. "I don't think you really understand the concept of ownership. The Lightning Stone was gathering dust when I found it." He swings his hands again, but this time, his blades are knives. "It's mine. I bought Voltaris Island for my own research. It's mine. It was my idea to design the serum that you want to destroy. The serum is mine." The static voice booms as he speaks. I search the smoke frantically for her shape. Nothing. Just an overwhelming ringing pain.

Get out of my fucking head.

The tall silhouette stabs through a Primordialist with a sword. Where do all these weapons keep coming from? Another Primordialist reels over as a knife penetrates his flesh. Now it's a knife? One Primordialist grabs his friend and kicks the silhouette back. The injured Primordialist pulls out the knife and disappears into the smoke. The uninjured Primordialist swings an Arcblade at the silhouette. The sword drags across the Seeker's body without doing any damage. My ears feel like they're bleeding from the ringing. Show up already.

Someone runs past me, slamming into my side. I topple over. My open wound smacks against the dirty ground; searing pain floods my body. The ringing only gets louder.

"What I do with what I own is my choice," the robot voice says. "And if you try to stop me, then I have no choice but to put an end to your useless protest."

I squint through the haze to see the tall silhouette standing alone. The Primordialists have disappeared. I look down. Blood-stained bodies scatter across the floor. The Seeker leans over a corpse of a fallen Primordialist, rummaging through its robes.

The smoke thins enough to reveal the silhouette in full form. He is a spitting image of the Seeker Mark 2 drawing. The red undersuit is stained darker in some spots from gore. His Akorth armor blocks any light, looking like a hole in the air. The armor is sleeker than typical guard armor, allowing the man to move freely. His masked helmet is painted red in blood, but black chunks of armor peek through on his cheeks, chin, forehead, and nose area. Goosebumps form where the surprisingly cool air touches my neck. Next to me, Axle begins to hyperventilate. The ringing in my ears finally stops.

The Seeker's head cranes down at me. He stands up and lurks closer, holding two knives. He presses the hilts with his thumbs, and the knives telescope outward into long black blades. Islorr's Blood. He raises his hand and points one of his swords at me.

"That suit is mine."

"Sapphire, stop," Renna shouts.

Sapphire moves in front of me, running at the Seeker with her two curved blades at the ready. The Seeker swings a sword at her and she flips over it, narrowly avoiding the attack and landing lightly next to a dead Primordialist. She swings one of her swords at the Seeker. The Seeker blocks it with one of his.

"Sapphire ajj Termani," the Seeker's modulated voice growls. "You've been in the way for far too long. I should never have made that deal with your father. It wasn't worth it to hire you."

Sapphire snakes the edge of her other blade at the red bodysuit underlining the Seeker's armor, but he meets it with his free sword. The Seeker twists to slash at her neck, while still blocking Sapphire's first attack with his other blade. She parries the Seeker's swing and pulls away from him. The Seeker stops her by throwing his arm around her neck and pushing her down toward the ground. He grabs the back of her lab coat before she hits the concrete. Sapphire's coat begins to tear, slowly lowering her closer to the ground; she swings both swords backward up at the Seeker's neck. He drops his swords, catches both of her wrists, and lifts Sapphire up, twisting her arms behind her back.

"I haven't seen authentic Shifter Arcblades in a long time. Did you get those from your father?"

Sapphire wrenches her arms out of the Seeker's grip and spins around to face him. He kicks her to the ground, placing his boot on her chest and pinning her down. She tries to breathe, but the Seeker's foot cuts off her airflow. The Seeker leans forward, picks up his dropped swords, and flicks his wrist to turn the sword in his right hand back into a knife. He presses the knife against Sapphire's throat and slowly starts slicing into her neck.

Renna screams, charging forward at the man. He hits her with the dull end of his remaining sword. She flies backward and crashes into the wall. The Seeker releases his foot from Sapphire and kicks her limp body toward Renna. Renna immediately leans over Sapphire, tearing a chunk off of Sapphire's bloodied lab coat and tying it around her neck. She removes her mask. Tears drip from her eyes onto Sapphire's body.

The Seeker ignores them, moving toward another Primordialist body to search for the stone. He yells, sending more static into my eardrums. He scurries over to another body, with the same result. Nothing. Another body. Still nothing. Each time, he glances over at Axle, who looks rooted in place. The armored man's eyes scan the room as well. He picks up a fallen Plasmar with the light on orange.

"Where is the Stone?" the Seeker screams, standing up yet again. He kicks a body in front of him, sending it spinning and spraying blood through the air. His mask's eyes face us. "One of you must have it. And if not, at least I get to watch you die." He turns his knives back into swords, slowly stepping toward us. His mask tilts to face Axle. "You first. You escaped the testing. You would've died anyway. I shall resign you to your fate."

Axle steps back away from the Seeker. Renna continues crying over Sapphire's injured body. There are so many bodies on the floor. So much blood. So much death. My ears start ringing again. I look back to Axle as the Seeker approaches him. Then back to the bodies, to Sapphire's body. One of the Primordialist's bodies near me still has a sword lodged in his chest. An Akorth sword. I clench my fists, now staring at the sword, and the ringing ceases. Grunting, I push myself up to my feet. Pain penetrates my side, but I remain standing nevertheless.

"Get out of here," I whisper to Axle.

"What?" he murmurs.

"I said get out of here. Leave. Now," I order, still watching the sword. The Seeker's head shifts to face me, then back to Axle. He lunges in a sudden sprint.

"Leave," I yell, running forward to intercept him. I grab the sword from the corpse's chest. Just as the Seeker turns to me in surprise, I stab him just below his right shoulder. Mechanical whirring accompanies my arm's movement as the sword pierces right through the black armor, which shatters and splinters around the wound. I pull the chipped blade out and dark red blood pours out of the wound. A blood curdling inhuman scream is ripped from the Seeker's throat, modulated so that it feels like needles digging around in my ears.

"Lukas!" Axle screams. Adrius speeds past us, picking up something from the ground. The Seeker throws a punch at my face. I spit blood back into the Seeker's face. His head cranes to face Adrius, and his sword telescopes inward to form a knife. I grab his arm and pull back. I hear gears rotating and straining in both our suits, and the Seeker's arm resists my pull. I grab him with my other arm, dropping the damaged Akorth sword. Adrius makes his way back to Axle, grabs his arm, and drags him toward the metal trapdoor. "What are you doing?" Axle yells.

Renna wipes her tears and pulls Sapphire's limp body toward the trapdoor as well. "Lukas…" Axle whimpers, struggling to get back to me. Adrius pulls out a Plasmar on blue and shoots him in the chest. He goes unconscious. The man throws Axle down the trapdoor, and helps Renna carry Sapphire. The Seeker plucks his hand from my grip and throws a knife at Adrius. It slices his shoulder; he winces but continues to carry Sapphire. Renna goes down the trapdoor and Adrius hoists Sapphire down after her. He turns to me, nods, and hops down. The trapdoor creaks shut.

Now it's just the Seeker and me.

The Seeker's head turns back to me.

"You idiot," he screams, and static overwhelms my ears. "What have you done?"

The Seeker unsheathes another knife, turning it into a sword to match his other hand. He swings one of his swords at my head but I just narrowly dodge the blade. I glare at him, grabbing the damaged but usable sword from the ground. Tightening my fists as I hold onto the sword with both hands, I swing down at the Seeker's head. The wound in my side is on fire. The robotic man blocks my swing with his two swords in an 'X' shape. I push harder with my sword, but he overcomes me, sending me stumbling backward. He steps forward, punching me in the ribs. A slight crack is quickly accompanied by a burst of pain. I grit my teeth, swinging my sword again. My body fails me, and I lose momentum. The Seeker bats the sword out of my hand with a flick of a blade. With his left hand he grabs the armor plate under my chin—while still gripping his sword—and pushes me to my knees. My eyes water and my vision blurs with hatred.

The Seeker stares down at me through empty robotic eyes, shoves me over so I sprawl onto the ground, and pins me down with his knee. He calmly places the blade of one of his swords against the armor beneath my right shoulder, the same place where I stabbed him. His entire suit whirs as he leans into the sword. The increasing pressure sends small cracks fracturing across the Akorth armor of the Mark 1 Seeker suit. The fissures expand, and the armor shatters around the blade. Shards of Akorth lodge themselves in my shoulder. I wince in pain as the damaged sword first makes contact with my arm, then the pain increases tenfold as the sword starts to slice through my arm. My skin hurts first, as blood pours out onto the ground. Then the sword reaches my muscle, filling me with overwhelming pain. The Seeker finally slices through my bone like it's butter. My arm drops to the ground, and my mind sears white hot with the worst pain I've ever felt. I look down at the severed arm on the floor, my vision blurring with every second, both from tears and from pain. My screams echo through the room, but they're drowned out by the Seeker's loud labored breaths.

I drop to my back on the floor as the Seeker leans over me. He punches the side of my face. Warm blood spurts from a cut and pours down my cheek. My vision continues to blur as the pain in my shoulder wracks my body. But my thoughts remain intact. I stare up at the Seeker's mask and spit. The spit misses and falls back down onto my face. The black eyes of the Seeker's mask stare at me as I slip into a painless sleep.

PART 2

To Shift Yourself is to Shift the World

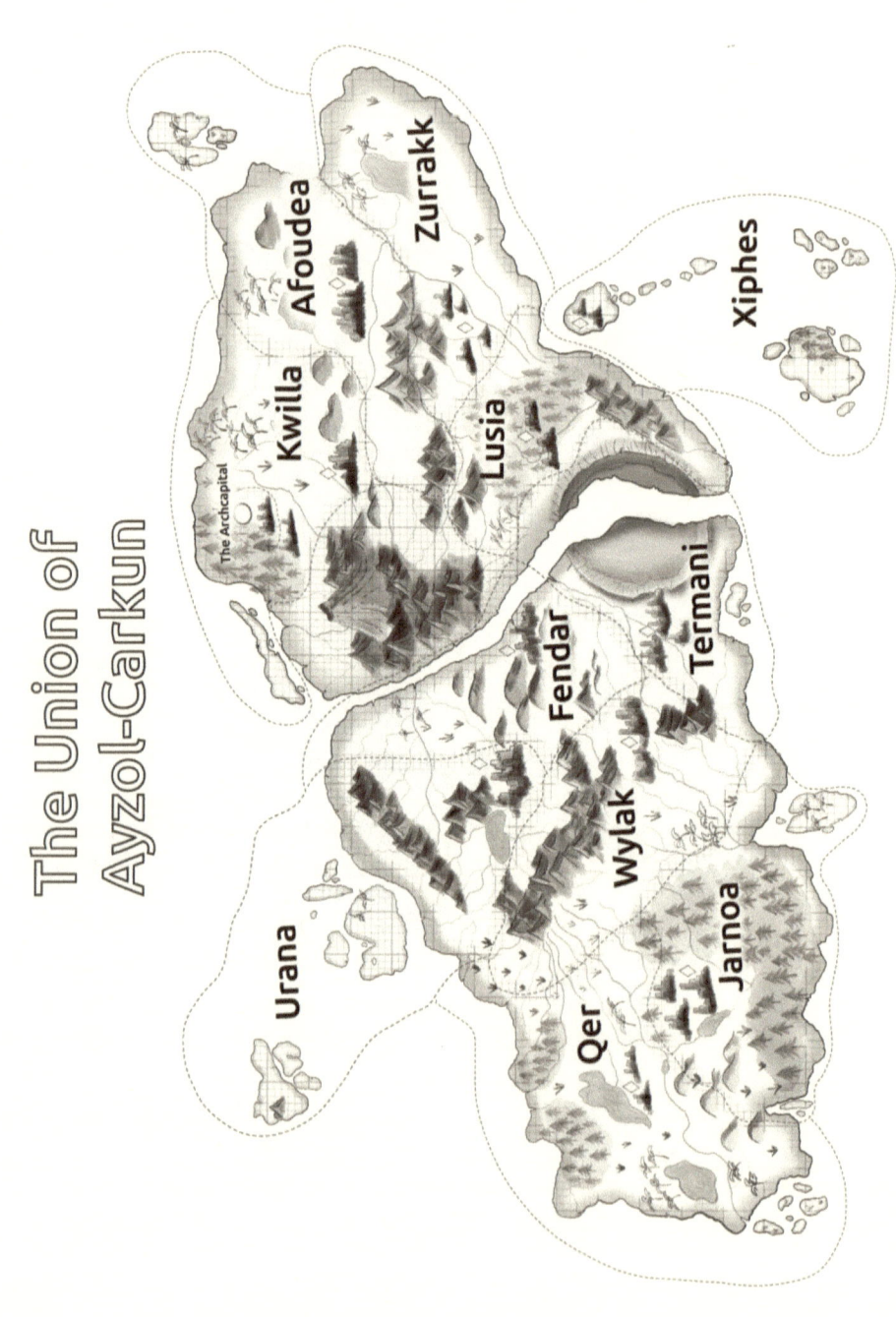

The Union of Ayzol-Carkun

Afoudea

Zurrakk

Xiphes

Kwilla

The Archcapital

Lusia

Fendar

Termani

Wylak

Urana

Jarnoa

Qer

CHAPTER 24

SAPPHIRE

I swing the door open and march into Voltaris Laboratories. Something's off. The lights above are still blindingly bright, but the desks are arranged in a different pattern. While evenly spaced as always, there's more walking room between them now. I try to look around more, but my eyes refuse to respond. What? I attempt to move my arm but it does not listen either. What is going on?

Without telling myself to, I step forward into the building. The over-whelming weight of countless stares pushes down on me. This is odd. I remember this. This was my first day at Voltaris.

Everyone who is... was working diligently just had to look up to see their new coworker. The scientists wore long white lab coats and worked with machines at their desks that I did not recognize. I didn't spend much time looking at them, since it was hard to avoid the weird presence of their stares.

With those strange masks, I couldn't tell if they were actually staring or not. They weren't the ordinary faceshields that I've heard of scientists using; I knew those were transparent. These masks were purposefully opaque, and covered anything about the scientists' faces that could be identifiable. Each mask was designed the same, a plain white circle with two big black circles that I could see my reflection in. A black covering masked the mouth area. I must have been staring at their masks for too long because eventually someone walked over and gestured toward the other side of the room. Having no idea what to do, I obliged and followed the masked man toward

135

two double doors with the text 'Voltaris Laboratories' plastered above them. He opened one of the doors, and I made to walk past him when he held out a hand to block me.

"You can't bring those in here," he ordered.

"Huh?"

"Your swords," he pointed at the two handles I had attached on either side of my belt. "You're not allowed to have them in the lab." I don't understand why he cared.

"I don't understand," I said, tilting my head. "I'm not going to use them."

"It doesn't matter. It's policy." The man reached his hands out to grab my Arcblade handles. I stepped back, resting both my hands on the handles.

"You are not going to take my swords." I glared at the man. "They are mine."

The man shrugged. "Well then, I can't let you in the tower."

"Ok, here's how this is going to work." I stepped closer to the man. "You've met my father, right? He kind of runs the place." The man's eyes widened, and he nodded. "I'm sure he'd hate to hear that some scientist refused to let his own daughter in the lab."

"S-Sorry ma'am," the man stuttered, moving his hand out of the way. "Right this way." I released my hands from my hilts and followed the man up a large spiral staircase. Underneath the spiral staircase was a bright white light that lit up the giant stairwell.

As we walked, the man pulled out a mask identical to his own. He stopped walking halfway up, forcing me to do the same. He turned to me and handed me the mask. "You have to put this on."

I shook my head. "That's ridiculous."

"We all have to wear the masks. Ever since Voltaris bought the lab a while ago—"

"I don't care that we all have to wear them. I still think it's stupid. I'm not wearing one." I stared into the eyes of the man's mask. He was a little bit shorter than me, so I had to tilt my head down to look at him.

"Listen, I may have been able to let you into the lab with your swords, but I can't let you go any farther without the mask." He moved his hand holding the mask closer to me.

"Do you want me to talk to my father?" I asked. The man shook his head.

"I'm sorry, you have to wear the mask. I'll get in trouble. Please just put the mask on..."

"Alright, whatever..." I grabbed the mask from his hand and put it on my face. It was humid underneath the mask, and I hated it.

The man stepped off the staircase and pointed.

"Down the hall, first door to the left."

I follow his instructions and end up at a door labeled 'Analysis.' He opened the labeled door, turned around, and disappeared back down the staircase. I looked through the door. It was a small room, with just one person in there and a piece of equipment that I'd never seen before. It was shaped like a box, with a small hole and a tube sticking out. The tube was filled with a viscous green liquid. The young woman in the room leaned against the side wall, her head tilted down. Her earpiece had a blue light, signaling to me that it was active.

Other than the woman and the strange machine on the desk, the room was empty. The walls were painted a dull gray color, the light occasionally flickered, and there was not even a chair for the desk. The desk was scratched up a bit with pencil markings. There wasn't even paper in the room. Whatever work the strange machine is used for must not be important at all.

The woman was wearing a lab coat that was too long for her.

"Hello," I said, standing in the door frame. The woman's head perked up and her head turned to me. "I was left here so I'm assuming I'm supposed to be here." The woman raised her hand and tapped a button on the earpiece, turning the blue light off.

"You're also an intern?" she asked, stepping off the wall and walking over to me, reaching out to shake my hand. I stepped past her, ignoring her attempt.

"No, I work here."

"You seem too young to work here. Are you sure you're not an intern?" she asked.

I scoffed. "Yes, I'm sure I'm not an intern. I got a message saying so."

"How old are you? I'm seventeen. I'm almost done interning, and I've been here for nearly a year."

"I'm sixteen," I responded.

"You're sixteen?" the woman exclaimed.

"Why do you keep asking me all these questions?" I walked over to the strange machine on the desk. "What does this do?"

"You're working here, and you don't know how things work?" I turned back to the woman, whose mask stared at me.

"Yes, so please tell me what this does, so I can find a way to be useful."

The woman continued to stare at me. "I'm Renna."

I tilted my head to the side. "I'm Sapphire. I'd appreciate it if you'd answer my question."

Renna sighed. "That analyzes a serum we've been working on in the lab. I don't know what it's supposed to do."

"How are you supposed to analyze something if you don't know what it's supposed to do?"

She shrugged. "I'm not sure. The machine does the work for us."

"Wait, we? You're not the only one working on this?" I asked.

"Everyone's working on it. It's been our only project for a while now."

"Do you really need that many people to work on one project?" I scoffed, pulling the tube out of the machine. The machine started to beep and displayed a bright red light, so I quickly put the tube back in.

"Yes, it's hard work," Renna said. I scoffed again. Renna scoffed in response. I turned back to stare at her. "Okay, what's your deal? Are you trying to feel cool, or are you just naturally a jerk?"

"What?" I tilted my head.

"See, that, what you're doing there… It's condescending."

"Since when was curiosity condescending?" I asked.

"*That* too," Renna raised her voice slightly. "Just try to be a little nicer."

"Nicer?" I tilted my head for the third time. Renna sighed. I slowly tilted my head back to normal. "I suppose, if we're going to be working together, I should accommodate your emotions." Renna sighed again and turned away.

"Uhh, tell me about yourself... I guess." Renna turned back, her head perked up. I gestured to her. "Go ahead... Speak."

"As you know, I've interned here for almost a year. I love lab work. It's exciting to—"

Although I allowed Renna to prattle away, I didn't really pay attention. Instead, I watched the green fluid as the machine analyzed it. I learned everything I needed to know about Renna as we worked together anyway. I forgot how long we've been working on this serum. We moved rooms too eventually, and then started making it in the main lab with everyone else.

This memory must mean something. This is when I learned about the serum for the first time. Why is my mind having me remember this now?

CHAPTER 25

LUKAS

A familiar ringing throbs in my ears. Of course. I cough. Mucus and dirt fly out of my throat and onto the ground. Ugh… I lean back against the wall behind me, my injured ribs aching. It's not dirt like the floor, but the concrete wall is covered in enough filth that I can't feel the surface underneath. If it weren't for the small gaps between thick metal bars replacing one of the walls, I would've sworn I was buried alive. Instead, I'm forced to accept the fact that I am still indeed alive, and trapped in this cramped cell.

In the cell is a small bed against one of the walls, if it can be called that. It consists of a rough wood plank on the floor with a few blankets draped on top. I don't know how long I've been in this cell, but the light gray blankets are fully brown with dirt. It has to be a couple of weeks at least. Sometimes I notice the smell of the room, or myself, but I'm mostly used to it. The ringing in my ears is accompanied by the droning echoes of a machine in the distance.

I turn to peek at my right shoulder, peeling back the thick cloth that is wrapped around my stub. Underneath the fabric, my wound has mostly scabbed over. Near the end of the shoulder, where my arm was attached, are too many stitches to count. The scars from the removal of the Akorth shrapnel are all but faded away. I pull the fabric back up and tie it back into a loose knot. I'm not used to using my left hand for precise tasks.

My ears finally stop ringing.

"You shouldn't have attacked him."

I close my eyes, raw from tears. My dry eyelids scratch my eyes as they close. It's painful, but I've gotten used to the pain. The physical pain, anyway. Without opening my eyes, I move over to the bed and collapse down on it. My chest collides with the wood; the dirty blankets don't protect me from the fall. The nearly healed wound in my side itches dully.

"If you hadn't attacked him, you wouldn't have lost your arm."

I pull the blanket up and wrap it around my body, especially my ears. The blanket rubs against my itching nub.

"If you hadn't attacked him, he would've left."

I moan. "And killed everyone else in the process."

"You don't know that, Lukas."

"Yeah, well neither do you!" I shout, shoving my face deeper into the blanket and using my left arm to wrap the blanket tighter over my ears. It doesn't shut her up though.

"You're worried about Axle. About all of them."

"You're in my fucking head, you tell me!"

Spit piles on the blanket and rubs against my face. I scoff, wiping the spit off my face on a dry part of the blanket. I sit up, looking around for the familiar silhouette of my mom. I find her through the bars, impressed onto the dirt wall on the other side. I grimace, and turn the rest of my body to face her.

"Are you mad you can't punch me?" she asks.

"I don't have an arm, how would I punch you anyway?"

"You have another arm."

"Why are we talking about this?" I press my palm to my forehead, rubbing at the skin. "Why are you here?"

"You wanted me here," my mom's voice says.

"I don't want you here."

"Then tell me why I'm here."

I sigh, close my eyes for a second, and open them again. The silhouette is still there. "I... don't know..."

"Do you think they're dead?"

"The Seeker won't stop chasing them until he's killed them." I spit on the ground next to my bed. "And I'm stuck in this stupid fucking cell. I can't do anything."

"Axle could escape. He's always been resilient."

"Are you even listening to what you're saying?" I cry. My dried eyes are starting to water up again. "You sound insane."

"No, I don't exist. No one can hear me but you. You sound insane." I can almost hear my mom smiling, even though the silhouette doesn't have a face. "What if they all got away successfully?" she asks.

"I would be crazy to think that," I mutter. "I saw how easily the Seeker murdered the Primordialists."

I pick up a dirty rock off of the ground with my left hand and throw it through the bars. It hits the dirt on the other side where my mom's silhouette is and falls to the ground. As expected, the silhouette doesn't move.

"But what if—"

"What if what?" I exclaim. "What if what? The Seeker is out there. They have the Lightning Stone. He's not going to let that go. They will all die."

"You don't know that."

I sigh. "What I don't know is why the Seeker kept me alive. Why he put me in this cell instead of leaving my body with the rest."

"I don't know. But there's nothing you can do about it."

"Exactly my point."

"So why worry about it?"

"Why are you asking me this? Why? They're going to die now, why does it matter? Why does it—" I start coughing and reel over as more mucus and dirt come out of my mouth. "Why does it fuc—" I cough again and this time blood comes out. It hits my left hand and drips off onto the dirt. I wipe my hand on the blanket and lie down again.

"You can't do anything."

"I know," I cry. "I know."

"So, all you can do is hope they survive."

"They won't."

Tears well up in my eyes, pooling over my eyes with nowhere to go as I lie on my back. Instead of wiping my eyes, I just close them, and the tears course down the sides of my face. Axle smiles at me. I don't question it, just smile back with my eyes closed. My smile falters as blood starts dripping down his head and across his face. He keeps smiling as chunks of skin peel off of him, replaced by more blood. I hardly recognize him, but he's still smiling. I shake my head desperately, my hand quivering. I force myself to imagine him without the blood. It works for a split second, but then blood drips down his face again. I press my left hand against my eyes to dry them out, then force my eyes open.

"There's nothing you can do."

"I know. Will you shut up about it?" I cry. My eyes aren't dry for very long, as fresh tears well up.

"I'm saying it's not your fault."

I chuckle. Saliva and blood mix in my mouth, and I spit it off the side of the bed again. "I questioned myself too much..."

"You've always done that."

"If I hadn't, I could've reacted faster. I could have stopped—" I stop myself to wipe the tears.

"You don't know that. You saw how fast the Seeker killed the Primordial-ists."

"I could've bought Axle more time." I sigh. "I shouldn't have run to Voltaris Island. I should've confronted Prime Termani and freed Axle earlier. I was too scared. I was too damn scared. I'm a coward."

"You're not a coward, Lukas."

"Then what am I?" I ask. My mom doesn't answer. I look over at where her silhouette was, and it's no longer there. "Of course," I murmur. "Of course." I clench my fist and stand up, pacing around the room. My lungs tighten and my breath feels shallow. I force deeper breaths in rapid succession, pacing faster and faster. My whole body starts shaking. Even without my eyes closed, Axle's lifeless body appears unbidden lying on the ground surrounded by debris. My breaths speed up even more, and so does my pace. I attempt to swing my right fist at the wall, forgetting that it no longer exists. Instead, my imaginary hand phases through the wall and my right shoulder collides with the dirty concrete, sending an immense shockwave of pain through my body. I thought I had gotten used to most kinds of pain, but this is enough to force me to the ground in agony. I clench my left fist, my nails digging into my flesh. I grit my teeth so hard that they start to hurt. My body shakes even more. It's a cycle of pain, as all my nerves blur together until my whole body feels like I'm burning alive.

I fall forward from my knees, collapsing onto the ground. My face strikes the dirt. I close my eyes, waiting for the pain to go away. It doesn't. The pain only gets worse. Axle's lifeless body continues to plague my mind.

Why?

I try to scream, but don't have the energy.

Why?

The Seeker owns Voltaris. He is running Prime Termani's tests. Voltaris is everywhere. I was going to have them repair the hole I made in the wall. They own the SpeedTrains. They own the Plasmars. They own the screens. The Seeker owns Voltaris. The Seeker owns everything.

My head shoots up, and I open my eyes. The stinging persists, but I ignore it. Anger spills through my body. I position my left arm under my chest and push myself up onto my knees again. I grab a bar of the cell with my hand, and pull myself upright. I lean toward the bars, glancing in both directions, before stepping back again. My eyebrows furrow, and I glare at the image of the Seeker in my head. I am not at fault. You are.

CHAPTER 26

SAPPHIRE

I shuffled down the full hallway toward the door of my first class. Someone bumped into me, pushing me into the door. I quickly recovered my balance, grabbed the handle, and swung the door open. I walked through the tall door into a medium-sized classroom. Immediately, everyone turned to me, including the teacher. The teacher wore a large red dress that was somehow still too tight for her rotund body. Her short hair barely made it past her ears, and her eyes were dark brown. The teacher stood with a screen behind her. The blue-tinted screen displayed a Primordial Stone. The artificial stone was made of a bunch of overlapping metal folds. The metal on the image was purple-silver, like the Shifter Arcblades at home. I had read about the Primordial Stones, but never seen an image of what they looked like.

"I presume that means I am late," I said, walking past students significantly older than me toward the nearest empty seat.

"You must be Sapphire," the teacher smiled, gesturing to the same seat that I was already headed toward. "I'm sorry for the confusion. You aren't late at all. I asked the other students to get here early so that we'd have time to welcome you to the class."

"That seems a bit unnecessary, but alright." I pulled out the chair and sat down at my desk. The desks seemed a bit small for the other kids in the room but, since I was younger and smaller than most, mine fit me perfectly. I pulled a small notebook and pen out of my pocket and set them down in front of me. I looked up, and everyone was still staring at me, as if they were expecting something from me. The teacher gestured her hand in the air, which I assumed was a signal for me to speak. "I'm not sure exactly what you'd like me to say."

"Just tell us about yourself," she said.

"Well, my name is Sapphire. I'm ten years old. My mother is in business. I don't know much about her work. My father works at Vinn—Voltaris Laboratories as a chief scientist. I'm an only child. Both of my parents are also only children. I'm not sure about my grandparents. I've never had any pets. I was born on Vinn, sorry, Voltaris Island. My parents were born in—"

"Alright that's enough," the teacher interrupted me. "What do you like to do for fun?"

"Fun?" I asked.

"Yeah, like your hobbies. You must be a very smart girl to be in upperschool this young. Do you like reading?"

"It's alright. It was my father's idea for me to read so much. He seems to like it a lot when I read."

"What about you? What do you like doing?" the teacher asked.

"I don't know… Can we just start class?" I asked. My eyes were starting to get itchy, and my butt was feeling uncomfortable on the hard wooden chair. It wasn't just my butt.

The teacher smiled. "Sure." I leaned forward in my chair, flipping my notebook open to the first page. I clicked the pen and hovered it over the page. I glanced around at the other students. Some of them didn't have anything on their desks. Those who did used small electronic devices that I've never seen before. One student glanced at me. The second our eyes met, I turned away.

"Let's talk about the Saberren war," the teacher began. She clicked a button in her hand and the screen shifted to an image of a person being whipped. Blood coursed down the Saberren slave's back. I winced at the image. I had never seen such violence before. War. All Saberrens were enslaved by the Cortenians. The war sparked when a couple of Saberren slave riots sprang up across Ayzol-Carkun. Mind you, at the time, Ayzol and Carkun were still recovering from their extensive war with each other. They had just reached a stalemate, and were at relative peace." I raised my hand. "Yes, Sapphire?"

"Why do you say relative peace? Were they still fighting?"

"Not anymore. The war between Ayzol and Carkun had ended. I say relative peace because although Ayzol and Carkun were no longer fighting, the nations still disliked each other."

"That's not what relative peace means," I said. The teacher opened her mouth to speak. "Relative peace is when there are still minor disputes, but there is not an all-out war. Therefore, the word 'relative' is both unnecessary and incorrect. If you are looking for a way to convey Ayzol and Carkun's hatred for one another, there are many words to use. But I am not the teacher here, so I will be quiet and let you continue."

"Thank you," the teacher said. "As I was saying, Ayzol and Carkun..." I zoned out. I already knew the content of the class. Besides, if I kept paying attention, I'd have to correct her again.

The teacher got so many things wrong. This class was supposed to teach me about the Primordial Stones. I already mostly knew what they were and what they did. The Shifters made them. They gave abilities to Saberrens who used them. That's all the teacher had to say, but instead, she spent an entire class helping everyone else catch up.

I spun my pen in my hand, lightly tapping on my knee with my other hand. After a bit, I realized everyone was shuffling out. I followed suit. I closed my empty notebook, capped my pen, and walked out the door.

"*That's* not what relative peace means," someone said in front of me, enunciating every word with a mocking tone. Idiot. He laughed, and the students surrounding him laughed as well. I shrugged, and picked up my pace, quickly walking past the group of friends. "The word *'relative'* is *both* unnecessary *and* incorrect." More laughter. I suppressed the urge to look back at them. I could feel my palms getting sweaty. "Oh, look. That must be the little kid right there," someone else said. *Kid.* My hands clenched into fists. Something in me wanted to whip around and beat them until blood poured from their disgusting teenage faces. *Kid.* My mind repeated the same word again and again. "How old is she anyway, five?" Even more laughter.

"I'm ten," I murmured, not expecting them to hear me.

"What did you say?" one of them snapped. I shrugged. A hand tapped my shoulder. I shuddered, quickly turning to face the small group of adolescent guys. "What did you say little girl?" I wanted to punch them so badly, but they towered over me. I wouldn't stand a chance. I just stared back at them and shrugged. "You said something, tell us what you said." One of the guys pushed me. I stumbled backward. They looked like fully grown adults. "Tell us what you fucking said."

"I..." I began, my hands shaking.

"She can't even speak, how cute," one guy said, and the rest broke out laughing again. I clenched my fists, furrowed my brow, and straightened my posture.

"I am ten years old, you imbeciles. Pay attention next time, and you won't have to ask."

I shouldn't have said anything. It never goes well when I speak my mind.

I turned around and walked away. Before I made it far, someone grabbed my leg and yanked it bank. I hit the ground face-first. I felt a crack in my nose, followed by numbing pain. I stood up, carefully touching my nose. My fingers were covered in blood, and more blood dripped out of my nose and onto the floor. I turned around, and the guys circled and hovered over me.

"Don't call us imbeciles," one of the guys said, and they all walked away laughing.

I sat on the ground, watching them disappear around the corner of the hallway. More students started swarming around me, exiting classrooms and rushing to others. Tears and blood dripped down my face. I rubbed my eyes and accidentally bumped my nose. Pain blossomed on my face and my eyes teared up even more. My whole body tensed up as I tried to push my sobs down. I finally stood up, and walked toward my next class. All I could think about were the two Arcblades at home that my parents never stopped talking about. I fantasized about stabbing the guys until they bled like I did. I clenched my fists and quickened my pace, looking for a towel to wipe my nose. As the pain kept burning on my face, I obsessed over the swords.

I try to open my eyes, but I remain trapped in reliving old memories. Why am I remembering this right now? First, the serum at Voltaris and now this?

CHAPTER 27

AXLE

The scene replays in my head once again. Lukas grabs the shadow-man's arm, holding him back. Adrius grabs the Lightning Stone. The one Voltaris employee, Renna, pulls the unconscious one, Sapphire, to safety. I stare at Lukas as sweat pours down his red face. His whole body shakes as his eyes beg me to leave. Adrius grabs me. I don't want to go. He shoots me in the chest.

The scene repeats. The shadow-man, the Seeker, attempts to move, but Lukas holds him back. The Seeker tries to throw a knife. He can't. My eyes water.

I rub my eyes, knocking dirt loose and smearing the grime caked on my face. I attempt to open my eyes, but my gritty eyelids scratch on the inside like sandpaper. I flinch and close my eyes again.

"Aal" a voice says. It sounds like someone distant calling out.

"Aal."

"Axle."

I force my eyes open, despite the stinging pain that follows. I need a shower. Renna hovers over me with eyes red from constant tears. She reaches out a hand and I take it, pulling myself to my feet.

"You're up early," I mutter, glancing back at my makeshift bed. It's dirt, like the rest of the maze of tunnels down here, but I made sure to pat it down extra. I should've smoothed out the ceiling too, so dirt wouldn't drop onto my face when I was asleep.

"No," Renna responds. "You slept late."

I shrug, looking around the tunnel. Sapphire is wrapped up in her torn lab coat. Still unconscious. Her neck is caked in blood and wrapped with fabric stained a deep red. The ends of her brown hair are clumped together in dried blood. Adrius is nowhere to be found.

"Where's Adrius?"

"He went to work on the carts," Renna says.

"Already?" I ask. My stomach growls. The Primordialists placed enough food down here, but Adrius is the only one who knows how to navigate the labyrinth of tunnels and find the stashes.

Renna nods. "He says he's nearly figured out how to use the Lightning Stone to recharge the carts."

"He's been trying to tap into the energy reserves for days," I grumble. "Weeks even. How do we know it'll work this time?"

We're interrupted by Sapphire's groaning. Renna bolts over to Sapphire, lightly shaking her.

"Come on Sapphire, you can do it... Wake up."

"Islorr's Blood..." Sapphire faintly whispers. Her face flinches for a split second, then goes back to rest. Renna sighs, then stands back up.

She shakes her head. "Nothing. Just talking in her sleep again."

I pause. "How long until Adrius is back?"

"Who knows?" Renna shrugs. "It won't be long before we have to relocate again. The Seeker's been intensifying his search. Adrius said he saw even more footprints last night."

"And why can't we just go up?" I ask.

"We've already been over this many times. Prime Termani is probably waiting up there for us. He's running the experiments with the Seeker, after all."

"We can walk down the tunnels until we find another exit."

Renna sighs. "We have to carry Sapphire. And what happens if the Seeker shows up? He'd kill us in an instant."

"So we just wait here, keep moving locations in this damn maze for who knows how long until either Adrius fixes the carts or the Seeker finds us." I kick at the dirt. "Renna, it's been weeks since Lukas gave up his life to save ours. I don't want his sacrifice to be worthless."

"We have no choice!" Renna whispers. "He had one. We don't."

"We always have a choice. I know that now." I pick up the guard armor from the ground and put it on piece by piece. "After this is all over. If Adrius's plan works. If we get out of Termani. What will you do?"

Renna glances back at Sapphire. "I'd probably go back to Lusia. That's where I'm from anyway. I could stay with my grandparents for a while. Then, when I'm all but forgotten by the Seeker, I'll go back to Voltaris."

"Are you serious?" I put the helmet on. "You would go back to work for the company that you *know* directly led to the deaths of hundreds of innocent people? I had friends at graduation. Like me, like everyone in that building, they were taken for the testing. I never found them. Never got to say goodbye. Now they're dead. Or if, by some miracle, they aren't dead, then they will be soon. How can you know about their murders and still consider going back to work for those who caused it?"

Renna pauses. She stares at Sapphire and wipes her eyes. "My family has been working for Voltaris since it was Islorr Manufacturing. Not everyone at Voltaris is evil. Maybe I can make real changes to the company. And I can't just leave my family behind."

"You wouldn't be leaving them," I say. "You aren't indebted to your family. If they're good people, if they love you, then they'll support your decision. If they don't, then that's their problem." I look down at the dirt floor by my feet. "I used to not make my own decisions at all. I was held back by what I thought Lukas was pressuring me to do. But it wasn't him. It was all me. I didn't really want to leave Termani with Lukas. I wanted to go to overschool. I just never told him that. When I know that the testing is over for good, I will go to overschool. I'll do what I want to do."

"I don't know, Axle. It's hard to leave everything behind."

A series of loud booms echo through the tunnel, each one closer and louder than the last.

"It's the Seeker. Help me grab Sapphire," Renna says. I nod, rushing over to Sapphire's limp body. Renna grabs her legs, and I lift her up by the shoulders.

The two of us shuffle down the tunnel as fast as we can. The booms continue to draw nearer, and the time between them shortens.

"He's gaining on us," I exclaim. I glance back, as someone turns the corner. It's not the Seeker. It's Adrius.

Adrius stares at Renna and me with bloodshot eyes, illuminated by a flashlight attached to his stolen guard helmet.

"I did it," Adrius says through strained huffs. "I fixed the carts."

* * *

Renna and I hoist Sapphire into one of the carts. Renna hops in the same one, resting Sapphire's head against her legs. Her and Sapphire's masks are stuffed next to Sapphire's still legs.

I get into a second cart. The two carts have noticeable wires sticking out where Adrius had attached the Lightning Stone. He jumps into the cart with me, his hand ready on the lever.

"You ready to get outta here?" Adrius asks. Renna and I nod. Adrius is about to pull up on the lever when he pauses. His earpiece light turns blue. Adrius raises his hand up to his earpiece and his eyes widen as he watches something that's projected onto his eyes. He turns off the earpiece and turns to face Renna and me.

"What happened?" I ask.

Adrius lets out a heavy breath. "Prime Termani. He's just abducted the next batch of people. He's starting the testing again."

"What?" I shout. "We have to save them."

"There's nothing we can do," Adrius says. "We have to get the Lightning Stone as far away from the Seeker as possible. Eventually he won't be able to make any more serum."

"You don't know that," I say. "You even said it yourself. They could have another Primordial Stone. Or maybe they don't even need the Stones anymore. But what we do know is that there are people who need our help." I turn to Renna. "This is your chance to make a choice."

"Let's go save them," Renna says.

"It's too risky," Adrius says. "We've stayed alive for so long because we didn't fight. Lukas trusted me to keep you alive. That's what I'm doing."

"Why did you save me in the prison?" I ask.

"You were going to die."

"See, you know that going back for them is the right thing to do. That Stone is not worth the lives of innocent people, and you know that."

Adrius hesitates. I see a vision of Lukas dying in my head. He's surrounded by the corpses of both Primordialists and innocent students who were murdered by the serum. I remember being in the prison, cramped in that room. I remember the graduation party, and seeing my friends there for the last time. I can't leave people to die. Lukas might be dead, but I can't let more people die. I can't let the Seeker do any more damage. I close my eyes, and tears drip down the sides of my face.

Adrius takes a deep breath, and I open my eyes again. A sly smile appears on his face. "Let's go back to the prison."

CHAPTER 28

LUKAS

I lie on the dirt floor of the cell. My eyes are dry and crusty; all tears long since spent. My shoulder is numb from the pain. All I feel there now is an itching tingle like I slept on it. I did not. I don't know how long it's been since I actually slept. The last good sleep I remember was before Axle's graduation. I'm used to it now. It's a strange feeling to be both exhausted and wide awake all the time. It's a war between my body and my mind; one wants sleep, the other does not. Every so often I'll drift off for a bit, but then I'll wake up again—feeling worse off for it. I can hear my own deep breaths as I try to calm myself. The breaths are long and full, accompanied by a deep static ambience. Wait. I hold my breath for a moment. I can still hear the crackling breaths. It's separate from the constant droning of the distant machine. I sit up, and standing right in front of the cell bars is the Seeker.

"What do you want?" I ask, my eyes barely open. His mask's eyes, on the other hand, remain permanently open.

"Is that really how you want to talk to me?" The Seeker chuckles, and the ensuing static screech forces me to cover my ears. With my right arm gone, I'm only able to cover my left ear. My right ear rings in protest. "I'm just here to talk."

"Why?" I mutter, lowering my left arm. "You've probably killed Axle. You really expect me to do anything for you?" I turn and spit on the ground.

"You're making a lot of assumptions. I'm not asking for anything."

"Then why are you here?" I scoff. "Why did you spare my life but take

155

everyone else's?"

The Seeker sighs, and static morphs it into something reminiscent of a chuckle. "How about I give you a tour of my work? Get you out of the cell for a while."

"Do I have a choice?"

"You're smarter than I thought." The Seeker flicks something on the outside of the cell bars and they swing open. I stand up and step out of the cell. The Seeker turns to look at my right shoulder. "You seem to be healing well." He stares at me, as if waiting for a response. When I don't reply, he sighs. "Alright, follow me."

The Seeker leads me down the dirt hallway. The hallway is rounded at the top, with long horizontal metal bars lining the ceiling. The bars are rusted, with some suffering large enough cracks they look moments away from snapping. Whatever this hallway was intended for, it's clear that it was made a long time ago.

"I understand you may want to know why I'm taking you around—"

I ignore the Seeker's incessant prattling. Instead, his robotic voice blends together into a deep ambience. I glance back. Besides my cell, numerous other cells line the hallway as it stretches into pure darkness. With my eyes somewhat adjusted to the gloom, I can just about make out a construction snaking across the floor of the strange hallway. Rusted metal tracks stretch its entire length, toward

"This is a mine," I murmur. The Seeker turns around and stops walking. He faces me, and his mask's black eyes stare at my dirt-ridden face.

"How observant," the Seeker growls. "I'd like to show you something." He pulls a knife out of his belt and holds it up for me to see. The black knife looks just like the one he used to kill Zeke. Without much light, I am unable to pick out any details on the knife, making the blade seem wrought of shadow. Akorth. I step back, and the Seeker chuckles—luckily soft enough that I don't need to cover my ears. "I'm not going to stab you. Just look." I lean in toward the knife. "There are two main uses of this material. One is for armor and weapons. This knife is made of Akorth, one of the strongest materials on all of Ayzol-Carkun."

I scoff. "I know what Akorth is. I saw your little display."

"Good." He pulls the knife back and sheaths it. The Seeker then points to his armor. "Then you know that I've covered myself in it." He pauses. "But Akorth is not only useful for physical structures." The Seeker points his arm to the ceiling and presses a button on the arm of his suit. A bright light shoots forth and illuminates the dirt room. "Ideally, I would use the material from the Crater. It's highly magnetic and a fantastic energy absorber. But the Council of Primes has a lock of sorts on the Crater. I just can't afford drawing attention to my use of the material." The Seeker sighs, and chuckle-static fills the air.

"However, if I were to find a similar material in a place where no one dares to go, my problems are solved. I would be sacrificing a small amount of efficiency for complete secrecy. Akorth handles high-energy absorption nearly as well as Cratermetal, and it has the added benefit of blocking the relentless immune cells found in pure Cortenian blood. It just so happens that Akorth has only been discovered in one place, which was closed and forbidden to access after the Saberren War. Perfect for secret experiments."

My mind flashes back to the fragment in the lobby of Voltaris Industries. The voice mentioned mines. I didn't get a chance to hear the rest of the sentence. There's only one place where the Seeker could've gotten all of his Akorth.

"Mount Islorr..." I mutter.

"Yes."

"They closed the mines because they were too dangerous."

"That is what they said, yes. That is not why the mines were closed." The Seeker steps closer to me, and I step back. "They closed the mines because they knew that the material, Akorth, was a threat to the Saberrens. The Saberrens had just won. Why would they want anyone to create something that could rival their powerful Primordial Stones?"

It all makes sense now. "Islorr's Blood."

"Precisely. Akorth, the Blood of Mt. Islorr."

The Seeker tilts his light-emitting arm down to reveal a strange mechanism connected to the side of the tunnel. The mechanism is connected to rails overhead and has twenty drills lined up in parallel. That must have been the mechanical noise I was hearing. The drills are attached to thick translucent tubes that carry miniature chunks of Akorth ore from the drill bits to a metal box. The metal box vibrates so fast that without the light I would have thought it was completely still. A multitude of wires protrude from the vibrating box and lead back to the rail system above.

"This machine grinds the metal into a fine powder. I then send it to the laboratory on Voltaris Island, where the metal is processed into this." The Seeker pulls a glass vial filled with a green fluid out of his belt. I recognize the color. Sapphire's lab coat was stained green. My heart starts racing. Axle said the prisoners were injected… Is this what he was talking about? My head is filled with screams, both from Axle and from people I've never met. My eyes start to water, and my left hand starts shaking. "This fluid is quite useful, and it allows me to—"

I grab the nearest tube connected to the massive machine and rip it free.

"Stop!" the Seeker yells from behind me. The static in his voice pounds at my ears. I resist the urge to cover them. I smash the tube across the wires and the thick glass shatters. The wires snap, and the vibrating metal box freezes. A small hole automatically opens up at the base of the box. Sparks from the wires cascade down over the box. Green flames erupt from the hole while black powder spews out of it, raining down on the tunnel floor. Powder meets flames, and a massive green blaze engulfs the machine.

The Seeker stares at me, his whole body trembling in rage. "What. Did. You Do?" He steps closer to me, and I back away from the machine until I am pressed up against the opposite dirt wall. "WHAT DID YOU DO?" the Seeker yells, blasting the tunnel with a screaming static that brings me to my knees. My ears ring like never before. Still screaming, the Seeker's fists clench and gears whir as he punches me with a suit-enhanced strike right in the ribs. I immediately fold in half and collapse onto the ground. The Seeker's boot comes down. Everything goes black.

* * *

I wake up to the sound of a door slamming wide open. The Seeker drags me into a room with only a table at its center. Heavy chains coil on its surface. He throws me on the table, grabs the chains, and wraps them around my legs and left arm. The Seeker looms over me, shining the bright light from his arm into my eyes. I shut my eyes and turn my head away. He ignores me. The chains are drawn taught on my limbs. The Seeker unravels the cloth wrapped around the stub protruding from shoulder. He examines the wound, then walks away.

As the Seeker leaves, my mind is instantly filled with a piercing ringing from my ears. It soon disappears, replaced with her silhouette. Except the silhouette isn't against a wall as usual. She stands in front of me, with a physical form. I can feel her eyes tracing over me, disappointed. I hear a deep static-filled breath behind me and my screaming stops.

The Seeker approaches from behind carrying a bundle of yellow wires tangled around a rusted and chipped hollow metal arm. "This will hurt." The Seeker pulls a knife from his belt and stabs into my wound. My scream returns, tearing my vocal cords raw. The Seeker digs the knife deeper into my skin, slicing through the knot of muscles that have grown around my stump. The blade strikes a nerve that sends a tingle of phantom pains down an arm I no longer. I start shaking uncontrollably, and the Seeker sets down the bundle of wires and metal arm on top of my chest. With his free hand, the Seeker grabs my neck and slams me down to pin my body against the cold table. A new type of excruciating pain wriggles its way into my brain. I strain my eyes to see the source of the new pain. The Seeker's knife is no longer in my arm, instead four faint gray strings dangle out of the incision that he had made. A sudden tension in the strings causes me even more extreme pain. I close my eyes and bite into my lip. My left fist is clenched so hard I can feel my nails digging deep into my palm.

After sheathing his knife, the Seeker picks up one of the yellow wires. Using a clip attached to the wire, he clips the end of the wire directly onto one of the hanging strings. The immense pain in my shoulder seemingly spreads downward into the yellow wire. My shrieks wrack my body with convulsions. The Seeker grabs the next wire. One at a time, he attaches the remaining three wires onto the nerves he dug out of my shoulder, adding even more pain with each new connected wire. Just as the pain finally starts to numb, the Seeker picks up the metal arm and shoves it onto my shoulder, letting the wires and strings snake through the hollowed-out interior. I watch as he uses a tool that I don't recognize to enter through a joint in the arm. He adjusts a mechanism and a faint wave of relief spreads through my arm. The phantom sensations of my missing arm intensify. I swear I can feel some of my fingers as if they were still there. The Seeker does the same thing three more times. He removes the tool. My arm is back. Not really, but it feels real. In a way, it is. The hollow metal arm is fully secured by a tight leather strap. So tight, in fact, that the intense pressure on my shoulder is nearly unbearable. Through the cracks in the joints, I can spot the yellow wires connected to small motors. I attempt to move my fingers and remarkably, the metal fingers move.

CHAPTER 29

SAPPHIRE

Tears coursed down my face. I instinctively try to raise my hands up to wipe them, but I can't move.

Of course, another memory.

I try to turn my head. Still no luck.

I don't cry very often.

When was this?

My eyes do... did move eventually, turning in the direction of a loud scream behind me. I turned around to face the man yelling at me. He was much younger than I remember. He had nearly black hair, with no signs of gray yet. His brow was furrowed deep. Wrinkles etched around his eyebrows revealed that he often wore this expression. His eyes were purple like mine, and his pupils were tiny as he stared at me. My hand moved up to wipe my tears; it was much smaller than I'm used to. The skin was still pale, but much smoother.

"Sapphire, you're supposed to be reading your book!" the man screams in my face, and more tears blur my vision. I remember this.

I sniffled. "I don't want to."

"Disappointing," he said, pacing around me. "I expected more from you." The man stepped away from where I sat. The chair was way too large for my small body. "Stand up."

I got up from the chair. I remained basically the same height. I was a lot shorter than my father back then.

My father walked over to the wall next to the dusty bookshelf, where two swords were sheathed in leather. He grabbed one of the swords by the handle, yanking it out of its sheath. I flinched as he swung the blade through the air. The sword was slightly curved and, while mostly silver, had a slight purple tint.

"I have never told you about these swords," my father said. "I think you are old enough now."

"I want to eat. Is Mommy making dinner?" I asked.

"Mommy's out on a business trip. It will just be you and me for a few days."

"You didn't tell me that Mommy was leaving." I cast my eyes down to the floor.

"Mommy is making money so that you can have a place to live."

"Will you make me food?" I asked. I shouldn't have said anything. Nothing I said ever changed anything.

"Listen to me," my father spat. Saliva hit my face, and I wiped it off. "This *Arcblade* belonged to a Shifter during the Saberren War. The Shifters were a group of Cortenians who made the Primordial Stones and helped the Saberrens win the war." He walked over to me, holding the sword out. "Here, take this."

I grabbed the handle from my father with both of my hands. It was heavy. My father walked to the wall and unsheathed the other Arcblade. He lunged forward, swinging the sword at me. I gasped and raised the sword to block. He swung the blade again, and I hid behind my outstretched blade The tip of his blade scratched my arm, I winced as blood dripped onto the

"Fight back," he demanded. "Don't let me scratch you again." He stabbed at me and I dodged to the side. Tears welled up in my eyes again. I ran toward him, swinging my sword at him. Without breaking a sweat, my father swatted the Arcblade out of my hand and onto the floor. He swung the curved blade over his head and down toward me. I didn't think he'd swing again. I scrambled for my sword on the floor and held it to block him. He pushed down, and both swords moved down toward me. I pushed back with all my strength, and he finally moved his sword away.

"You need to focus. There will always be people stronger than you. You cannot let that be your downfall." My father cut across my stomach without warning. Blood gushed out of the cut, spraying the carpet. I cry out and reach for the cut, but my father swung again. Tears streaming from my eyes, I desperately swung my sword to block him.

"The Shifters had a mantra that guided them during the war," he said, swinging the blade again. I blocked again. "To shift yourself is to shift the world." My father moved forward, yanking the Arcblade out of my hand. He held them both against my neck. "It means that if you can find a way to change who you are, then you can do better in the world. The Shifters changed, and gave up the old beliefs of many Cortenians. They decided to fight for the Saberrens. They changed the world by winning the war." He walked away from me, wiped the blades on his sleeve, and placed the Arcblades back into the hanging sheaths. I clutched at the cut in my stomach. "If you can change, if you can show me that you can learn and become a smarter person, those Arcblades are yours. They will remind you of your oncoming success."

I stared back at my father, tears starting to dry. He hurt me and said nothing. No apology. Nothing. He stepped toward me, and I stepped back. What is wrong with him? Why did he do that?

"Can I have a bandage?" I muttered. Why ask? There was no point. Nothing ever happened. He treated me like trash. Worse than trash. At least the trash was taken out. I was nothing to him.

"After you're done reading the book you started," my father said. "Sit back down."

I stepped backward and slumped down into the large chair, pain lancing through the shallow cut on my stomach. The book was next to me, pressed against the side of the seat. My father grabbed the book and placed it on my lap. Carved into the leather was the title, *Advancements in Modern Science*. With the book still on my lap, my father began flipping through the pages.

"What page were you on?" he asked.

"I'm not telling you," I whined.

"Fine. Then I guess you'll have to start from the beginning." My father grabbed the book from me and flipped all the way back to the first page, which had a slight tear in the corner. I hated that book. It was so dense.

"I don't wanna," I screamed. "I want food. I haven't had food all day."

My father ignored me. "Over many hundreds of years, Cortenian science has significantly impacted how we view the world. Whenever there was a problem or an unanswered question, we turned to science to gain knowledge that would help us solve that problem or answer that question. Due to the sheer amount of scientific discoveries across time, let alone in this century, we will only be focusing on scientific advancements during and after the Saberren War."

My father flipped the page. My eyes squinted.

Don't do this Sapphire. This is a bad idea. My little hand began to shake. No, stop. I try to move my hand away, but my younger self does not listen.

Please. No. Don't do this. Don't do this...

I grabbed the book out of my father's hand and threw it across the room. The book hit the wall, and the leather cover came partially undone. Several sheets of paper came loose and scattered onto the floor. My father looked at the tossed book, his face turning a deep red. He spun back to me with dilated pupils. In an instant, he stood up, clenching his fists.

"Sapphire!" he yelled. "I have been patient with you for too long." He marched over to the book and snatched it off of the ground, leaving the few torn out papers behind. I stared at him as he marched back over to me and slammed the book down on my legs, which hurt a little bit. "You are not allowed to do anything else until you finish this book." Tears started welling up in my eyes. "Do you hear me?" I nodded. "I said do you hear me?"

"Yes... father," I said, opening the book.

Why did I throw the book? Why did I have to throw the stupid fucking book? Why did he care so much about that damn book? He cared about it more than me.

As if automatically, I turned to the page that I was on before our argument. Tears dropped onto the page, but they were not enough to blur the ink.

I began to read. Why did I listen to him? I should've run away. My mother was never here, and my father treated me like I was never there. I would've done better in the damn streets.

'The Saberren War, like other wars in the past, encouraged scientific and technological development. When the Shifters created the Primordial Stones, Cortenians attempted to harness another material to create their own version. They found the material deep in the mines of Mt. Islorr, a material that they had already been using to create their armor. When ground up into a fine powder and dissolved, this material could theoretically be injected into the body, despite the Cortenians' stronger immune systems. The material had a property that miraculously allowed it to stabilize in Cortenian blood. The Cortenians named this material Akorth, after an ancient word for blood.

'The so-called blood of Mt. Islorr was never fully harnessed to its maximum potential. The Cortenians were unable to complete their research, as the war had ended and the mines were shut down.'

Akorth... It was Akorth. The powder in the serum is Akorth. The Seeker must have reopened the mines in secret.

CHAPTER 30

AXLE

"Come on, let's go," Lukas whispered, running in front of me alongside the tracks as the SpeedTrain slowed down. The magnetic tracks angled downward and the train lowered closer to the ground. The tunnel swarmed with people boarding and exiting trains. Dirt coated the SpeedTunnel walls. A graffitied mural of the old Prime's long face dominated the wall behind the train coming to a stop in front of Lukas and me.

"You know this is a terrible idea, right?" I said.

Lukas turned back to me, a large grin on his face. "It's gonna be great. Finally somewhere other than Crathenos." Wind rushed around me as the train finally came to a stop, and Lukas and I ran up to the door. He chuckled and stepped onto the train's entrance, coming face to face with a guard. The guard stepped off the train, forcing Lukas back and blocking our path. Compared to our small frames, the guard was a giant, especially with his massive, shiny armor.

"I didn't see you purchase tickets." The guard pointed toward the robot in the center of the SpeedTunnel. I opened my mouth to speak, but Lukas spoke before I had the chance.

"Right... tickets," Lukas muttered with total confidence. He had a plan. The guard glared at Lukas. "The ticket prices are a bit high, don't you think? Nine ferrings? They used to be five."

The guard furrowed his eyebrows. "How old are you?" Lukas hesitated.

"Listen kid, maybe if you were older, I'd let you get on alone. As it is, you're far too young to travel on your own. I'm sure your parents will take you two somewhere if you ask them nicely."

"Mom?" Lukas yelled, looking away from the guard and the train.

"She's not h—" Lukas cut me off with a raised finger. I shut my mouth. He tilted his head at the guard, who was looking off in the direction Lukas called. Lukas beckoned for me to follow him toward the doors. We scurried past the guard. Just as we got on the landing, the guard whipped his head around.

"Hey," the guard shouted, moving toward us. Lukas kicked the guard back and pushed me through the door. The guard raised a fist, staring at Lukas.

"You wouldn't hurt a child, would you?" Lukas smiled, stepping backward onto the train. The doors hissed shut, leaving the angry guard behind. Laughing, Lukas led me toward two seats, and we sat down on the train just as it started moving.

* * *

I lean forward, bracing myself against the front of the cart as it rapidly decelerates, swerving off of the intentionally broken rail. The cart lurches to a halt. Adrius jumps out of the cart, looking up toward the hole. Or where it was. The hole still goes up through the dirt, but it stops suddenly at a large metal plate. Renna and I clamber out of our carts. I help her lift Sapphire out and set her down on the ground.

Adrius pulls out his Plasmar, the light switched to orange. He points it up toward the metal plate, then hesitates. His head swivels to face Renna and me.

"Here's the plan. I'm going up first, because I have a weapon. Axle, you come behind me and grab the nearest Plasmar. Renna, you'll come last, since you have to carry Sapphire. Do you need help with that at all?"

Renna shakes her head. She squats down and picks Sapphire up over her shoulders. She grunts, but is able to straighten her legs. Sapphire's tall body flails across Renna's shoulders and upper back.

Adrius turns back to me. "We can't leave any guards conscious. Let's go." He squeezes the trigger and blasts the metal plate. He jumps out of the way. The hot plasma slowly melts through the relatively thin plate. The hole is too small, but the glowing hot metal around the edges droops downwards, increasing the size.

Soft footsteps echoing above soon follow the creation of the hole. They grow louder. Closer. The hole widens. By the time the metal around the hole's edge cools and stops sagging, the footsteps stop as well. Adrius steps forward again, aiming his Plasmar straight up through the hole. The head of a guard peeks down the hole and Adrius fires another blast. The guard's head explodes backward. Gravity takes effect and blood, brains, and skull shards rain down through the hole. It drenches Adrius's armor and pools on the ground at his feet.

Adrius removes his belt, saws it in two with a pocket knife, and wraps the two pieces tightly around his fists. He grabs the metal around the hole, wincing from the residual heat. Adrius hoists himself up and through. More footsteps pound above. Adrius's Plasmar shrieks. Silence. His head briefly appears in the hole, and he signals for me to come up, tossing down the leather scraps. Wrapping my hands, I grab the metal around the hole. It's hot to the touch, but it doesn't hurt. I bend my arms, reposition, and pull myself up. My head clears the opening. I swing my legs up and slide across the floor above the hole. I immediately stand up.

Adrius holds his Plasmar in front of him. Two guards lie splayed out on the floor close by. One of them is missing a head and another an arm. I turn down to face Renna at the bottom of the hole.

"Give her to me," I say. Renna nods. She crouches next to Sapphire, hoists her onto her back, and then rises up, straining her back and legs to raise Sapphire higher. Adrius drops his Plasmar to the ground. He and I each grab a shoulder to hoist her up. Adrius picks up the Plasmar again, I throw Renna the leather scraps, and Renna climbs up. She leaves the leather scraps by the hole.

"Take this." Adrius grabs a Plasmar from one of the dead guards and hands it to me. The light is orange. I flick the switch to blue. As Renna squats down and lifts Sapphire back onto her shoulders, Adrius beckons me forward slowly.

I move slowly, retracing my steps toward the door that Adrius had closed when we fled the prison. As I approach the door, I notice the large heap of bloodied bodies stacked in front of it.

Some heads are severed completely, others still dangle from tissue and bone. Limbs twist at wrong angles. Blood pools from stab wounds, from mouths and eyes—guards and Primordialists alike.

I pick my way through the corpses, shoving bodies aside with my legs so that I don't have to step on them. Step by step, I move through the hallway of bodies to the door. With each step, I hear more footsteps moving around me. The two behind me make sense, but are there more footsteps ahead? We're not alone.

The door swings open, pushing more bodies out of the way. Standing on the other side is a group of guards. I count eleven of them. They all raise glowing orange Plasmars. They don't care about stunning people anymore.

I seize the moment of surprise and shoot the guard nearest to me. The stun blast hits his lower abdomen. The guard reels over and the guard behind him fires at my neck. Adrius pushes me to the side, raising his Plasmar. It's on orange. Adrius shoots the guard in front of me, sending guts exploding onto the guards around him. I wish I was fazed, but I'm not. I've seen so much death.

The remaining nine guards all point their Plasmars at Adrius. He shoots two of them before a third fires a shot straight at his chest. Adrius dives out of the way but the blast still sears his side. He falls with a grunt, dropping the Plasmar. Another guard fires a blast at Adrius's head. He rolls to the side. The blast grazes his leg, and a piece of skin flies off of him. He screams, snatches up the Plasmar again, and fires off another shot. The guard dodges the poorly aimed blast with ease.

A loud cry behind me startles everyone. Renna charges past Adrius and me, Plasmar blazing blue. Her scream doesn't stop. Sapphire is no longer on her shoulders. The majority of the guards turn to her. She fires a stream of wild shots at as many guards as she can. Her barely-charged shots mostly miss, but a few guards drop onto corpse piles. Adrius raises his Plasmar and shoots a distracted guard in the face. The guard's head explodes, and blood flies into the nearest guard's eyes. Adrius shoots the lone remaining guard, and he collapses in a spray of gore. Renna swings back and lifts Sapphire from the floor.

"Adrius…" I murmur. He groans, pushing himself up to his feet. He winces when he steps on his wounded leg, and I grab him, helping him limp alongside me.

My breaths grow heavier as I approach the room that I was nearly forced into. I turn to the door. I reach for the doorknob but pause. My hand freezes.

"Open it," Adrius says.

"I am opening it."

"No, you're not." Adrius sighs and grabs the doorknob.

"No, don't," I cry.

Adrius turns the knob and swings the door wide open. I am met with countless gazes. One person stares at me with wide eyes and a foaming mouth. Blood pours from her bloodshot eyes and mixes with the white foam, turning pink as the two intermingle. Another's neck is sliced open, his head wrenched backward at an impossible angle. One corpse's mouth hangs open, revealing another body behind her through a hole in the back of her throat. That's only three out of hundreds of dead bodies. The bodies stack from floor to ceiling. No walls visible. Only flesh and death. I feel cramped, because anywhere I look, I'm met by the gaze of a dead man. These bodies are fresh. How many were killed during the previous batch? So many lives were taken. All of them were murdered by the Seeker.

CHAPTER 31

AXLE

"This is what the serum did?" Renna gasps, pointing at someone with a foaming mouth. "This is what Voltaris made us work on for years?" Renna's eyes fill with tears, and my vision blurs as well. Renna squats down, placing Sapphire on a small patch of bloodless ground. She examines Sapphire's neck wound, then looks up at the decapitated men and women. "The Seeker... I can't believe he did this. Why?"

I turn back to Adrius, whose blank eyes show no sign of emotion. He blinks a few times, then turns around, wincing as he steps on his mangled leg. "Let's check the other rooms. See if anyone hasn't been tested on yet."

"Why would Voltaris do this?" I ask.

"Why does anyone do anything?" he responds. "They want to stop the Primordialists. They want the Primordial Stones for themselves. They will do whatever experiments they can in order to achieve that goal."

I stare back at the students, at Renna, at Sapphire, then follow Adrius as he slowly limps out of the giant room. "There are good people out there. There have to be."

"Good people suffer far worse than innocents. Unlike innocent people, good people get in the way on purpose. Lukas is a good example."

I clench my fists, following Adrius down the hallway. He swings open the first door, the room I was held captive in. My fears are confirmed. Empty.

"Why did you join the Primordialists then?" I ask.

Adrius sighs, approaching the next door. "I was once a guard in this prison. I moved here from Lusia to make a living. A guard post seemed like a good opportunity, given Termani's insane security budget." Adrius swings open the door. Another empty room. He doesn't even bother to close the door, limping past it. "I was assigned to guard a woman who was an especially dangerous prisoner. She was a Primordialist. She was one of the few survivors of a protest at Voltaris, before the Lightning Stone was hidden. Zeke was another." Adrius opens the next door, glances into the empty room, and continues. "She told me about the Primordialists, about their plan to reclaim the Primordial Stones from Voltaris. I didn't agree with her at the time. Those who made the Primordial Stones were long dead. I believed an energy company like Voltaris had a right to the Lightning Stone." We round the corner and continue down another hallway. "But then I heard about this man in a suit who murdered almost everyone at the protest. I realized then that Voltaris should not be allowed to keep the Stone. If they had responded differently, I may have never become a Primordialist."

"What happened to the woman you were guarding?" I ask.

Adrius swings open another door, and the room is empty like all the rest. "She was killed with a spoon while eating. A Voltaris supporter did it. He gouged her eyes out with the spoon and forced her to choke on her own eyeballs." Another empty room. "I killed him in retaliation. I was fired on the spot. They would have imprisoned me if I hadn't escaped. I found Zeke, following instructions that the woman had told me before she died." Adrius comes to another door, but stops, turning to face me. "It's no use anymore. It's not worth fighting for a useless cause. I'm done with the Primordialists, and I'm done trying to be a hero."

"You came with me to the prison," I say.

Adrius chuckles. "I suppose I did."

We turn another corner, and hovering over me is the fearsome mask of the Seeker.

"Hello, Axle," the Seeker says, a sigh-chuckle suffusing the air. "I spent weeks searching for you. I thought I'd find you down in the tunnels, but you came to me instead. How convenient."

I glare at the shadow-man. "You killed them all!" Next to me, Adrius grips his Plasmar.

"Primordialist scum," the Seeker says, staring at Adrius with his mask's black eyes. He takes a step forward.

Adrius limps away from the Seeker, raising his Plasmar. The Seeker unsheathes two knives, dashes forward, and stabs Adrius in his side. Adrius reels over, finger on the trigger to fire a shot at the Seeker's armor. The Seeker knocks the Plasmar out of Adrius's hand, and stabs him in the same spot a second time. Adrius's mangled leg fails, and he pitches over, crunched around the blade in his side. Adrius hits the ground with a thud, clutching at the new wound. The Seeker steps forward, sheathing one of his knives and using the free hand to lift Adrius by the scruff of his neck, dangling him. Adrius groans. The Seeker positions the knife in his other hand at the bottom of Adrius's spine and drops him for a brief second, letting gravity pull Adrius onto the blade. Adrius screams as his spine cracks. The Seeker pulls the knife out and sheathes it in his belt. He drops Adrius, leaving him to stare blankly up at the ceiling.

"You killed him," I yell.

"He's not dead... yet."

I run forward and grab Adrius's Plasmar off the ground, aiming it at the Seeker. The Seeker steps back, grabs the Plasmar, and crushes it with one hand. He drops the useless weapon to the ground.

"Which one of you has the Lightning Stone?" The Seeker steps over to Adrius's body, rifling through his pockets. His hands come out empty. My right pocket weighs heavy against my hip. I reach into my pocket and grab a ball-shaped object. He put it in my pocket. I didn't notice.

I clench the Lightning Stone and pull my hand out. I take a deep breath, clenching the Stone even tighter; the folds cut through my skin and blood begins to drip on the ground. The Seeker lunges at me, grabs my bleeding hand, and pulls my fingers away, taking the Lightning Stone out of my hand.

"What? No!" the Seeker exclaims.

He unsheathes his swords, extending them out into long blades, and pointing them directly at me. The new cuts begin to ache and itch, and I can't resist the urge to dig my nails into my flesh. The pain is overwhelming, but I continue to rip into my own hand to relieve the itch. The localized itching and aching subsides, but a deep pain persists, slowly spreading up my arm and across my body. An explosion of pain blossoms in my head. I stumble away from the Seeker, who still points his swords at me. However, he now holds the swords looser than before.

The Seeker chuckles; the static is even worse with my headache. "You just got yourself killed." I stare at him, his mask's black eyes return an unblinking gaze. "Right now, a genetically modified virus is latching onto your brainstem, which is causing your headache. There are three things that can happen now." The headache gets worse and worse by the second. My vision blurs and I stumble backward again. "It depends how strong your immune system is. If you are a mix of Cortenian and Saberren, your immune system will destroy your own mind trying to kill the virus. You will die. If you have a superior Cortenian immune system, it will destroy the virus, but you will faint for long enough for me to kill you. You will also die. Finally, if your immune system is primarily Saberren... you may gain the powers that my serum attempts to recreate. I can still kill you then. So let's see which one happens."

I stagger about. All that's keeping me from keeling over backward are the convulsions making me double over and vomit in front of me. Blood drips onto the floor. "I can't—" I stutter.

"You can't what?" the Seeker chuckles again. The static screech nearly forces me to my knees.

"I can't let you win." I swallow my vomit and force my body upright, staring directly at the robotic man through blurry vision.

"You. Don't. Have. A. Choice." His mask doesn't move, but I know he's smiling underneath it. The thought makes me furious. I take a step forward, pause for a wave of convulsions, then take another step. He only stands and laughs. My ears continue to ring out. The hallway swims. I blink, trying to focus. I glare at the man, forcing my feet forward in increments. My legs give out with no warning. I collapse backward onto the ground with a thump. I glare at the Seeker, who turns his swords back into knives and sheaths them. He steps past Adrius's motionless body. "I will make sure to

174

tell Lukas that you have actually died."

He's alive.

I grit my teeth. A strong tingle races from my head, down my back, and spreads through my limbs. My convulsions stop and my symptoms slowly fade. My headache fades away and my vision clears. More than that, the fatigue from the past weeks fade from my muscles. The Seeker leans over me, his mask staring at my eyes. The tingling sensation intensifies, turning into a buzzing hum centered around my hands and chest. My heartbeat races faster and faster. The buzzing crests, becoming electric. Energy crackles in my hands. The shock should burn. I should be screaming. But this is exhilarating. I look down at my hands; sparks of lightning arc between my fingertips. The Seeker slips a knife free from his belt with one hand. With his other hand, he grabs my neck. The instant he touches my skin, tendrils of electricity surge out of my chest, hands, and neck. They strike the Seeker with a blinding flash, blasting him through the air and across the hallway.

The Seeker sags on the ground, his labored breaths filling the air with terrifyingly deep static. He groans as he stands up to face me. "I'll admit, I was wrong. I assumed you were a Cortenian." He pauses. "No matter, I can still kill you easily." The Seeker flings a knife at my head. I snatch the handle out of the air a hair's breadth from my face. "Interesting."

The Seeker unsheathes two more knives, flicking them out into long blades. He lunges at me, swinging his swords. I scramble up and dodge out of the way, attempting to scurry past him. He aims a kick at my ribs, and I grab his leg before it hits me. More sparks spider down my arm and onto his leg. The Seeker gasps with an inrush of static, cool air spilling over me. He twists in my grip and swings one of his swords at my arm. I release his leg with a shove, and he jumps back away from me. The Seeker grabs his wounded leg. He lets out an earsplitting deep screech. The sound tears the air and then fractures, replaced by the higher-pitched scream of his real voice. He stumbles over onto the ground. I approach him, sparks gathering on my hands. I reach for his sword-wielding hands when thick smoke billows between us. I hear a familiar crackle near his legs, like that of a Plasmar. The crackle ignites again from the Seeker's boots followed by plumes of plasma.

The Seeker propels up, blasting through the roof of the prison, leaving a pile of concrete in his wake. I look down and stare at my hands, my fingertips still crackling with sparks.

CHAPTER 32

SAPPHIRE

T
he room is small and dark. Cracks weave across the dirt covered ceiling. My body's drenched in sweat from the stuffy heat. I suck in a ragged breath, stinging my throat as air flowed in and out. I don't recognize this room. I don't remember this memory.

I try to look around. My eyes actually move when I tell them to. What? I sit up and survey the room. The walls are lined with dead bodies who are, in turn, covered in blood. Some of the corpses have charcoal hands surrounded by crumbling powder on the floor. Eyes dangle from their sockets where heads lie separated from their bodies. Where am I?

There is someone standing in front of me, facing away. She whimpers, and raises her hand to wipe her tears. Her hair is brown and curly. It's Renna. I reach my hand behind me and push myself up to my feet.

"Renna..." I rasp, and my hoarse throat burns. A fit of coughs racks through me, and I have to brace my hands on my knees to steady myself. Renna turns around, her bloodshot eyes wet with tears.

"You're awake..." Renna blinks, then rubs her eyes with her dirty hand.

"What?" I croak. Tears burst from my eyes and begin streaming down my face. What is happening? Renna steps toward me and I reach forward, clutching her in a tight hug. "I'm sorry."

Renna grabs me as well, reciprocating the hug. "For what?" she mutters.

"I treated you horribly."

"It's fine."

I step back away from her, my vision blurring from my unexpected tears. "No, it's not."

"What happened when you were unconscious?" Renna asks. "You were mumbling a lot."

I sigh. "I relived some memories that I wish I'd forgotten." I step around the room, making sure not to step on any of the corpses. "Where are we?"

"This is the prison. It's where Axle was almost tested on," Renna says. "We came to save the next batch of test subjects. It's been weeks since the students were tested on. These are all new."

I crouch down, my eyes meeting those of one of the dead prisoners. I tap my earpiece to initiate a scan of the room. "This is what the serum does?"

"I don't think it's supposed to."

"There are decapitated heads. I think you're right. The serum didn't kill these people, at least not all of them." I point to a prisoner with foam surrounding her mouth. "I think she was killed by the serum."

"So the serum only works on some people?" Renna asks. "But who?"

I turn to Renna. "The Primordial Stones only worked for Saberrens. I think the serum is the same way. But it's not supposed to be."

Renna sniffles. "What does this have to do with the Primordial Stones?"

"I figured out what the serum is made of. It's made of Akorth, from Mount Islorr."

Renna's eyes widen. "But Islorr was shut down."

"I know. The Seeker must've reopened the mines. The serum interacts with blood. So does Akorth. It's the only material I know of that exhibits the same properties. And it is special because it bypasses the strong immune systems of Cortenians." I close my eyes, picturing the magnified image of the serum that I analyzed. "Remember when I told you about the organisms in the serum?" Renna nods. "Why would the Seeker be so obsessed with retaining the Lightning Stone? I'm sure Voltaris would have other methods of generating power. But if the Stone served another purpose, if it provided the organisms needed for the serum... I think the serum is supposed to replicate the effects of the Primordial Stones, but without the same restrictions. Adding Akorth should theoretically allow the serum to work with all immune systems."

"Why would he want to recreate the Stones' powers?" Renna asks.

"I don't know," I say. "But the Seeker was willing to kill people in order to do so," I scoff, stepping toward the metal door. I kick the door open and step out of the room.

"Where are you going?" Renna asks.

"I'm getting out of here. I can't find the Seeker if I'm in prison. And then, once I have enough evidence, I'm going to the Archcapital to expose him. I'm gonna raze Voltaris to the ground."

"You can't," Renna cries, grabbing my arm.

"And why is that?"

"You don't even know what's going on." Renna pulls me back into the room and shuts the door. "The Seeker likely killed Lukas. Axle and Adrius came here to free the prisoners. You almost died. I took you with me to save your life. I saved your life, and we don't even know how to find the Seeker."

I pause. Renna's eyes glisten with fresh tears. "Thanks." I grab the door again.

"You need to rest. Your neck isn't healed yet," Renna cries. I lift my finger up to the fabric around my neck, push it slightly out of the way, and glide my finger across the ragged gash. It's unbearably sensitive. I pull the fabric back up. Looking at my finger, I can tell that there is no trace of blood.

"It's healed enough." I pull the door open once again. "I'm going."

A pause. I turn back to Renna, who is trying to swallow back sobs. "I can't let you." I tilt my head to the side. "Stop it with that stupid head tilt. I know you're not actually confused."

I return my head upright. "But I am..." I continue holding the door, staring at Renna.

"Then you do not pay attention."

My eye twitches. "I assure you; I pay attention to everything. I have watched every single tear that has left your eyes. That does not mean I understand why they are there."

"You almost died."

"I didn't."

"It doesn't matter. Do you understand how stressful that was for me?"

179

Snot drips from Renna's nose. She wipes her face with her arm. "Sapphire, you're my best friend. I cannot let you die again."

I start to tilt my head again, but stop myself. "But I didn't die. How would it be again?"

"I don't want to lose you, Sapphire."

"You won't. I won't die," I turn away from Renna and toward the door.

Renna sighs. "Then I'm coming with you."

I pause, turning back to face her. "No, you're not."

"What?"

"I know you believe that you chose to come with me, to help me fight against Voltaris, but you didn't. It was an illusion. I pressured you into coming with me, because I didn't want you to turn me in." I reach for Renna's shoulder, stepping closer to her, but pull my hand back. "I'm done dragging you along. I told you I treated you horribly. I refuse to do that anymore."

Renna sniffles, her widened eyes watching me anxiously. "What do you mean?"

"You are not prepared for the dangers of fighting the Seeker. My father taught me to fight at a young age, skills passed down from our Shifter ancestors. You do not have that experience. If I let you come with me, Rosaea knows if you'll survive… and I cannot guarantee I'll succeed either."

"Sapphire, I don't understand…" Renna wipes her face again. "I helped break into the prison while carrying your unconscious body. I can fend for myself."

"It's more than that. You will hold me back. You would be dead weight. There's too much on the line for me to risk it."

"Dead weight?" Renna cries. "Sapphire, I kept you alive!"

"And I am returning the favor," I force a smile, which Renna does not reciprocate. I step away from her and back out of the door. "Goodbye, Renna. I will see you again."

Taking one last glance at Renna's teary eyes, I shut the door behind me. Something tells me to turn around and go back to Renna, but I ignore it.

Leaning against the wall of the large hallway connected to the door, I pull the stolen vial of serum out of my pocket. I'm surprised it didn't break. The serum emits an eerie green glow. I move the vial back and forth, and the serum slides cloyingly along the inside of the glass vial. Why make this? Tears fall from my eyes again, and I turn back to the door. I shake my head, clenching my fist around the vial. It doesn't matter. I have to put an end to it. I have to stop the Seeker.

My neck throbs with pain. The once hardly noticeable fabric now scrapes my raw wound like sandpaper. I grab the fabric and tear it off. There's no blood coursing down my skin, but it feels as if there were. No one knows the Seeker exists. Except Voltaris... and Prime Termani. If I can prove that Prime Termani is working with the Seeker, then I can get Prime Termani removed from office. Then I can focus on destroying Voltaris.

I push myself away from the wall, heading down the hallway. I don't know where to go, but I just keep walking anyway. I'll find my way out somehow. I round another corner, continuing down the barely lit hallway. I place the serum in my pocket again, and grab the handles of my Arcblades. I speed up, jogging through the hallways. My neck still hurts, but I ignore it. As I walk, I notice unconscious and dead guards lying on the floor. Blood drips out of fresh and old wounds alike. I step over the guards, continuing forward. Just beyond the pile of guards, the floor is littered with rubble leading up to a gaping hole in the ground.

Releasing my hands from the hilts of my swords, I lean down and grab the ledge of the hole. I swing my legs under me and into the hole. I take a deep, painful breath, and drop down into the hole. I'm in a large tunnel that stretches off in both directions. Dim light filters from the hole to reveal walls of tightly packed dirt. On the floor are metal rails going in both directions. Right next to me, sitting on the rails, is a large metal cart.

I look up at the cooled metal globs drooping from the hole. This must've been how we got in the prison. I turn back to the cart, staring in the opposite direction that the cart is pointing. I know what these are. These tunnels were built before the SpeedTunnels. They were used during the war. If I go far enough, I should get to Islorr. I just hope there's enough power left.

I pull the cart off the rails and carefully rotate it around, dragging it back on the rails again. I grip the edge of the cart and hoist myself in.

CHAPTER 33

My eyes are tired, but not from a lack of sleep. They're tired from tears. I wipe my eyes with my new arm, wincing in pain as the rough metal gouges my skin. In all the years that I'd spent living with Axle, all the times that I refused to leave, I told myself it was to protect him. I thought—*no, I knew*—that he wouldn't survive by himself. And then he did. He had survived the attempted murder by the Seeker and Voltaris, as well as being chased down. But now he's dead or about to be. Dammit. Hot blood trickles down my face instead of tears.

I swing my fist at the rock in front of me and it cracks from the blow. I also *knew* that I could do things on my own. But I guess it was because I was never really alone with my mom haunting my mind. I swing my fist again, and the metal crashes into the rock, widening the crack. I grab the shattered chunk of rock and pull it free from the wall. I spin around, throwing the rock into a large metal bucket in the middle of the cave. Attached to the bucket is a blazing torch that illuminates the cave. The back wall is pocked with holes from where I've torn chunks of rock free.

Why did I have to break the stupid machine?

I step farther away from the bucket toward an untouched part of the wall. Something pulls at my legs, and I fall forward. I throw my arms up to protect my face as I strike the ground. I push myself up. My flesh hand—not the metal one—bears a new scratch among dozens of others. Each one from catching myself. I turn to what tripped me up, two large chains

183

wrapped tightly around my ankles. The chains lead up to rails along the ceiling. The rails are blocked after a short distance on either side, keeping me from moving too far. Scratched into the blockers are the words 'Islorr Manufacturing'. These mines really are old.

I reach for the untouched wall once again.

"Hey Seeker," I call out, disgust in my voice. "I need you to move the rail blockers. I've run out of space to do your dirty work." I wait in silence for a response. Nothing. "Seek-" I start to say, when a hand grabs my mouth from behind. I spin around, swinging my metal arm at the attacker. She flies back, unsheathing two curved Arcblades. The attacker runs forward at me, slicing at my legs. I jump out of the way, and the swords barely miss the chains on my ankles.

"I see how it is. Hit me while I'm already down..."

She swings one of her swords at my legs again, and I grab the blade with my metal arm. In the torch's flickering light, the Arcblade gives off a familiar purple-silver tint. I barely have time to look at the sword, before the attacker twists the hilt of the sword, sliding it out of my grip. The blade flies behind me. She catches it effortlessly and swings at my legs again. I don't have time to react. Luckily, she misses my legs, and the swords clang against the metal chains on my ankles. The metal barely leaves an indent.

"Akorth," she mutters, sheathing her Arcblades. "Like everything else."

She drops to the ground and grabs the chains. I swing my fist at her as she approaches me. She grabs my arm and twists it away before I can land a blow. I look toward her face, but she's already slipped behind me impossibly fast. Her hair obscures my vision as she pulls at my arm. I yank my arm free and throw myself at her, swinging my fist once again. She dodges my attack and grabs the chains, wrenching them toward her. I fall backward and catch myself with my right hand alone. I push myself back up and swing another fist, aiming for her a wound in her neck. Right before I hit her neck, she shifts back, holding up her hands.

"Lukas. It's me, Sapphire. Don't hurt me."

I pause, looking at her face through stinging blood in my eyes.

"Sapphire?" I step forward and indeed, it is Sapphire, standing right in front of me. I gasp and grab my forehead with my hand. "You died. How?"

Sapphire shrugs. "I'm not entirely sure."

"Is... Axle alive?" I say through shaking teeth.

Sapphire nods. "Yes. He's alive."

I lunge at her, embracing her in a tight hug. My breathing comes in gasps as sobbing wracks my body. After a few long seconds, I release her from the hug and step back again.

"You're a mess," she says.

I chuckle. "So are you," I say in response, nodding toward her wounded neck. Sapphire tilts her head, before straightening her neck.

"Your chains are made of Akorth. It would take too long to break them. Or to find a way to detach you from the rails above. I don't have much time here." Sapphire looks around at the holes in the wall. "You made those."

I sigh. "Everything here is made of Akorth, even the Seeker apparently."

Sapphire's eyes widen. "The Seeker is here? I have to go." She starts to turn away.

"He's not here right now. You don't have to leave."

"I'm sorry, but I'm not here to find you. I didn't think I'd find *you* at all."

"Then why are you here?" I ask.

She holds her hand out with the vial, and I take it in my left hand, holding it up to the light from the torch. The green fluid glows in the light.

I shrug, handing the vial back to Sapphire.

"Mount Islorr is the only place that Akorth has been found," Sapphire says. "Of all the places to find evidence of the serum's makeup, it would be here." Sapphire pauses, pacing back and forth, occasionally glancing at the chains around my legs and at the numerous holes in the walls. She stops, spotting the bucket full of rock and metal ore. She crosses over to the bucket and examines the debris. After a split second, she turns back to me. "Why are you mining all this?"

I sigh. "I broke his machine." I nod my head in the direction of the destroyed contraption.

Sapphire taps the side of her earpiece and steps over to the machine, pacing around it. The blue light from her earpiece shines onto the mechanisms

185

"And this is what mined the Akorth? Before you broke it?"

"It processed the Akorth into powder. He's using it to make the—" I'm interrupted by loud steps in the distance. "He's coming," I whisper, grabbing Sapphire's arm.

"I know what it's for." Sapphire whispers. "He's mining Akorth for the serum, right?"

I nod.

"I hope this recording is enough." Sapphire mutters under her breath, tapping the earpiece again. The blue light turns off. "But if not, maybe I can force Prime Termani to acknowledge the serum, then I can connect him to the Seeker directly." The loud steps thunder closer.

"You have to go," I whisper.

"And leave you?" Sapphire mutters.

"Just go," I whisper harshly.

Sapphire disappears down the tunnel just as the Seeker enters my view, blocking the seemingly endless cave behind him. The light from a torch on his arm is absorbed by his black armor despite being bright enough to light up rest of the cave. Even the orange light reflected by the chipped walls of the cave are lost to the shadows of the Seeker's Akorth armor. From what I can see, the armor is sloppily assembled. One of the shoulder pads slants off to the side more than usual. His mask is also angled slightly to the side, and his gloves are pulled on too tight. The Seeker's breathing is haggard, coming fast enough that I can hear his actual breaths beneath the static overlay.

The Seeker takes a step toward me, then reaches up to the blockers latched onto the rails. Using a strange key, he detaches the blockers. The burning torch by the bucket casts ominous shadows as he walks toward me. He stops just a few steps away from me and reattaches the blockers using the same key. He turns to leave without saying a word. He stops. His gaze drops to the floor. Gears whir as the robotic man leans down to glide his glove across the dirt, following footprints that I hadn't noticed earlier. There are two sets of prints, mine and Sapphire's. He expertly traces her path. Where my footprints are all mostly centered between the wall and the collection bucket, Sapphire's footprints disappear down the tunnel away from me. He follows the tracks, blurring away from the torch's light. I can barely see his head turn upward, pointing down the cave tunnel. The Seeker spins around and runs at me.

"Someone was here. Who was it?" he booms, his mask nearly pressed up against my face. His breaths escape the vent in his mask, spilling cool air along my face. I stay silent. I turn away, walking toward an untouched part of the cave wall. The Seeker grabs my metal arm and swings me around to face him. "Who was here?" he yells, and static assaults my ears. I make to cover them, but the Seeker intercepts, forcing my arms down. "Who was here?" The static pounds against my eardrums. A ringing explodes in my head that drowns out all thoughts. I still refuse to respond, and the Seeker bolts away down the cave in pursuit of the trespasser.

My mind flashes to Axle. He is still alive. The Seeker won't let him stay alive much longer. I look down at my metal arm, clenching my artificial fist.

I need to escape.

CHAPTER 34

AXLE

I stare at my hands as the sparks die down and fade away. I snap my fingers, expecting another spark, but it doesn't come. I drop to my knees, still staring at my hands. Placing my palms together, I rub them back and forth. No effect. I close my eyes and envision the Seeker hovering over me. I take a deep breath, and snap again with both hands. I don't feel anything. I peek through half-closed eyes at my hands. Nothing happens from applying friction with my fingers.

Clenching my fists, I stand up and punch at the air. My eyes dart around at the hallway, at the doors that still haven't been opened.

"Oh, shit." I turn to Adrius's lifeless body lying limp on the floor. I lean down and lift him up. I stand up as Renna runs toward me, her eyes bloodshot.

"Axle," she exclaims, her eyes jolting around the hallway. "What happened?"

I pause, glancing down at my hands, then at Adrius in my arms. "The Seeker took the Lightning Stone. Where's Sapphire?"

"She woke up. She said she was going to the Archcapital." Renna looks down for a split second, then back up. She reaches out her arm and holds it against Adrius's neck. "He's alive, but probably not for long. What are we gonna do?"

"Well, we can't stay here, that's for sure."

"What do you propose?" she asks, wiping away tears from her face.

I glance back at the unopened doors. "We have to see if anyone is still

188

alive." I lay Adrius back down and head over to one of the closed doors and swing it open. Just like the rest, the interior is completely empty. I grab the next door and swing it open. No one. Renna joins me, opening door after door along the other side of the hallway. I look back at Adrius's limp body. He's not going to die. Not on my watch. No one else is going to die.

I hear something coming from a door up ahead. Faint whimpers. I rush toward the door and swing it open. The room is packed with people.

"Please don't kill me." Someone drops to her knees, her hands clasped together. Her body is covered in dirt and her aged face is carved with tears. "I'll do anything, please."

Renna scurries over to me as more people drop to the ground.

"Please. I lost my family. I just wanna see the ones who are still alive..."

"Vermaiye have mercy..." Renna mutters in my ear.

"I haven't seen my kids. They were taken weeks ago. I want to see them. Please, sir." This man wears a white shirt with Prime Termani's face spray painted on it. His eyes are covered with painted 'X's. A few others wear similar shirts, and some have hash mark tattoos on their shoulders.

"I can't do this again," someone with a hash mark cries. "Please, I can't do this again."

"We're not here to kill you," I say, stepping closer into the room. The prisoners dart backward. "And we're not here to test you." The prisoners eye me the way prey eyes a predator. "This armor that I wear... it's not mine. I was in the first batch of testing. I escaped. I think I was the only one. But I won't be anymore. My friend and I are getting you all out of here."

"Are our kids dead?" someone asks, sniffling.

I sigh. "Unfortunately, yes."

"Where are their bodies?"

"I don't know. They've been moved. Replaced by the bodies of those in your group." I pause, looking at the unopened doors. "Here's what we're gonna do. I need each and every one of you to start opening doors. Every single door needs to be opened. I don't know how many others are still alive in here." The prisoners nod, and I step aside as they rush past me. They throw doors open. Most are empty. A few have some prisoners remaining.

"So now we get out of here?" Renna asks.

I nod. "Now we get out of here." I lean over Adrius's body and lift him up. I look down the hall at the prisoners. "Does anyone know where the exit is?"

* * *

Rosaea's light floods my eyes as I step out of the SpeedTunnel, leaving the prison far behind. I'm just glad they redirected reserves for the SpeedTrains. This is the first time I've been outside in weeks. The prisoners run past me on either side, rushing through the Crathenos cityscape. The city is different from the last time I saw it. Skyscrapers tower on either side of me, but the usual projections are oddly absent. The light poles are on though, so some power has been re-established. On the horizon, the diamond at the top of the capitol building glows under Rosaea's pink light. The interior light that typically illuminates the ornament is not turned on.

Massive CSD rollers are parked at every corner. Their wide doors are left open, and CSD workers patrol around them. Renna and I hurry to the closest roller. One of the workers spots us, and rushes over, screaming orders at the other workers. They pull a gurney out of the roller, and I lay Adrius down on it. As the workers tend to his body, I glance back at the capitol building. I have to put an end to the testing. Once and for all.

I turn to Renna. Her eyes follow Adrius's bloodied body, but her mind seems elsewhere.

"Renna." She whips her head to face me. "Make sure he stays alive." Renna doesn't say a word. She just nods and follows the CSD workers as they move Adrius.

I step away from Renna, from Adrius, and march in the direction of the capitol building. I can still recall the Seeker's black eyes, staring at me from the testing room. I watch as he injects the innocent student with the serum for the first time. This ends today.

I reach the capitol to find two guards posted on either side of the entrance. They nod as I approach, and move out of the way to let me enter. The guard armor proving useful once again.

The capitol walls are lined with a fake wooden texture similar to that of the school. A red carpet stretches the length of the central hallway, reminiscent of the deep red of Prime Termani's cloth face wrap. The carpet is dotted with many dirty footprints.

The narrow hallway of the building funnels toward two doors. One is a metal lifter door with a glowing orange arrow pointing up. The other is an ordinary door and, opening it, I find that it is the same room where Lukas, Sapphire, and Renna found us. I stare at the trapdoor in the center of the room. Underneath that trapdoor are the tunnels where I hid in for weeks. I expected there to be more guards in here, but I suppose so much time has passed that they're no longer at high alert.

I step toward the lifter. I press the button, and it flickers from orange to blue, then back to orange. The door squeaks as it slides across the ground. It staggers opens, rather than sliding in a fluid motion, and comes to an abrupt halt halfway. I manually pry the door all the way open.

The wall is filled top to bottom with silver buttons labeled from '1' to '50'. Above the '50' button is a slightly larger, golden button marked with a 'P'. I press the golden button and the lifter jerks upwards slightly, then stops again. I press it one more time, but the lifter's gears only groan.

I scan the lifter's interior and spot a small swinging door, too small for anyone to fit through. Above the door, a sign reads 'Emergency Use Only'. I swing the door open, revealing a thick metal chain. I grab part of the chain and pull down. As I pull, the lifter inches up. Finding a rhythm, I continue to yank the thick chain down. The lifter ascends at a steady pace. The blue flickering light switches from button to button, inching me closer to the top floor.

The golden button flickers blue, and I can't move the chain any further. The top floor is completely different from the first. The floor is covered in a wooden texture. The room is barren apart from a small desk at its center. The desk faces a large camera and light mounted to the right wall. Dark gray composite covers the walls.

The left side of the room opens up more as I fully exit the lifter. It extends farther out than the right, but it's empty, except for a massive pile of papers in a corner. I head over to the paper stacks and start rifling through. It's mostly just legal documents. I recognize key terms, like 'Primordialists' and 'Termani District', but nothing related to Voltaris. Nothing that can shut the testing down. It's like the Seeker doesn't exist.

I take deep breaths and pace around the room. I clench my fists, lean against the wall, and let out a deep sigh. My breathing quickens. I push off the wall, and lunge toward the camera. I scream, tearing at my hair with my hands. I look down at my hands; a chunk of charred hair rests in my grip. The stink of burning hair stings my nostrils. I drop the hair, grab the camera, and tear it off the wall. A blue light flickers faintly on the camera, then dies. I drop the device. I grab the desk with my hands and sparks cascade across the wood, burning fractal patterns across its surface. I stare down at my hands, my breaths slowing down again.

I turn back to the desk, ripping out the drawers. They're all empty. I scream again, picking up the wooden desk and flipping it through the air. It hits the wall, and flakes of composite break free. I turn back to where the desk was, and spot an upturned piece of metal. The wood around it does not line up with the rest of the floor's pattern. I grab the piece of metal and pull it. A trapdoor opens up.

The hidden space is too small to fit a person, but it doesn't seem like that's what it's meant for. Stuffed in the compartment is a bunch of black armor and a black undersuit. I drag it all out and lay it on the floor. Lukas was wearing that when fighting the Seeker. And now Prime Termani has it.

CHAPTER 35

AXLE

I tear off the stolen guard helmet and toss it across the room. It hits the wall and crashes next to the desk. Gripping the underside of the chestplate, I pull it upward and off of my sweat-drenched body. I remove my boots as well. The stench of the clothes underneath the armor is impossible to ignore. I've worn these clothes since the graduation party.

I grab the armor that Lukas was wearing. It looks like a prototype of the Seeker's suit. The black undersuit fits snugly over my clothes, and it traps the stench. I attach the armor piece by piece. The black armor is different from the undersuit. This is the first time I really had a chance to examine the metal. Unlike the undersuit, which reflects the dim light from above, the armor appears flat, with no highlights or shadows. The metal itself looks like a shadow. When Lukas was wearing it, it vaguely took on his shape. Without a person to conform to, the metal looks like an abyss, like a hole. I guess that's why I thought the Seeker looked like a shadow-man in the prison.

I pull the last piece of armor onto my body and pick up the helmet. I turn it around to face me. The empty black eyes stare at me, almost through me. I close my eyes, reminded of the day that Lukas found me in that room downstairs. I open my eyes again, turn the helmet back around, and place it over my head.

The inside of the helmet stinks worse than the weeks-old clothes I've been wearing underneath the armor. Unlike the clothes, the helmet smells as if it had never been washed before. It probably hasn't. It's also hot inside the armor, and my body breaks out in fresh sweat. This thing needs a ventilation system. The eyes of the armor are strange as well. I'd expected the vision to be darker, like wearing a pair of UV glasses. Instead, my eyesight is clearer than usual, albeit with a strange green undertone.

I step inside the lifter and grab the chain. I push the chain upward, and the lifter shoots down at immense speeds. The chain flies up at the same speed. I brace myself against the walls of the lifter until it finally slows. The last bit of its descent felt like trudging through syrup, likely part of an emergency braking system. I step out of the still-open lifter door and walk into the hallway of the capitol. I take a deep breath and run for the giant entrance door.

I push the door open and step outside. Immediately, a blast of plasma flies at my head. My head swerves to the side with inhuman reflexes. How did I dodge that? The plasma bolt sears through the guard on the other side of the door. Her head explodes and blood splatters the armor of my left side. I look to the right at a guard with an orange-lit Plasmar pointed directly at me. His finger quivers over the trigger.

"He's back," the guard whispers. His finger twitches forward, and I lunge at him, yanking the Plasmar free from his grip. I point the weapon at his head, switch the light to blue, and fire. His face droops and he collapses.

Dozens of guards emerge out of hiding. Some come out of random buildings around the capitol. Others exit from the capitol. They all fire their Plasmars at me in unison.

Oh, shit.

My reflexes kick in again. As plasma burns through the air, my body swerves out of the way of each incoming blast. My movements are on autopilot, as if something else is controlling my body. I strain to listen if it's the suit, but there's no mechanical whirring like what I'd heard from the Seeker's armor. This is something inside me.

I fire more shots from my Plasmar and stun a few other guards, but I don't think my fast reflexes will last for long. One guard lunges at me, Plasmar holstered. She grabs my shoulders and pulls me down. Another guard steps forward and pins my legs in place. A third guard presses down on my chest, holding me against the ground. I attempt to pull my arm free. This time the suit does whir to life, and I fling the guard behind me out of the way. Another fires a shot at my hand. I move my arm away from the blast and it explodes against the ground next to me instead. The burning smell fills my nose. Yet another guard runs forward and pins my shoulders back down. The remaining guards circle around me, their Plasmars pointed at different parts of my body. They all fire blasts at the same time. Time seems to slow down, and I perceive each bolt of hot plasma streaking towards my body.

This can't be how it ends. My mind flashes to the prison, to my fight with the Seeker. It flashes to Lukas, telling me to run away. It flashes to the graduation party. To my friends. They all died after that party. I lived.

"Good people suffer far worse than innocents." Adrius's voice echoes in my head. *"Unlike innocent people, good people get in the way on purpose."*

You're wrong. I may be in the way, but I am *not* going to suffer for it.

Huge sparks erupt from my body, arcing at the guards holding me down. They fly through the air before the electricity tears their bodies apart. I roll out of the plasma's way just in time and return to my feet.

I turn around, away from the capitol. Plasmars from other guards fire continuously, a storm of fiery plasma following my footsteps as I flee. Just from the crackling sound in the air, I'm able to react and avoid each and every shot that comes my way. The sound ceases. I spare a glance behind me. The guards have stopped firing and are now running at me in hot pursuit.

The last time I ran from someone was in the prison. I could feel my heart rate rising and my whole body heating up. This feels different. My heart rate feels strangely steady, and I don't feel any warmer than I did before I started running. My fingers twitch, and I look down at my hands. Sparks fly between my fingertips. Cool air rushes by on either side of me; I can feel it tug at the gaps between the armor. The air howls as it speeds up. I glance behind me again. The air isn't moving faster. I am. I'm leaving the guards farther and farther behind as I accelerate with a growing intensity. I spot the SpeedTunnel, and have to wrench my whole body to redirect my insane momentum down into the tunnel. I lean back and my legs eventually slow down to a walk.

The SpeedTunnel is empty, as I expected. The overhead lights are on, but dim. Just like in the capitol. Power's coming back to Termani. I just don't know if it's the Lightning Stone, or if Voltaris has other means of producing electricity. I doubt the Seeker would use the Lightning Stone this soon after losing it. I approach the robot at the center of the station.

"Where would you like to travel?" the robot asks.

"The Archcapital."

The robot's eyes, small sensor devices placed to mimic people, flash blue. "That will be fifty-seven ferrings."

I don't have my earpiece.

"Damn it," I mutter under my breath. I look around at the display signs above. They're flickering every couple of seconds. 'Lusia', 'Fendar'. I move past the sign for Lusia, toward the labels for the Carkunese districts. 'Zurakk', 'Afoudea', 'Kwilla'. Found it. Right next to the sign labeled 'Kwilla' is a smaller one reading 'the Archcapital.' The SpeedTrain parked on its track is shorter in length than the other trains in the station, limiting the traffic to and from the Archcapital. I walk up to the door. There aren't any guards. Instead, a sensor tries to scan my earpiece. I wave my hand directly in front of it, my fingers are still carrying residue sparks. The sparks hit the sensor, and the closed door slides open. I step onto the SpeedTrain and sit down, waiting for it to take off. It's meeting day today. I just need an audience with the Council of Primes.

CHAPTER 36

SAPPHIRE

I stab my swords up into the dirt ceiling of the tunnel. Dirt crumbles and falls on either side of me as I keep loosening the heavily packed soil overhead. I stand on the rim of the cart, which is partially bent out of shape. Getting the cart to start was a pain, but I was able to tap into its electricity reserve. However, the cart was not built to handle the immense speeds that the backup power put out.

Continuing to dig into the ceiling, I look at the rails on either side of me. In one direction, the rails head back to Termani, probably past it all the way to the edge of Ayzol. The other leads directly to Mount Islorr. I glance up at the loosened dirt just as a giant chunk falls onto my face. I squeeze my eyes shut too late and dirt worms in under my eyelids. I rub at my eyes as more dirt collapses down onto my head and upper back. I keep my burning eyes tightly shut and leap out of the way as the rest of the tunnel roof caves in. The cart clangs as chunks of rock bounce off its interior. I rub my eyes again before opening them. A massive dirt mound covers the cart. My eyes sting as I walk forward again. I squint up through the dust cloud at pieces of concrete pushed together and secured by a thick dried paste.

I lower one of my swords into the handle and clamber on top of the dirt pile to reach the concrete above. Using my free hand, I push up on the concrete. It doesn't budge. Gripping my extended Arcblade with both hands, I stab the blade up through the paste between two of the chunks. I am barely tall enough for the tip of the blade to pass through. I swing the sword in

197

an arc to cut through the glue-like paste. I sheathe my sword, and use both of my hands to push up on the concrete. Unlike before, the two connected pieces now shift and grind against each other. I rise onto the tips of my toes, pushing up as hard as I can with my whole body stretched and strained. The concrete chunks shake until both pieces break loose and fall down. I duck, allowing both the pieces to slam against my back, sending me tumbling down the dirt mound. I wince in pain. I gingerly stand up straight and lean back to stretch my back; it cracks as I move.

I look up again to aww blue sky above me. The bright light forces me to squint. I have been underground for so long that daylight burns my eyes. My eyes water as I scramble back up the dirt mound, jump, and grab the concrete on either side of the hole. I strain to pull myself up, but my joints give out, and I fall back down.

Come on Sapphire.

I grit my teeth, jump up again, and pull as hard as I can. The muscles around my partially-healed neck wound sear with the effort. I make it a bit farther up before my arms give out again. As I fall, another piece of concrete breaks loose and crashes on my foot. I whimper out loud. Damn it. I lean over and push the piece off of my throbbing toes. Tensing up my muscles, I jump again and grab the concrete on each side. The hole is now wider, allowing a better purchase to spread my arms push over the ledge. The concrete starts to slip in my hands, but I'm able to throw my legs up in time. For a moment, I'm awkwardly splayed over the hole. I stiffen my legs and arms and roll to the side and onto the ground. Letting out a deep breath, I finally stand up on the surface.

The blue skies are more beautiful than I remember. The bright light triggers more tears, which flushes out the dirt from my eyes. I adjust to the glare and am tempted to stare at the vibrant sun. Shaking my head, I turn away from the sky and toward the city sprawling out in front of me. Though the city is technically in Kwilla, it isn't under the jurisdiction of the district, or any others. The Archcapital is an independent entity that houses the government of the entire Union of Ayzol-Carkun.

Although the city is small, it radiates power and authority. Immense buildings of white marble accented in gold are laid out in a neat grid with large streets between them. Most people roam the streets wearing embroidered robes. A few tourists are easily spotted in their normal clothes. Considering that most people who choose to live here work for the government, the formal attire makes sense.

Though I've never been to the Archcapital, I've seen enough maps to navigate it with relative ease. I know that the city is structured in a unique format: large apartments on the outer rim, then hotels, then museums, and finally the capitol building in the center. The giant building in which people decide the fate of the Union is easy to spot. Not only does it tower over the rest of the city's massive edifices, it's also ringed by giant statues of historical figures. On the far left of the capitol, carved from a deep gray stone, is a statue of the tall and ominous Carkunese General of the Saberren War. He's known partly for his battle strategy, but mostly for his role as the first Carkunese Archprime of the Union of Ayzol-Carkun. On the far right is his counterpart and previously sworn enemy, the Ayzolian General. He was also the first Ayzolian Archprime of the Ayzol-Carkun Union. No one remembers his role in the war, but he's infamous for being driven to insanity by some unknown cause. Both generals fought against the Saberrens, but their statues were kept after the war.

The middle of building is dominated by a larger statue, flanked on both sides by sets of double doors. It depicts a confident man with a knowing gaze. His gaze is fixed on the horizon. The man's two hands are held out on either side of him, like a scale balancing Ayzol and Carkun. He's the Archprime who reformed the Union around fifty years ago. The first Archprime of *both* Ayzol and Carkun. Only after his ten-year term did people largely consider the Union of Ayzol-Carkun one society.

I stride through the double doors on the left of the former Archprime's statue and into an ornate chamber bustling with government workers. A few tourists pass through the doors behind me, and others are already ogling at the chamber within. The chamber is made of stone, with massive pillars holding up the glass dome ceiling. The pillars are layered, with carved-out cracks filled with gold. Engraved into the stone floor of the chamber is a map of Ayzol-Carkun. Each district is carefully outlined with thick gashes, and the finer details of the map are the width of a hair. I've never seen anything so imposing yet delicate at the same time.

Positioned at the other end of the room is another set of double doors. Either side of the doors are staircases going to the upper level. It is inside those double doors where the Council of Primes conduct their scheduled meetings. I walk toward the doors. People stare at the blood on my neck, some whispering to each other. Blocking the doors are two guards dressed in silver-tinted armor unlike the dark gray of the Termani guards. The guards have different versions of Plasmars holstered at their belts too.

"What is your intention?" one of the guards asks as I approach the doors.

"I need to speak to the Archprime."

"The Archprime is busy right now," the guard says. "As are the other Primes. If you have a question or request, please go upstairs and speak with the representatives."

"I have evidence to present regarding Prime Termani's unlawful actions," I assert. The guards stare blankly at me.

"What evidence?" the other guard asks.

"I have captured footage of the mandatory testing in the Termani District." I can't mention Mount Islorr until I'm in the room. They won't let me in if I tell them I've been there.

"You may enter," the guard says, gesturing to the doors. I open the doors and step forward. The room on the other side is filled with chaotic chatter. I dart behind one of the giant pillars in the room before anyone has a chance to notice my presence. The timing of my accusation must be just right.

The vast room is mostly empty, except for the giant pillars arranged in a circle. Twelve large chairs are positioned in front of the pillars, forming another slightly smaller circle. The chair opposite the double doors is the largest of them, adorned with vines of gold crawling up its frame. Most of the chairs are occupied. A man's gruff laugh thunders in the expansive room. I can't see who it is; he's seated in the chair in front of the pillar I'm hiding behind. Next to him is a stout elderly man with thin gray hair. The countless wrinkles on his loose skin gives him a serious expression. He wears an assortment of bracelets around his two thin wrists. Seated opposite the man with the gruff laugh is a thin woman with beautiful, glossy skin and a large flurry dress. Atop her shoulders rests a fur coat. The rest of the Primes each sport their own unique attire. In large adorned chair sits a woman with wavy golden hair and an equally wavy white gown. Tightly gripping the armrests of the chair, the Archprime of Ayzol-Carkun casts quick glances around the room. Her eyes settle on an empty chair two seats to her right.

"Where is Termani?" the Archprime asks. Everyone else shrugs and returns to their side conversations.

"I'm right here," a static-filled voice booms from a side entrance. I peek around the edge of the pillar. Prime Termani enters the room with a barely noticeable limp in his left leg. He's dressed in his usual white and red suit and accompanying cloth mask. Prime Termani waddles forward with an ornate black cane, gripping the golden orb at the top. As he reaches the chair, he grabs the nearest armrest and pulls himself into the seat. With his other hand, he continues to hold onto the cane, using it to straighten his posture. "I am sorry for the delay. I had business to attend to." Everyone leans back in their chairs.

"You've claimed this meeting, what do you want?" a large woman with a barely-fitting suit says. She sits two chairs to the left of the Archprime, mirroring Prime Termani.

"I am here to ask for your support. We have allowed the Primordialists to persist for far too long. They have taken too much from us. They have taken our power, they have killed our people, and they may even have influence over members of this Council." Chaos erupts after Prime Termani finishes his last line.

"This is outrageous," the gruff voice in front of me exclaims. "You accuse us of terrorism?"

Prime Termani sighs. "I am merely stating a possibility. The important part is that I want your support."

"In what way?" the woman with the fur coat asks.

"Great question." Prime Termani twirls his cane, then stands up from his seat. The Archprime turns to glare at him, and he returns to his seat. "I am asking for your armies."

"That's preposterous," the stout man cries. "You have given nothing to us, yet you expect our armies?"

"Thank you, Kwilla," Prime Termani says. He pauses, looking around at everyone, who all look back at him. "Yes." Before the Prime has the chance to continue speaking, the other Primes stand up, yelling incomprehensible words. Prime Termani leans back in his chair, twirling his cane again.

"Silence," the Archprime yells. All the Primes cease their yelling and return to their seats. "Termani, you may continue." She gestures to the calm Prime.

"Thank you, Archprime," Prime Termani nods. "Ayzol-Carkun is at peace. The Primordialists threaten to destroy that peace. Do you want to spend the rest of your terms cleaning up after their messes? Do you want your precious peace to destroy your districts? Termani is already in shambles from the power outage. If we continue to allow the Primordialists to ravage Ayzol-Carkun, who knows what could happen next? We must act fast and eliminate the threat before they eliminate us. I would like to hold a vote."

The Archprime waits for a brief moment. "Motion to support Termani." The woman with the fur coat raises her hand.

"Thank you, Wylak," Prime Termani says. The woman nods. One after another, hands slowly raise. I must act now. Before the last hand raises, I run into the center of the room. Everyone turns to me.

"Who are you?" the Archprime asks.

"My name is Sapphire ajj Termani. I work for Voltaris Industries. I am here to prove to you that Prime Termani is conspiring with Voltaris Industries to kill innocent civilians."

"This is a private meeting. You should not be here," Prime Termani says.

I face Prime Termani, who leans in, the eyes of his mask glaring at me. "You are a Prime, you should understand the law. As long as I have evidence to present, I am allowed to remain in this room."

"You may present your evidence," the Archprime says.

"Thank you." I look around the room at all the Primes. "Voltaris Industries is run by a man who hides his face. A man known as the Seeker." I point to my injured neck. "He did this to me when I tried to interfere with his work."

"Assuming Voltaris is killing people, for which we still require proof, how does that connect to Prime Termani?" the Archprime asks.

"The answer lies in Prime Termani's mandatory testing," I say. Prime Termani's non-cane holding hand clenches. "I have seen the prison where he took the students. They're all dead. Some of the corpses appeared to be fatally affected by the testing, and others had their heads manually severed."

The Archprime raises a finger. "Given that you have not brought any physical evidence, I cannot accept what you say as fact."

I turn on my earpiece and project an image onto the floor. Everyone stares down at the scan I took of the testing room. Many of the Primes gasp in horror, including the Archprime herself.

"Turn it off," the Archprime orders. I cancel the projection.

"What you just saw represents only one of Prime Termani's mandatory testing rounds."

"That image could have easily been fabricated," Prime Termani says.

"Termani makes a good point," the Archprime nods. "Can you prove to us that this image is not a fabrication?"

"You can go to Termani and look for yourself. The evidence is there."

"You still have not explained how Prime Termani and Voltaris are connected. And who this... Seeker is. Without probable cause, I am unable to interfere with Prime Termani's orders."

I sigh. "I do not know who the Seeker is. But Voltaris Tower has an unlabeled room with designs of the Seeker's suit. And I have seen him in person." I pause. "But I know that isn't enough evidence for you." I pull the vial of serum out of my pocket. Prime Termani taps his foot, still clenching his fist. "I took this vial from Voltaris Laboratories, where I work. This is the serum used for Prime Termani's testing."

"May I see it?" the Archprime asks. I nod, walking forward and handing her the vial. She leans back in her chair, examining the serum.

"I have analyzed this serum. You should know that one of the main components of the serum is powdered Akorth."

"The mines of Mount Islorr were closed," the Archprime says. "No one can access them anymore."

"Not legally," I add. "However, the underground tunnels that lead to the mountain still exist. Voltaris has very carefully guarded that fact. I became suspicious of the serum when we were told to fabricate it in large quantities by hand in the lab. Simple work that a machine can do. But a machine would have to be registered. And if the serum was produced outside of the Termani district, then the shipments would have to be registered. My suspicions deepened when we, the lab scientists, were forbidden to analyze the contents of the serum. I had to figure that out myself." I pause for a moment, then project the image of the broken mining machine Lukas pointed out. The Archprime's eyes widen. "I know I can be imprisoned for admitting to illegally entering Mount Islorr, but I am willing to take that risk. This machine was used to mine and process Akorth into powder. This kind of machine is too advanced to date back to when the mines were legally open."

"Another fabrication," Prime Termani adds. "This means nothing unless you can prove it to be true."

"What if you're wrong about the serum?" the Archprime asks. I turn off the image.

"Archprime, if you compare the components of the serum with Akorth, you will find that they are identical."

"What does this serum do?"

"I believe that it is meant to recreate the effects of Primordial Stones."

Audible gasps ripple across the room. Prime Termani whips his head around the room, then turns back to glare at me.

"What evidence supports your claim?" he asks.

"I have no direct evidence for that theory. All that I can do is speculate based on the perceived side effects of the serum. What matters more is that the serum is killing people under your sanctioned testing."

Prime Termani turns to the Archprime. "Due to the lack of evidence, I recommend that she be removed from this room immediately."

The Archprime nods. The doors swing open and a man walks in, wearing the prototype Seeker suit. Everyone turns to watch as the Mark 1 Seeker approaches the center of the room.

CHAPTER 37

AXLE

"This intruder should not be allowed in this room," Prime Termani declares, jolting up from his seat. The Prime's white suit is dirtier than when I last saw it on the screen at the school. The wrinkled, off-white suit clings to his body as he steps toward me. His white overcoat billows behind him. He paces around the room with a black cane in his left hand, favoring his right leg over his left. He raises the cane, gripping its golden orb, and waves it at me. He stumbles and lowers the cane to catch himself.

Sapphire turns to me with wide eyes. Her head tilts to the side, then snaps back up. She's still wearing her dirty lab coat. The bloodstains are now mostly obscured by brown stains from dirt. Her hands slide beneath her coat to rest by her belt.

"You may leave," a woman orders from across the room. She has long and wavy blonde hair that flows over a white gown. Just like the other ten seated Primes, she occupies her own chair, though hers is larger than the others'. The Archprime's seat is carved from white marble, matching her gown.

Sapphire turns her head to face the woman. "Archprime, if I may, I do not believe you fully understand the evidence presented."

"You. May. Leave."

"Yes, Archprime." Sapphire bows, her head tilting to stare at me. I see a glimpse of purple-silver metal glint from one of her Arcblades as she begins to slide it out of its sheath.

"Archprime, I have more evidence," I say, the helmet's modulator makes my voice deeper and unnatural.

"He should not be allowed in this room," Prime Termani repeats, raising his cane at me again. He falls forward, and catches himself with the cane. "Dammit," he mutters under his breath.

"You shall return to your seat, Termani," the Archprime orders. Prime Termani limps back to his wooden chair and takes a seat. "As for you," she points at me, "you are allowed to present your evidence. Once you are done, if it is determined unsuitable, then you shall both leave immediately. Sapphire ajj Termani, you may stay for now." Sapphire nods. The Archprime turns back to me. "State your case."

Smirking under my helmet, I step closer to the Archprime. I glance at Prime Termani, who leans forward in his seat. The goggles over his cloth wrap follow me as I move.

"People call me the Seeker," I say with a robotic voice. Prime Termani clenches his fists. "I run and own the energy company operating as Voltaris Industries. With Voltaris Industries, I helped design and create the serum that was used in Prime Termani's mandatory testing protocol. This serum has several disastrous side effects, including death. I fully confess to working with Prime Termani on the testing, and to the murder of thousands of innocent civilians in the process."

"You know you will be imprisoned for life for this confession, right?" the Archprime asks. She reaches up and presses a button on her earpiece. Rustling erupts from a door behind the Archprime.

"I am fully aware of the consequences of my actions. I am also fully aware that these actions were condoned and ordered by Prime Termani."

"That is not the Seeker!" Prime Termani slams his cane on the ground. The perfectly placed diamond pattern of the floor cracks beneath the blow. All the Primes turn to face Prime Termani, still silent.

I grin widely beneath the helmet as I turn my whole body to face the Prime. "How do you know?"

Prime Termani slams his fists into the armrests of his chair. He drops the cane to the ground, his hands shaking.

"I wear a mask. How do you know I am not the Seeker that you've been working with?"

Prime Termani pauses, allowing his hands to steady. "If I can prove he is not the Seeker, then his claim about our partnership is invalid, correct?" The Prime glances around the room. The Primes nod in response. He looks at the Archprime, who nods as well. "It's your voice. You sound different."

"So, you've met the Seeker?" I ask.

"Yes, I have met the Seeker," Prime Termani admits. Everyone turns to stare at him. "That does not mean I worked with him."

I sigh. "How would you know my voice is different? I modulate my voice, just like you I might add."

"This… Seeker makes a valid point," the Archprime says. "If he cannot prove he is the Seeker, you cannot prove you are Prime Termani."

Prime Termani's gloved hand grips his armrest. "I retract my statement."

"So, you are claiming you cannot prove this man is not the Seeker. Therefore, we have to consider his confession as potentially valid," the Archprime says.

"I know he's not the Seeker," Prime Termani states.

The Archprime takes a deep breath, looking around the room. Sapphire keeps her hands on the hilts of her hidden Arcblades, but her stance is more relaxed. She continues to stare at me.

"Let's introduce some certainty into this discussion, shall we? If you will, please remove your masks."

Prime Termani scoffs. "I will not. You are not allowed to require me to."

I smile. "I will." I reach up and grab the helmet, taking it off. Sapphire's eyes widen as she stares at me. She releases her hands from her hilts. I turn to Prime Termani, who's masked eyes glare at me.

"That is Axle ajj Termani." Prime Termani says. "He was selected for the mandatory testing, yet he claims he helped run the testing. That is a contradiction."

"You're right. I am not the Seeker." Gripping the helmet with both hands, I step closer to Prime Termani and meet his mask's dark stare. I roll the helmet to his feet. "I believe this belongs to you."

Prime Termani grabs the helmet from the floor and throws it across the room, standing up and marching over to me. "This is outrageous," he exclaims. "How dare you claim that I killed people? How dare you claim that I am a murderer?" He storms at me, his cane lying forgotten on the ground. The limp is all but gone.

"Termani, please return to your seat," the Archprime says.

"You have been in my way for far too long, Axle. You should be in the prison, like the rest of the students."

"So, I should be dead?" I ask.

"More murder? More accusations? Who are you to say that to me? I am Prime Termani. You are nothing."

"Termani, return to your seat now," the Archprime orders in a louder voice.

"You're just like Lukas. You get so involved in what doesn't affect you."

I freeze. My hands clench, and I spit on the floor in front of Prime Termani. He raises his fist at me.

"Prime Termani has never met Lukas," Sapphire says. I turn to face her, and so does everyone else in the room.

"And why is that relevant?" the Archprime asks. The other Primes pass confused glances between them.

"Prime Termani is comparing Axle to Lukas, a man that Prime Termani has never met. But the Seeker has met Lukas. The Seeker severed Lukas' arm, took him to Mount Islorr, and forced him to mine Akorth." Sapphire turns to face me. "Fortunately, he is still alive."

What? I stare at Sapphire, my eyes wallowing up with tears. Thank Lokx. The Seeker didn't kill him. He isn't dead. I look back at Prime Termani. The Seeker. My fists clench.

"Is this true, Termani?" the Archprime asks. The Seeker's cloth mask remains focused on me, his back turned to the Archprime. "Is it true that you have never met Lukas?"

"There is no right answer to that question, Archprime."

"Answer my question," the Archprime demands.

"Being a Prime has so many responsibilities that I could never have predicted. Sometimes I wonder if it's even worth it." I watch as the Seeker grabs a knife hidden underneath his overcoat. "I can't let anyone know too much."

"What are you talking about?" the Archprime asks. Prime Termani whips around, swinging his knife hand in the Archprime's direction. I grab his arm in time and the knife misses the Archprime. The Seeker turns back to me, unsheathing another knife. Sapphire moves to block his attack with one of her two Arcblade.

"I hated being a Prime," the Seeker spits, stabbing at Sapphire with another knife. He steps back, and the two knives shoot out into long swords. Sapphire blocks his attacks, and swings at the Seeker. "So many rules, so much to do. There were silver linings though. When I became Prime, I could finally go over your father's head and send my guards to pluck your meddling nose out of my affairs."

Sapphire snarls. She kicks the Seeker's injured leg, and he drops to a knee. "Everything you need is in Mount Islorr," she yells to the Archprime. "You'll find Lukas there. He can tell you more."

The Archprime nods, reaching up to her earpiece. "I need you to conduct a search on Mount Islorr immediately."

The Seeker's eyes dart between the Archprime, me, and Sapphire. His sword turns back into a knife, which he throws at the Archprime. Sapphire sprints to intercept and shoves the Archprime out of her chair. The knife chips the back of the marble seat and falls to the floor.

"You are revoked of your duties as Prime Termani," the Archprime yells, hunched over on the ground. The other Primes sit frozen. The Seeker's head cranes around the room. He looks back at me, and at the helmet he threw across the floor.

I watch the now-former Prime as he flees through a side door.

CHAPTER 38

LUKAS

I hunch down by the chains wrapped around my legs, holding the metal rungs in my hands. Gripping one of the chains in my left hand, I use my metal hand to grind at the Akorth chain. Despite my efforts, I only manage to scratch my arm. The chain remains unmarred. Gritting my teeth, I grab the other chain with my right fist and clench as hard as the joints of the mining arm can handle. The chain shifts slightly in my grip, but it doesn't break.

"Ugh..." I sigh. I drop the chain and lean back, lying flat against the coarse dirt and rock. My eyes close, and I drift unwillingly into an exhausted sleep. In my head, I watch as the Seeker tries to throw a knife at Axle over and over again, my arms barely holding him back. I thought, after my failed attempt to stop the Seeker, that he would surely go after and kill them all. But they survived.

I pry my eyelids open with my hands. The metal fingers of my right hand scratch my eyelid, and a small drop of blood drips down my face. I wipe it with my left hand and lean forward onto the chains again. I pick the length of chain up in my hands and march toward the torch, wrapping the chains even tighter around the wooden pillar. I turn around and walk away from the post. The chains resist my movement, pulling at my legs. I strain forward anyway, but the chains refuse to budge, and I pitch over onto the ground. I claw at the ground in frustration. I delve my metal fingers into the ground and tear at the rocky dirt beneath. I start to crawl forward, relying purely on the strength of the mining arm. A loud crack peals in the air behind me. I grimace at the chains digging into my ankles, but I keep crawling forward with all my strength. A series of cracks follow then stop abruptly. I hear a large thump shakes the floor and the cave is plunged into darkness. I turn back; the torch is no longer lit. I stand up and run. Free. Then the chains rip my feet out from under me again. I crash to the ground with a smack to the head.

"What?" I exclaim, forcing myself back up to my feet. With my hands as my guide, I trace the chains back to find a small metal rod with cracked wood around it. "No." I lie back onto the ground, closing my watering eyes.

Just as my sobs quiet down, a loud scream tears through the cave. The deafening sound assaults my ears. The scream is followed by a tumultuous clanging as things shatter in the distance. The scream peals through the air again with increased ferocity. Yet another series of crashes follow. The pattern persists, each scream louder and more intense than the last as they close in on me. They almost sound like pain. If I can hear him that close... I take a deep breath to scream, then hesitate. Even if he comes over here, he won't do anything... Unless I'm injured. I turn to my shoulder, staring at the tight leather strap connecting my arm to the rest of my body.

I reach with my left hand toward the strap. I pull the leather up. Relief floods through my back muscles as the pressure releases from my shoulder— a weight I'd stopped noticing until now. I stand up, scrunching my eyes tightly closed. I take a long and deep breath and release the leather strap. The detached arm drops like a stone for a split second, before the artificial nerves abruptly pull taut. The sudden tension sends an overwhelming release of pain cascading through my whole body. I drop to my knees and let an animalistic shriek tear from my throat. Behind my sealed eyes, I force myself to see Axle and the prisoners he mentioned, all murdered. I maintain my scream. I see Sapphire, limp, with her neck torn open. My throat's raw, but the pain in my shoulder is exponentially worse. I see Prime Termani above the bodies, the Seeker by his side. I clench my left fist, digging my nails deep into cuts I had previously gouged in my palm.

Footsteps thunder closer until they come to a stop, replaced by the deep robotic static of the Seeker's breaths. I open my eyes, still screaming in agony. The Seeker leans over the chains and starts sawing at them with his Akorth knife. Most of his armor is missing, and the red undersuit wrinkles and bunches at his joints. The pieces of armor that are present, his shoulder pads, boots, and part of his chest armor, are hanging loosely by their straps. His helmet is the only thing unchanged. The red parts of his mask and armor are lit up by a small flickering torch. The Seeker's breaths are labored. The first chain snaps, freeing my left leg. I look over at the limp metal arm as the pain starts to numb. I turn back to the Seeker again. The second chain snaps.

I take a deep breath as the Seeker stands up to face me. I move my left arm as fast as I can, grabbing the leather strap and yanking it back in place. The metal arm is instantly responsive, and I throw an uppercut at the Seeker's chin. My fist strikes the Seeker's mask, his neck snaps back, and his whole body flies back and crashes onto the ground. He turns to me, and I can feel his rage as he glares beneath the mask. The Seeker stands up and unsheathes another knife. Both blades extend into swords with a snick. The Seeker swings at me with both. I block with my arm, but the force of the blow sends me stumbling backward. The blades leave deep cuts in the metal of my mining arm, revealing the orange and blue transmission wires underneath, reminding me of the display in Voltaris Industries. The Seeker swings again with the same attack. I block again and am slammed back into the wall behind me.

"Why are you doing this?" I spit in the Seeker's face. He moves his sword-wielding hand up and wipes my saliva off of his mask.

"I'm saving my work. Your Primordialist friends want to take the Lightning Stone away from me. The Stone I found all by myself."

"You killed so many," I yell, my vocal cords hurt as I speak.

"You cannot comprehend my goals." The Seeker turns his swords back into knives and presses both at my neck, forcing me to stay against the wall. "If I can remake the Stones... If I can make them work for Saberrens *and* Cortenians, then the precious Lightning Stone will mean *nothing*!" the Seeker screams in my face. The static triggering a familiar ringing in my ears. Not now. "That is, nothing to the fucking self-righteous terrorists. It won't be their special trophy anymore. *It will be mine.*"

My ears throb as they ring. Please, not now. I swing my leg up to kick the Seeker away from me. He grabs my leg and cuts along my thigh with his knife. I wince in pain, attempting to pull my leg free. With his other hand, the Seeker holds his knife at my neck. I gasp for air, and my ringing ears become unbearable. Get out of my head. Get the fuck out of my head.

I yank my leg free, forcing the knife to glide along the wound again. I snatch the Seeker's knife away from my throat, slipping free from the wall. I throw a punch at the Seeker's back. He turns around and grabs my metal arm, holding it in place.

"I am *done* with your nonsense." The Seeker slices into the flesh of my left arm. I try to wrestle my metal arm free, but the Seeker tightens his grip on my fist. He twists my arm, throwing me over and flipping me onto the ground. The wind is knocked from my lungs. I stand up gasping and throw another punch at the Seeker. He blocks with one knife and slashes down with the other. Another cut spurts blood from my injured leg. I wince in pain, swinging to punch him again. He grabs my metal arm and pulls it behind my back, sliding the leather strap off my shoulder. He starts pulling my arm off, drawing the wires taut and inflicting the same immense pain from earlier. My body shakes uncontrollably. The mix of intolerable pain and the ringing in my ears is too much to handle. Please... get of my head.

"Your friend, Sapphire. She's smart." The Seeker takes a step forward. "So is Axle. But you... you've been the biggest thorn in my side."

"You can't just do all this," I exclaim. "This cave, the lab, the prison in Termani."

"Oh, you idiot," the Seeker chuckles. The static sounds distant through the pain. I reach over with my left hand and slide the leather strap back onto my shoulder. Just as the Seeker notices, I yank my arm free and swing a left hook at him. He catches my fist with one of his hands while still wielding his sword. I thrust up my clenched metal fist, aiming a punch at the bottom of the Seeker's mask. The static cuts off abruptly.

The Seeker releases my fist, stumbling backward. "What did you do?" His voice is no longer robotic, and I hear his higher pitched actual voice. He reaches up underneath his mask and pulls out a metal device trailing severed wires streaming out from small holes. He tosses the modulator to the side and turns to me. The ringing doesn't stop. It crescendos to a terribly high pitch. I grab my ears. The Seeker marches toward me, turning the knife in one of his hands back into a sword. He swings both swords at me, and I jump back. I grab the large bucket filled with Akorth ore and tilt it, dumping the rubble out onto the Seeker. He walks through the debris, slicing through the air at me with one of his swords. I dive to the side. My breathing becomes panicked gasps.

I hoist the bucket overhead and smash it down onto the Seeker's head. His head ducks to brace for the impact, and his hand snakes out to snatch the bucket's rim while still holding his sword. I grip the bucket even tighter. My ringing ears spike into a migraine. I shudder, and the Seeker seizes the moment to yank the bucket free from my grip. He tosses it across the cave. It collides with the cave wall, knocking pieces of ore to the ground.

I ready my fist for a punch, but the Seeker moves too fast to keep up with. He lunges at me. throws his arm around my neck, and spins my body around. I'm frozen in a chokehold. "Nice try, Lukas ajj Termani." The Seeker manually deepens his voice as he speaks. I grab his arm with my metal arm, but whirring gears resist me. I can't pull his arm away from my neck. "Do you really think I would give you something that could beat me in a fight?"

"How... d-did you g-get Prime T-T-Termani involv—" I stutter, gasping for air.

"I am Prime Termani!" The Seeker yells, cutting me off. My ears throb from the ringing. Get out of my head. My vision blurs. I need to breathe. I manage a few short shallow breaths.

"How?" I murmur, the loudest I can speak.

"It was easy. You Termans care so damn much about safety, you didn't even question me when I ran for Prime. Strange guy in a mask shows up, promising safety. Nobody cared who I was. Nobody bothered to ask. I marched right into the office of Prime Termani."

"The t-testing..." I stutter.

215

"Mandatory testing..." the Seeker chuckles. "That was a lovely excuse. I just needed test subjects." The Seeker tightens his choke, and my vision darkens. I stare forward at the holed wall, trying my hardest to take a breath. The ringing stops.

What?

Standing right in front of me, fully materialized, is my mom. No longer is she an obscure silhouette. Her golden hair flows down her face, and her bright green eyes meet mine. Her expression is neutral at first, but as she approaches her eyes squint at me with disdain. I try to speak as she walks closer to me, but the chokehold makes it impossible.

I clench my fists. My lungs scream for air. But I need to speak. "Get... out... of my head," I mutter, the words an incomprehensible garble.

My mom steps away from me, crossing her arms. She frowns, her eyes glaring down at me.

"Get... out... of my head," I say with my last reserves of air. The image of my mom flickers briefly before solidifying again.

"What?" the Seeker asks. He loosens his grip slightly. I steal one blissful breath of air before he quickly tightens his grip again. I don't know how much longer I can hold out.

My mom continues to stare with the same disapproving frown. I miss the silhouette. At least the silhouette didn't show her emotions. I guess they're my emotions. Her eyes start to water, becoming bloodshot as she refuses to blink.

"Get... out..." I try to say but my voice won't let me finish speaking.

"What are you saying?" the Seeker asks. My mom looks at me as if asking the same question.

I clench my fists tighter than they were before. My mom starts to flicker in and out of existence as she circles around the Seeker and me.

I try to take a deep breath, but it fails. Again. It fails. My vision goes black. I flare my eyes open.

"Get out of my head!"

I tear at the Seeker's arm and pitch forward with the force of my entire body, yanking his grip free. I spin around and punch him in the chest,

216

sending him reeling backward toward the cave wall. The Seeker's body flies through my mom, shattering her image. The Seeker collides with the wall, slumping to the ground. He shakily gets to his feet, staring at me with his empty black eyes and readying his swords. I run at him, landing a punch under his mask that lifts him into the air. As he falls back down, I slam my fist down, driving him into the ground. I pummel at the Seeker's armor.

"Who are you?" I yell.

I repeatedly thrash his face. A crack spreads from the mask's left eye. Sudden pain flares as his knife stabs into the open wound on my leg. Gritting my teeth, I throw punch after punch at the mask, snapping his head against the floor. The crack expands with each punch. Summoning all my strength, I smash my fist onto the cracked eyepiece. The piece finally snaps free and falls into the mask. Without the piece of Akorth-glass in the way, I can finally look the Seeker in the eye. His eye is light gray, or at least it is supposed to be. The sides of his eyes are bloodshot, dying them a deep red. My bloody face reflects in his small pupil. The eye jolts back and forth, then settles on my face and squints. The Seeker reaches for something on his lower legs. The air crackles, plasma erupts from his boots, and he blasts off, speeding down into the gloom of the tunnel.

I stand still, staring off at the dusty trail left in the Seeker's wake. My throat still hurts, but at least I can breathe again. As I continue staring at the windswept dust, guards filter into the tunnel around me, all wearing silver armor. The guards have older, non-Voltaris EM-Plasmars drawn, and they each wield large torches.

"It's done." I turn to my left. Sapphire stands next to me, her purple-silver Arcblades sheathed on either side of her waist. Next to her, Axle wears the Mark 1 Seeker suit. Holding the helmet in his hands, he attempts a smile, but I just stare back at him, taking in a ragged breath. "The Archprime has removed Prime Termani from office. Termani is free." I do not respond, still staring off in the direction that the Seeker flew. Sighing, Sapphire walks past me to address the guards. I stare at Axle and, taking another deep breath, smile back.

CHAPTER 39

AXLE

I sit at my desk in a small wooden classroom. The desk is barely large enough to fit my notebook. Surrounding me are students of various ages from different districts. The professor, a lanky man with large round glasses, is rambling on about the ethics of letting robots run specific aspects of society that would otherwise be vulnerable to bias. The topic, while interesting, is not what I signed up for when I joined the robotics class at Termani Overschool.

I glance down at my notebook. Instead of lecture notes, it is filled with doodles of the Lightning Stone. At the center of the page, the Stone is depicted in two different states. The first depicts the Stone as I remember it, with all of the folds closed up around the spherical ball. The one next to it is what the Stone looked like when it was open. An expanded cross-section of the splayed open folds showcases my interpretation of what the modified virus that the Seeker spoke of might look like. The organisms carry clusters of tangible sparks with them, as if the arcs were solid objects. I signed up to this robotics class in hopes of gaining insights into how those enhanced bugs could manipulate energy like that. Instead, I'm subjected to an endless stream of ethics lectures, a topic that I already understand.

I grab my pen to sketch an up-close representation of the modified bug, then hesitate; I don't know what they look like. I sigh, putting the pen back down. I place my hands on the notebook instead, letting sparks of lightning flicker between my fingers.

"Axle," someone whispers from across the room.

I close my fists, letting the energy dissipate. I look up at the professor, but he's still wrapped up in his monologue. Totally oblivious to anything else in the room. I glance around at the rest of the students before noticing Lukas leaning against the doorframe. His metal arm is different from before. Gone is the rusted metal mining arm. His new arm is made of solid cast metal, polished to perfection. The arm consists mostly of metal pieces connected seamlessly at every joint. The joints themselves are concealed by small, curved extensions of metal, making it near impossible to see the desaturated yellow nerve-wires snaking through tiny holes at the joints. Lukas notices me staring at his arm and flexes the joints on the fingers. I knew that Lukas was tinkering with a new metal arm, but today is the first time that I actually get a good look at it.

"What do you want?" I mouth. "The professor will see you." I point over to the professor, who is still distracted by his own lecture. Lukas pulls out my earpiece from his pocket and tosses it across the room. I snatch it out of the air and carefully place it on my head.

"See you at lunch," Lukas mouths, grinning as he scurries off along the hallway. I smile, discreetly turning on music in my earpiece.

Acknowledgments

I remember when I was in first grade, all alone on the playground at the park, when I first came up with *Super Ethan*. It was a superhero story centered around the hero, Super Ethan, fighting against different villains. This book has been decades in the making, and I owe its existence to many people.

The first person I'd like to thank is Liam, my best friend in elementary who joined me on the adventures that I created. He inspired me to keep working on the story and to flesh it out into a real novel.

It was in fourth grade when I transformed *Super Ethan* into *Metalfist*. Metalfist, otherwise known as Lucas Mystery, was a hero who fought with a powerful metal arm. Through many restarts and revisions, I spent countless hours over many years workshopping *Metalfist* into the story that I now call *Islorr's Blood*. But if it hadn't been for Zechariah in fourth grade, who inspired me with his own projects, I don't know if I would have ever committed so much effort to this story and the *Voltaris Saga* as a whole.

I also would like to thank the many sounding boards in my life. Each chapter of my life and rewrite of my book introduced me to new friends who agreed to listen to my new ideas. These friends helped me shape my story, turning the once corny Lucas Mystery into the heroic Lukas ajj Termani.

Next, I'd like to thank everyone who supported me on Kickstarter. Your support allowed me to afford excellent editors to transform my novel into what it is today. Speaking of editors, I'd like to thank Gary Smailes (https://bubblecow.com/) and Ben Espach (https://www.linkedin.com/in/ben-espach/). Gary was a fantastic first editor, providing me with not only detailed comments on the document itself, but also offering a thorough review of the book. Gary, your comments were immensely helpful, and I cannot thank you enough. After Gary, Ben served not only as a copyeditor, but as a second developmental editor. Ben, I thoroughly enjoyed our chats about my novel, and your feedback was instrumental to finalizing the story. I'm excited to see what both of you can do for books two and three.

Between Gary and Ben working on my novel, I also had a few people (friends, family, and otherwise) kindly agree to beta read the story for free. Your feedback was highly informative, and gave me much needed insight into the readers' perspective.

For the cover and map designs of the novel, I would like to thank Elyse Royer (https://www.instagram.com/lous_artbook/). Elyse was incredibly patient with my nitpicking, and she delivered exactly what I wanted. Elyse, I look forward to working with you for the future books.

Finally, I would like to especially thank everyone who has been there for me throughout the entire process. Thank you to my mom and dad, who raised me to become the man I am today. Thank you to my best friends, who encouraged me to keep working through all the writer's block. Thank you to my sister, for playing Super Ethan with me when I was younger. I love and appreciate all of you, and I hope you enjoyed reading this book as much as I enjoyed working on it.

About the Author

Ethan A. Gerber has been writing since he was a child, spending over a decade refining his craft and transforming early creative experiments into the epic science-fiction world of the *Voltaris Saga*. A student of aerospace and nuclear engineering at Purdue University, Ethan balances rigorous technical studies with his passion for storytelling, reading, musical composition, guitar, and bass. *Islorr's Blood* marks his debut novel, with the second book of the series already in progress.

You can connect with me on:
- 🌐 https://sites.google.com/view/ethan-a-gerber
- 🔗 https://www.linkedin.com/in/ethan-a-gerber